Veils

How Far Would You Go
to Claim an Inheritance?

JOSH LANGSTON

More books by Josh Langston

Novels:
Resurrection Blues
A Little Primitive
A Little More Primitive
A Primitive in Paradise
Primitives in Peril
Treason, Treason!
The 12,000-year-old Whisper
Oh, Bits!
Voices
Greeley
Zeus's Cookbook
Garden Clubbed!
A Season Gone to the Dogs
Hyde and Zeke

Novels with Barbara Galler-Smith:
Druids
Captives
Warriors
Under Saint Owain's Rock

Short Fiction Collections:
Mysfits
Christmas Beyond the Box
Dancing Among the Stars
Who Put Scoundrels in Charge?

Textbooks on the Craft of Writing
Write Naked!
The Naked Truth!
The Naked Novelist!
Naked Notes!

Dedication

This book is dedicated to Annie Langston—my wife, my compass, and my passion. Without her love, her patience, and her encouragement, I'd never get anything written.

Thank you, Annie, for making my life complete.

Acknowledgements

I am honored to claim membership in two amazing writer's groups: the **Verb Mongers** and the **Soleil Critters**. The members of these two gangs have gone out of their way to help me improve my work, an ongoing process for sure. So, hat's off to these marvelous Mongers: Doris Reidy, Pam Olinto, Betty Smith, Sonya Braverman Cooper, Don O'Briant, and Joe Kalcso.

Among the Critters, the following have been brutally helpful: Jack Bowie, Erika Passantino, Brad Ballish, Fred Cruser, Lou Knight, and Brian Paley.

When it comes to critiques, everyone in both groups came through for me.

Lastly, I want to thank one additional First Reader who waded through my efforts all during development and helped me turn a work in progress into a readable and hopefully enjoyable tale. My thanks go to Don Wolf, a great friend, a careful reader, and a pretty good golfer, too!

Chapter 1

"I enjoy slaughtering beasts, and I think of my relatives constantly." –Roger Zelazny

When his Aunt Edna's estate was liquidated, Lenny Gianella presumed most of the proceeds went to pay off her debts. As her sole surviving heir, he became the reluctant recipient of the meager surplus. This consisted of a small, heavily sealed envelope she had entrusted to her attorney, a shoebox full of photographs, and a large, shaggy, and mostly white dog of dubious lineage. The attorney showed them out of his office, and Lenny dutifully took his "inheritance" home for further examination.

At the time, he would have been content with just the photographs, even though he didn't know a single soul in them.

According to one of the tags on his collar, the dog's name was Ebenezer. Lenny had no idea what Edna actually called him; he didn't know Edna even had a pet. They weren't close, a condition espoused by his late father, who urged him to stay the hell away from her lest he somehow contract her feeble grip on reality. His father never bothered to mention why he felt that way.

The envelope was addressed to Leonardo, although the ink hadn't fared well in the transition from paper to packing tape, a heavy band of which kept it safe from prying eyes. He sliced one end of the envelope open and shook a safe deposit box key into his hand. Dear, clever Aunt Edna hadn't bothered to mention from which bank the key hailed. A call to her attorney failed to generate any additional information about the key's origin.

While pondering this issue, he discovered Ebenezer had a bladder condition.

Lenny didn't think of himself as a mean person. He liked animals. He often admired them when strolling through Piedmont Park, which was just visible from the patio of his apartment—his 28th-floor apartment. But, he reasoned, was it fair to think Ebenezer would ever be able to negotiate the elevator and several blocks of heavily traveled city streets to find relief? Repeatedly, throughout the day?

Lenny didn't think so. And neither did the nice lady at the animal shelter who accepted Ebenezer the following day along with his donation in support of the outfit's good work. All the way home, he kept telling himself his Aunt Edna would understand, and that this was the absolute right thing to do. By the following day, he'd stopped thinking about the dog altogether.

A few days later he got a call from Edna's attorney, Norb Putzkin. "Mr. Gianella?" he asked, somewhat breathlessly. "Mr. Leonardo Gianella?"

"I go by 'Lenny,' but yeah, it's me."

"I've been trying to reach you."

"Congratulations," Lenny said, "you just did." He stepped gingerly between the carpet stains Ebenezer had left behind and opened the patio doors. The weather was perfect, warm and dry with a gentle breeze.

"I'm sure you remember calling my office the other day about the key left to you by the late Ms. Gianella."

"I do. You told me you had no idea which bank it came from."

"That's true," Putzkin said. "However, a clerk here in my office found a second envelope from Mrs. Gianella which had been misfiled with another client's papers. It was addressed to me with instructions that it only be opened after her death."

Lenny waited patiently while the lawyer covered all his bases. "And?"

"It contained a message for you. In light of the delay, I thought it prudent to call and read the note to you."

Lenny settled into a chair on the patio, his cell phone in one hand, a beer in the other. "Fire away,

Mr. Putzkin. I'm all ears."

The lawyer cleared his throat and said, "The note reads as follows: 'The key is from my bank in Alabama, and the deposit box fee has been paid in advance for the next couple of years. For secrecy's sake, I won't include the bank's name or branch here. But, Ebby knows which one it is, and if my nephew is the sort of man I hope he is, he'll find it and make good use of its contents.'"

"Who the hell is Ebby?" Lenny asked.

The question clearly caught attorney Putzkin by surprise since he only produced monosyllables in response.

"Please," Lenny said, "tell me she wasn't referring to that dog, Ebenezer."

"Actually...."

"Yes. Go on."

Putzkin cleared his throat again. "Uhm, actually, I think that's exactly who she meant."

"The *dog* knows which bank in Alabama has her safe deposit box?"

"According to her note, yes."

"Have you any idea just how many banks there are in Alabama?"

"Quite a few, I imagine."

"That's my thought, too. Thanks so much for the update."

Veils

Lenny killed the connection and immediately dialed the animal shelter only to hear a recording that detailed their hours of operation. It seemed poor Ebenezer would be spending another night in doggie jail.

He hoped the dog wouldn't hold that against him in light of his new-found concern for the animal's well-being.

~*~

Life looks different when one is between jobs. Lenny's job as a customer relations agent had been replaced by a computer program. They came up with a machine which could answer calls and piss off customers 24/7. They called it artificial intelligence. It never called in sick, never asked for a raise, didn't have a 401K, and could lie as fluently as middle management.

When it happened, he felt an immediate sense of panic.

How far can I stretch my severance pay? How long before unemployment benefits kicked in? How long would they even last? And finally, how likely would I be to find a cheap place in the burbs since I'm no longer able to pay for my upscale apartment in Midtown?

The bag his Aunt Edna left him holding did, however, offer a hint of hope. *What had the old lady stored in her safety deposit box? Jewels, perhaps? Stocks? Bonds? Cash?*

In all likelihood, it would turn out to be

something mundane—a marriage certificate maybe, a diploma, or an autographed photo of somebody he'd never heard of. But then, why would she feel the need for secrecy? He knew very little about her beyond the obvious. She married his uncle Max, and the two of them spent most of their lives traveling. Lenny wasn't sure how they could afford to do that, but they did. His father didn't approve of what he called their "gypsy" lifestyle. Lenny had adopted the same attitude since he had nothing else to go on.

He kept going back to the simple fact that dear old Aunt Edna had a safe deposit box.

And only the damned dog knew which bank it was in.

The following day he returned to the animal shelter intent on restoring Ebenezer's freedom and determined to earn his trust. He encountered the same woman who had so graciously accepted the dog and his donation a few days earlier.

"I've had a change of heart," he explained. "It's been a difficult decision, as you can imagine, but I really need to get Ebenezer back."

She looked at him with utter disdain. "You know," she said, "it's amazing how many people think they can drop off a pet and expect us to care for it while they traipse off on vacation. And when they return, they're always shocked if they discover someone has adopted their beloved family member." She made quote marks in the air with both hands when saying "beloved." She managed a level of scorn he'd only seen in movies and on TV.

"That's not what I've done," he said. "Seriously. I've simply changed my mind. My late aunt left the dog in my care without giving me any warning. I wasn't prepared to care for him. I didn't know—"

"Him? You didn't even notice that Ebenezer is female?"

"Ebby's *female?*"

"Indeed."

"Wow. I... Uhm...."

"Are you sure you gave us the correct name?"

"Yes! Of course. It's the only name I had. The attorney—"

"Oh, don't get me started on lawyers," she said. "Did you know that roughly forty percent of the people in Congress are legal eagles?"

"No, actually, I never—"

"And we wonder why nothing ever gets done." She gazed briefly up at the ceiling. "They're all too busy running for re-election."

"You're right, I'm sure. Now, about Ebenezer. What do I need to—"

"Do?" She sighed. "Look for another dog. We've got a bunch you can choose from. Real cuties, too."

"I don't want *another* dog. I want Ebenezer!"

She exhaled slowly. "Sorry, pardner. Someone

beat you to it. Ebenezer was adopted the day after you left her here."

Lenny was surprised his jaw didn't bounce off the cement floor. "You've got to be kidding. Someone adopted *my* dog?"

"Yep. I filled out the paperwork myself."

"Who?"

"Me."

"No. Who adopted Ebenezer?"

"I don't recall," she said.

He found it increasingly difficult to control his temper but managed a marginally subdued response. "Would you be kind enough to look it up?"

She shook her head from side to side.

"Does that mean you can't, or you won't?"

"We aren't allowed to give out any of that information."

"But—"

"What I can tell you is that a young woman came in the day after you dropped the dog off and claimed her. We check every animal left with us for a microchip. It's the safest and best way to assure owners can be contacted when a pet is lost."

"I doubt my—"

"Even when owners abandon their pets, we check for microchips. That way we can change the registration when someone adopts them."

"But—"

"In Ebenezer's case, the name on the registration wasn't yours."

"It must've been my Aunt Edna's. She—"

"It belonged to the young woman who picked her up. When we called, she was overjoyed to learn her pet had been located."

Lenny's mind spun. "*Her* pet? But that's— Are you saying I wasn't Ebenezer's rightful owner?"

"I can't prove I'm right," she said, "but if someone asked me, I'd guess you stole the dog." She looked at him without blinking. If eyes could give off venom, he thought, he'd have shriveled up and died on the spot.

"But—"

"If you think for one tiny moment that I'd give you the name of the real owner of that dear, sweet pooch, you're crazy. Now, get out of here before I sic some seriously unhappy pit bulls on you."

He caved. Speechlessly. And clueless.

~*~

Three weeks earlier....

Samantha Everton patted the big, white, fluffy mutt at her side. She'd fallen in love with the dog at first sight. Delivered to the law practice where she handled the filing, the dog came straight to her as if they'd been lifelong pals. She remembered the occasion clearly.

"Sam, I've got a huge favor to ask of you," said her boss, Norb Putzkin, as he strolled into the windowless file room at the back of the office.

Samantha was so entranced by the dog, she paid little attention to what her employer was saying. Putzkin's law clerk, Myra, stood behind him, and when she cleared her throat, it broke the spell. Samantha looked up quickly and smiled at the overweight, balding attorney. "Yes, sir? How can I help?"

"I need someone to care for this animal until I can arrange a transfer to the man our client wanted to give it to. You remember Edna Gianella, don't you? She is—well, *was*—quite a character."

"Yes, sir. Nice old lady from somewhere in... Alabama, wasn't it?"

"Right," he said. "We went to high school together actually, back in the day. I used to think of her as a..." He paused; his lips twisted. "Well, that's all in the past. So, never mind." He shook his head as if to clear it. "She came in here a while back to tie up the loose ends of her estate."

"Not that there were that many," observed the law clerk, a pinch-faced shrew of a woman who appeared to have logged more years than Putzkin and the late Mrs. Gianella put together.

"I'll be happy to care for the dog," Samantha said, reaching for the animal's leash. "Is there anything I need to know?"

"I don't have anything to add," Putzkin said.

"His name's Ebenezer."

"*His* name?" Samantha asked, checking quickly to make sure she hadn't been mistaken about the dog's gender.

"Oh! Well, I just thought... You know, the name... Edna never ceased to amaze me. She could make things appear so..." He waved his hand in dismissal. "Whatever. You won't have to care for the dog very long. The man we're trying to find is Mrs. Gianella's nephew. He lives here in the Atlanta area somewhere; we just need to track him down."

"We don't have his contact information?"

The attorney shook his head. "Mrs. Gianella wasn't sure about it."

The law clerk muttered, "Don't you just love it when clients can't even tell you how to reach their next of kin?"

Samantha remained quiet for a moment, chewing her gum and thinking how happy she was not to be related to the law clerk.

"So, can you handle it?" Putzkin had asked.

"Sure," Samantha said, rubbing Ebenezer's jowls. "I've got this."

She and Ebenezer had been together for a few days when Samantha took her to a local veterinarian who assured her the dog was neither chipped nor spayed. Samantha opted to have Ebenezer microchipped. She listed herself as the owner, though a decision to have her spayed would have to come later, presumably by whoever adopted her; something Samantha hoped would never happen.

In any event, if the dog got loose, or Mrs. Gianella's relative didn't want her, Samantha was quite ready to step in.

Chapter 2

"Dogs are better than humans because they know and do not tell." –Emily Dickinson

Lenny would readily admit, if anyone asked, that his second visit to the animal shelter didn't qualify as a shining moment. But he wasn't guilty of doing anything wrong. He hadn't stolen the dog, and he certainly hadn't dropped him—*or her it seems*— off in order to take a vacation without paying a boarding fee.

There was something weird going on, and he aimed to figure out what. The logical place to start, he presumed, would be with Edna's attorney. After ruminating in the parking lot of the animal shelter, he cranked up his car and headed for the aging lawyer's office. The chip on his shoulder weighed heavily on him at that point; he didn't feel the need to be the least bit civil.

Putzkin's   practice   occupied   what   had

formerly been a single-family home. Commercial real estate prices in the area had gone nuts in the 80s and 90s, and converting homes to office space became quite common. The conversion made the place less formal, and to him, less intimidating. He cruised right in.

Putzkin's book-lined office sat dark and vacant. His secretary and a much younger gal—her great-great-grandchild, maybe?—manned the fort. He didn't recognize either of them; the older one, however, recognized him.

"Mr. Gianella?" she queried in a gravelly voice.

"Yes."

"Mr. Putzkin is out of the office today. Is there anything I can help you with?"

"Probably, since I don't need any legal advice. I just need a little information about my late Aunt Edna. You see, she—"

Rather than respond, the woman shook her gray-haired head. "You'll need to talk to Mr. Putzkin about that. His dealings with clients must remain confidential."

"Of course. I just need to know—"

She waved him off. "He has a cancellation first thing in the morning. I can work you in at 8 a.m."

"Fine," he said. "But honestly, I—"

"I'll have your aunt's files pulled and ready for him when you come in," she said. "You'll have about thirty minutes." She then gave me a mirthless smile and added, "Regular rates apply."

He thanked her and left, his mood still dark. Since he had the rest of the day to himself, he started looking for a new job and another place to live. The high-rise in Midtown his father left him had been a blessing, but it carried a mortgage he couldn't cover without a steady income.

Sadly, he struck out on both employment *and* housing which only increased his desire to find and explore Edna's safe deposit box. He spent the evening alone and depressed, but by the next morning felt somewhat better.

Though not looking forward to another encounter with the woman guarding Putzkin's inner sanctum, Lenny was eager to meet with the lawyer and pulled up to the modest parking area beside his office.

The lot, however, was choked with police cars, an emergency vehicle from the Fire Department, and an ambulance. He was directed to a neighboring lot, where he left his car and hurried back to Putzkin's office.

The two women he'd seen the day before stood outside the building while a uniformed officer from the Atlanta Police Department struggled to erect a barrier of yellow, plastic "crime scene" tape without the benefit of trees or bushes in the front yard.

"What's going on?" Lenny asked when he reached the two women.

Both were upset, but the younger of the two, an attractive twenty-something brunette, appeared to be taking it much worse than her companion.

The older woman said, "Norb is... I— Uhm. Oh, Gawd. I mean, Mr. Putzkin is... *dead*."

"What? How?" He suspected a heart attack; Putzkin hadn't looked too healthy during their only encounter.

"I don't know. He came in after hours, sometime last night—"

"I thought he took the day off."

"He did!" She wore a pained, desperate look. "There must've been some kind of emergency. We found him at his desk when we got here this morning."

A heavy-set detective stepped between them and shouldered Lenny aside. "I have to ask you some questions, ma'am," he said without bothering to apologize for the interruption.

Lenny watched him as he extracted a notepad and pen from his breast pocket, checked the time on his watch, and scribbled it down. He seemed bored with the process, his manner more resigned than intrigued; just another dead body in the big city.

Lenny knew it would be impossible to look like he wasn't listening in when standing beside the people having a conversation, but he did his best. He didn't learn much.

The cop asked for the senior woman's name and contact information, then requested the same from the younger female at her side. After a yawn and a shoulder roll, the cop wanted to know when they had arrived at the office and how much time had elapsed before they called 9-1-1. The answers came quickly: just before 8 a.m., and about two minutes.

"Did you see anyone leaving around that time? Maybe hanging around the parking lot? Walking by? Anything?"

"No," they both said.

"Do you know what he was working on? Any big cases?"

The older gal turned, looked at Lenny, and frowned thereby drawing the detective's attention.

"Him," she said. "He had an early appointment. Claimed he wanted information on one of our clients. He was quite insistent when he showed up at the office late yesterday." She paused and squinted at him as if he was shrouded in fog. "If you ask me, he looks suspicious as hell."

"Step aside, sir, and stick around. I have a question or two for you, too."

Suddenly, Lenny found himself a suspect in… what, exactly, he wasn't sure.

He waited and tried to appear inconspicuous, a good trick after the old crone all but accused him of killing her boss. He glanced at the twenty-something brunette at her side, pleased to see she was shaking her head and rolling her eyes as theatrically as if she'd been on stage. But it definitely made him feel better.

After the detective got his contact info and quizzed Lenny about his need to talk to Putzkin, he ignored Lenny and focused on the girl. Lenny returned the favor she'd paid him and rolled his eyes, shook his head, and even shrugged his shoulders in an attempt to make it known he was on her side, whatever that was, and that the cop was wasting both his time and theirs.

The older gal, who had continued to glare at him, cleared her throat and tapped Lenny on the chest. "There's no reason for you to hang around. Your appointment's been... you know... cancelled."

The girl did another eyeroll which had a magnetic effect on him. He stepped past the old grouch and addressed her colleague. "I can see you're upset. Why don't you let me take you somewhere less... stressful? There's a coffee place nearby."

"Cleo's," she said with a nod.

"How's that sound?" he asked. "I'm buying."

"Sam," the older gal said, "we don't know this character at all. I don't think it'd be very smart of you to—"

"Sam," Lenny said. "Samantha, is it? It's up to you, but you don't need to follow her lead anymore.

I'm not a bad guy; I just want to help you calm down a bit, and a change of scenery sure wouldn't hurt. Fair enough? I promise you; I'm harmless."

He backed that up with the most innocent smile he could muster. "Seriously," he said. "I don't mean you any harm. None." He even nodded at the senior woman. "She can come along, too, if it'd make you feel any better."

"I have a car," Samantha said. "How 'bout I meet you there, at Cleo's?"

He sealed the deal with a wink. "Five minutes? As long as Sherlock Holmes here is done."

She managed a tenuous grin, checked with the detective, and got his permission to leave. Lenny walked her to her car, then continued on to his own. Within a few minutes they were sitting in a coffee shop two blocks away.

~*~

Cleo's café wasn't part of a huge national chain like Starbucks or Dunkin' Donuts. It was a hole-in-the-wall spot just off Peachtree Street that offered only two kinds of coffee and some pastries simply called "sticky buns." The owner actually operated the shop, and everyone knew Cleo usually ran out of pastry by mid-morning. Without any of her signature buns available, she didn't bother to open for the lunch crowd. Fortunately, Sam and Lenny arrived long before the buns were all gone.

Once settled in with pastries and java, Sam took a deep breath and wiped her eyes with a napkin. "My gosh," she breathed, "I must look like... like hell."

"If so," he said with a chuckle, "hell doesn't seem like such a bad place."

She thanked him for dragging her away from the attorney's office, though she clearly hadn't gotten over the grim discovery she and her colleague made that morning.

"Myra, the woman I work with, said she thought Mr. Putzkin was in pretty good health."

"Heart attacks can happen to almost anyone," he said. "That's what killed my dad, and he used to run every day." He paused, hoping to lighten the moment. "And that's why you won't catch me jogging!"

Sam rewarded him with a giggle, then immediately grew serious. "I'm sorry you didn't get to have your meeting today. Myra said you didn't want legal advice; you just wanted to look at your aunt's file."

"I'm surprised she remembered that much," he said. "I was pretty sure she wasn't listening to me."

Sam gave her head a little shake. "That's just the way she is. She does things one way—*her* way. It can get annoying."

"Trust me, we've both known people like that, and you're right; it is annoying."

She suddenly looked stricken. "If Mr. Putzkin

is dead, then I'm out of a job."

"But you've probably got some great skills. How long have you been a law clerk?"

"I'm not," she said, still glum. "I'm a file clerk. I pulled the records you wanted to look at."

Suddenly it dawned on him. "You're the one who found the misfiled note from my aunt about her dog and the bank where her safe deposit box is."

She looked sheepish. "Yeah, I guess so. I don't know how that happened; I just—"

"You know about her dog, Ebenezer."

"Well, of course I do," she said.

"According to the note, Ebenezer knows which bank it is." He gripped his head as if to keep his brains from bursting out and moaned, "But I no longer have the dog."

She sat quietly for a very long moment, then said, "You gave her up. You left her at a shelter. If no one had adopted her, she might've been... I don't even want to think about it."

"But when I went back to get her, they said she'd been adopted the very next day! That's what blows me away. I mean, the next day? C'mon."

If Sam looked sheepish before, her expression went fully hangdog. "What's the matter?" he asked.

"I've got her," she said. "Ebby is my dog now."

~*~

Sitting in a small, dark gray car directly across from Cleo's Cafe, a woman who went by the name of Millie Abraham watched the two people who arrived by separate vehicles from the office of the late attorney, Norb Putzkin. Millie didn't know him, had never met him, but she knew about the person who killed him—the man who applied pressure to the old lawyer's left forearm until both bones in it snapped.

Millie hadn't observed the torture, but she found the body a few hours before Putzkin's employees did. The shock and pain of the brutal interrogation "technique" probably caused the old man to have a heart attack. She felt certain that if he hadn't died, he would have suffered even more.

On the other hand, Putzkin's death may have been intentional. If his attacker obtained the information he wanted, he may have killed the old man to keep him quiet.

The attorney's death was merely another that cried out to be avenged; Millie had vowed to be the one to do it. And the best way to keep track of *her* target was to keep an eye on *his*.

Chapter 3

*"The only things you can truly depend on are gravity and greed." –*Jack Palance

Lenny felt blindsided, and Samantha's words, "Ebby is my dog," rattled around in his head like marbles in a can. At length he managed, "She is? Really?"

"Yes."

Sam didn't appear the least bit sheepish anymore. "How long have you—"

"She lived with me from about the time your aunt died until you came to pick her up. And, as you well know, she ended up at the shelter a day later." She paused for just a moment, as if summoning courage for her final statement. "She's absolutely, definitely, hands down, no-questions-asked, *mine*, Mister Gianella."

"*Mister?* Please. I go by Lenny."

"Okay then, Lenny. But Ebby is still *all mine.*"

He tried to swallow his shame for giving up on the dog as quickly as he had. Rather than offer up some sort of shallow apology, he shifted gears. "And I thank God you took her in!"

"You're not... I dunno... upset?"

"Are you kidding? No! If anything, I'm grateful." He took a breath. "Does he—I mean, she—still have the... you know... bladder thing going on?"

Sam looked at him as if he'd just sprouted a fern garden for a mustache. "*Bladder* thing? What are you talking about?"

He had no idea how to put it nicely. Instead, he took a massive bite of sticky bun and tried to look pensive, an almost impossible combination. He held up his index finger pleading for time while he chewed, all the while trying to figure out how to say it politely. "Look," he continued between swallows and napkin swipes at the sugary residue on his lips and chin, "the poor thing couldn't... you know... hold it for very long. She needed to go outside constantly."

"Seriously?"

He nodded.

"Hmpf."

He had no idea how to read that. "Are you suggesting she just holds it all day while you're at work?"

"Well," she said, a bit sheepishly, "I've got a doggy door."

He wagged a finger at her. "That's kinda like cheating, isn't it?"

She shrugged. "You tell me."

He switched tactics again. "Here's the deal. I need Ebenezer's help. I've got to find that safe deposit box, and she's the only one who can identify it."

"*The box?*"

"The bank."

"Oh." She tapped the table with her nails. "How in the world could she do that?"

"I don't know!" He had both hands extended, palms up, the universal symbol for being dumbfounded.

"Sounds crazy to me," Sam said. "The bank's in Alabama somewhere isn't it?"

"I think so, but I can't be sure. It's why I wanted to read my aunt's file. As far as I know, she lived out of a travel trailer. Where she even collected her mail is a mystery to me. I thought Mr. Putzkin might know."

"For someone who knows so little, you seem awfully eager to get your hands on that safe deposit box." She paused briefly before once again tapping her fingers on the table. "So, what's in it?"

He took a deep breath and prayed she wouldn't think he was bluffing. Telling the truth seemed like the best option. "Honestly? I don't have the slightest idea what's in it."

She gave him a look that screamed, "Liar!"

"It's true," he said. "I don't know what's in it. What I *do* know, is that she went to great lengths to keep its location a secret. She trusted the dog more than anyone else on Earth."

"And you believe *Ebby* knows where it is?"

"Yes, according to the note my aunt wrote to me—the one you found."

"And you seriously believe her?"

He shrugged. "What choice do I have?"

She had her mouth twisted to one side as if trying to decide just how much bullshit he'd been spreading and whether or not she needed hip waders.

"Look," he said, trying not to sound whiney. "I need your help."

She shook her head, no. "You need *Ebby's* help."

"Well, okay. Yeah. Definitely. I need Ebby's help."

"You can't have her," she said.

He exhaled in frustration. "I know! You've made that abundantly clear. Ebby is your dog. Completely. I've no claim. None whatsoever."

She sat quietly for the longest time before she spoke, and then it was in a low tone, delivered while she leaned across the table toward him. "Here's the thing. I'm out of a job, and you need my dog's help. That means you need my help, too. We're a package deal. So, what's in it for me?"

He hadn't anticipated that. "I uh... Well, y'see...."

She cut him off. "I want half of whatever's in the safe deposit box." She said it quite matter-of-factly.

"*Half?*"

"Yep."

"But... But there might not be *anything* of value in there."

"On the other hand, it might contain the Hope Diamond."

"I'm pretty sure that's in a museum somewhere."

She pursed her lips in dismissal. "Whatever. If there's nothing of value, then so be it. But if there's something in there that *is* valuable... Well, I want half. Agreed?"

Knowing he had no other choice, he gave in. "Agreed."

"We need a contract."

He felt as if he could hear his own eyeballs rolling around. "For real?"

"Yeah. Myra can do it. She wrote up that kinda stuff all the time for Mr. Putzkin."

"Fair enough," he said, and they shook on it.

He had no idea if he'd made a dreadful mistake or not. There was only one way to find out.

~*~

Millie waited as patiently as she could for Gianella and the girl to leave Cleo's. She tried, unsuccessfully, to ignore thoughts of the coffee and sticky buns available inside. Since they didn't look like they'd be leaving anytime soon, Millie gave in to her cravings. If they left before she finished eating, she'd take any leftovers with her and finish them later.

As she expected, they paid no attention to her when she entered. She placed her order and took a seat in a corner where she could keep an eye on them. The place wasn't crowded, but she sat too far away to eavesdrop on their conversation. Instead, she kept her eye on the entrance in case her nemesis chose to enter.

As if on cue, they got up to leave just as Millie took the first bite of her sweet, sugary pastry. Stifling her emotions, she waited for the pair to leave, then quickly packed her purchase, left a few dollars on the table, and made her way to the exit. She didn't leave the shop until both of them were in their cars. She then made a quick but casual saunter to her own vehicle, got in, and drove after them. When Gianella's car pulled away from the girl's, Millie followed him.

~*~

Veils

Dak Heller never intended to become a killer-for-hire, but he realized in his mid 20s that he wasn't very good at anything else. Certainly not anything that paid as well. Most of his hits were quick and easy—in and out, done. And not having a conscience definitely helped. Sometimes, however, his employer required him to do other things. For his current assignment, he wasn't required to kill anyone, unless of course, they got in the way of him reaching his goal—easily the strangest goal he'd ever had.

He had been hired to steal a camper, but not just any camper. He had to find the one used by Edna Gianella, a woman his employer called a witch. Or maybe it was bitch. He couldn't remember, and he hadn't asked for clarification.

His employer—whoever it was; he/she/it whatever, *they* remained anonymous—and gave him no idea what the camper looked like, how big it was, or where he might find it. None of that mattered, according to them, as long as he found it and delivered it at the appointed time and place. All he really knew was that an early delivery would earn him a bonus.

Putzkin, the attorney who handled the Gianella woman's estate, claimed he didn't know anything about her camper, even though Dak provided ample encouragement for him to give up the information. When the bones in the old man's arm snapped, Dak realized he'd probably been telling the truth. But then the old fart died on him. Dak went through the lawyer's file cabinets, but couldn't find anything about his client. The Gianella folder sat empty, not a single document.

He had nothing new to go on other than the name and address of the woman's heir, Leonardo Gianella. That much Putzkin volunteered early on. It seemed unlikely that the woman's heir would have mob connections, but with Italians one never knew. Dak had little taste for dealing with anyone in organized crime; they had long memories and far too many associates who did the same things he did. For that reason, he planned to take his time confronting the younger Gianella. A GPS tracker placed in the undercarriage of his crappy little Toyota would do Dak's work for him. That bit of handiwork would be completed soon enough, though not before Putzkin's corpse cooled.

It would do; at least for the time being.

~*~

When his cell phone rang, Lenny glanced at the number and exhaled. It read "Unknown Caller."

But just as he was about to dismiss the call along with all the other annoying and anonymous rings he got daily, he wondered if it might be Sam. So, he took a chance and answered it.

"Lenny?" asked a familiar female voice. "I've got it!"

She caught him slightly off guard. "You've got what?"

"Your Aunt Edna's file. You know, from Mr.

Putzkin's office."

"How'd you—"

"It was in my desk. I was supposed to give it to Norb when you came in for your appointment. Myra will have an absolute fit if she finds out I took it when I went to clean out my desk. So," she said, "I don't have much time. I've gotta return it as quick as I can. Now, what were you hoping to find in it?"

"I dunno. Anything that would help me figure out where that bank is."

He heard a bit of paper rustling over the phone, then Sam spoke up. "The only address I see in here is a post office box in Camp Hill, Alabama."

"Camp Chill?"

"*Hill!* Camp Hill."

"Never heard of it," he said.

"Me, either. But we can look it up online."

"And then go there!" he added.

"You driving?"

"Sure," he said, though he wasn't sure how much gas he had left, or how much more he could afford. "You've gotta bring Ebby along, too. She can sit in the back."

"And just like that, you're ready to hit the road? We don't even know how far away this Camp Hill place is."

"I think Camp Chill sounds better," he said.

"And yes. I'm ready to go. I'm tired of packing up my stuff, especially when I have no idea where I'll end up."

"That doesn't make sense," she said. "Why are you moving?"

"'Cause I'm nearly broke, and I can't afford the payments on this place. Problem is, without steady income, nobody wants to rent to me."

"What kind of work do you do?" she asked.

He wasn't in the least bit eager to talk about it. "I'll explain in the car, okay? How soon can I pick you up?"

"I need a little time," she said.

"What's your address?"

She hesitated before responding. "Uhm… Why don't you just pick us up at Cleo's? You already know where that is."

He didn't know what that was all about but decided to play along. In the meantime, he needed to figure out how in the world to get to Camp Hill, Alabama.

Chapter 4

"The Bible and several other self-help or enlightenment books cite the Seven Deadly Sins. They are: pride, greed, lust, envy, wrath, sloth, and gluttony. That pretty much covers everything that we do, that is sinful... or fun for that matter." – Dave Mustaine

Rather than spend time on hair, makeup, or a selection from her pitiful wardrobe, Sam opted for cut-off jeans and an Auburn University T-shirt. The weather was warm, and she hadn't made up her mind about Lenny Gianella. He seemed like a decent sort, and he was reasonably attractive, but aside from one off-hand but complimentary remark, he hadn't shown much interest in her. Shrugging off further thoughts about him, she decided that digging up some information on the town of Camp Hill was a better use of her time.

She quickly realized there wasn't a great deal going on in the tiny, southeast Alabama town. Based on recent census data, the population was shrinking, and would likely dip under four digits before long.

She couldn't even be sure the post office there was still in operation. But, it appeared to be the only lead she and Lenny had. Hopefully, someone in Camp Hill would remember dear, old Edna Gianella.

When the doorbell rang, Sam answered it and led Myra into her house. "Thanks for coming," she said.

The woman nodded and handed her a document. The single sheet of paper bore a centered line at the top which read: "Contract." Myra had balked when Sam first approached her and asked her to create something that would bind Lenny to his promise of sharing whatever his aunt had left in her safe deposit box.

"It's not greed," Sam had said. "It's more like desperation. You know, with Mr. Putzkin gone—" She had to pause and swallow. "I no longer have a job. I can't go back to being a teaching assistant. That ship not only sailed; it sank. And what if I can't find anything anywhere else? I've got to have something to live on, something to keep me going."

Myra softened at that. "You're right. You do deserve it. But don't you go gettin' too close to that Gianella character. I don't trust him."

"Why not?"

She shook her head. "It's nothing specific, mind you, other than him giving away the dog." Her lip curled up in a brief snarl. "He's just— I don't know, shifty-looking."

Myra went on to say something about

Richard Nixon, but Sam ignored it while Myra attached three copies of the document to a clipboard, ready for signatures: hers, Lenny's, and Myra's as an official witness. Everything went into an oversized purse. Myra gave a little laugh as she snapped the bag shut.

A growing sense of guilt however, was not easy for Sam to set aside. What, after all, did she really *deserve* from Lenny?

Ebby wandered into the room and plunked down next to Sam. The dog settled her huge, shaggy head on Sam's thigh. Sam stroked her lightly, her lips twisted to one side. "I'm conflicted, Ebby."

The dog focused her large, brown eyes directly at Sam.

"Yeah," she went on. "I'm conflicted. But then, when the heck am I not conflicted?"

"Get yourself together, young lady," Myra said, standing and tapping the face of her watch. "I'll be outside waiting for you."

"Okay. I'll just be a second." Alone again, Sam chastised herself for not giving Lenny her address and instead asking that he pick her up in front of Cleo's Café. It was a stupid thing to do. Yes, she was a bit embarrassed that she still lived with her parents. And yes, the house was small.

And old.

And needed repairs. In truth, lots of repairs.

But it was where she grew up. So what if her

parents weren't rich? They loved her, and they had taken to Ebby with nearly as much enthusiasm as Sam had.

She resolved to tell Lenny—if, that is—he turned out to be the sort of guy she wanted to befriend. The thought made her smile. Maybe he'd become more than a friend. Maybe....

She abruptly got to her feet. "Time to go."

~*~

Lenny didn't sleep well after his first encounter with Sam, and it wasn't simply because he'd agreed to give away half of whatever might turn up in his Aunt Edna's safe deposit box. The events of the day kept sloshing around in his head, and he floated between his attraction to Samantha and his resentment of her co-worker. One incident in particular had injected the woman under his skin.

His attorney had died suddenly, and as far as he knew, mysteriously, a short time before he was scheduled to meet with him, and the woman who served as his primary assistant had suggested to the cops that Lenny had something to do with the poor man's demise. What a lovely way to begin a relationship!

"Thanks, Myrtle. Or Melba. Or whatever the hell your name is. Mudd, maybe?"

He liked the last option, not that he'd ever mention it to Sam. One should never rail on a friend of someone of interest, and the more he thought about Sam, the more interested he became.

Veils

The drive to Cleo's went smoothly, and he parked right out front. Sam and Ebby were waiting for him. While she put the dog in the back seat, he watched her meddling, accusatory co-worker leave the café and walk toward them. *Oh, great. It's Miz Mudd in all her smarmy glory.*

He glanced at Sam. "What's she doing here?"

"Just taking care of a little paperwork."

"She's *what?*"

"Leonardo Gianella?" Mudd asked, then continued without waiting for confirmation, "I need you to sign this. And the two copies." She shoved a clipboard at him with printed pages attached.

"What's this all about?" he asked, staring at the clipboard as if it were a bag of Ebby's droppings.

"You agreed to enter into a time-limited partnership with Miss Samantha Everton. This is the contract covering the arrangement. As soon as you've both signed all three copies, I'll notarize them. There's a copy for each of you and one which I'll maintain until such time as it's no longer needed."

Sam's mouthed curled up on one side, a half-smile that would have been endearing if she hadn't just ambushed him.

"Go on," Sam said. "Remember? You promised me half of—"

"Yeah, I remember. But—"

"Okay then. C'mon, Ebby," she said, opening the door and signaling to the dog in the back seat that it was time to leave. "We're done here."

"Wait!"

"Why?"

"Because... 'Cause I'm not backing out of anything." He felt he had no choice. Without Ebby, he'd never find his aunt's bank.

"Then," she said, "sign the papers."

"Okay. It's just— Y'all kinda took me by surprise."

Mudd looked at him with undisguised suspicion and once again shoved the clipboard at him. This time he accepted it, quickly scanned the text, and signed all three copies. Before handing it back, he reread one of the sentences which mentioned something about "future value obtained." The wording felt as awkward as he did.

"This part," he said, pointing to the passage. "Makes it sound like Miss Everton has a claim on any future value I might get from the contents of the box."

"That's correct," Mudd said. She pursed her lips before explaining, as if to a child. "Let's say the box contains a gemstone. Are you a jeweler, Mr. Gianella? Could you somehow split the stone without ruining it?"

"Obviously not," he said.

Veils

"Well, that's the reason for that little clause. It ensures that you won't be able to cheat my client—"

"Your *client?*"

"Precisely." With that she grabbed the clipboard and passed it to Sam.

"Thank you," Sam said as she added her signature and waited while Madam Mudd signed and punched each document with her notary gizmo.

The scowling Notary handed him a copy, grunted, and stepped closer to Sam. "Be careful with this clown. I still don't trust him."

"I'll be fine," Sam said and climbed into the passenger seat of his car. "Thanks for giving me and Ebby a lift. I owe ya."

Mudd waved and walked away, probably in search of a troll hole in which to crawl. Lenny glanced at the young woman in his car, still unsettled about the way she'd engineered their contract. But, he realized, how could he stay mad at someone so pretty?

Sam strapped herself in, checked on the dog sprawled on the back seat, and smiled at Lenny. "Do you know how to get to Camp Hill?"

"Sorta."

"Fear not," she said and extracted a sheet of paper from her purse. "I looked up the town online and printed out the directions." She checked her watch. "We'd best get a move on. I want to be home before nightfall."

"Why? Are you afraid of the dark?" He feigned a worried look. "You aren't likely to turn into a werewolf or anything, are you?"

She shook her head. "I'm way more worried about being with you after dark." She then extracted a small spray can from her handbag. "And just so you know, Myra gave me this handy-dandy can of pepper spray in case you try something."

His opinion of Mudd took yet another hit, but seeing the expression on Sam's face, a mixture of uncertainty and determination, actually calmed him. He smiled at her. "You've got nothing to worry about," he said. "I promise."

He had no idea that promise would become empty way too soon.

~*~

Millie's plan to keep an eye on the killer of Norbert Putzkin, Esq. hadn't worked quite the way she had hoped. He hadn't shown up at the coffee shop where the two young people she'd been following had dined. She felt sure the man's target was the male half of the couple, a fellow named Leonardo Gianella.

She'd worked for months to narrow down the hit man's identity: Dak Heller, an average man with a big reputation and no presence on social media. If not for help from an unofficial source, she'd never have discovered who he was. She didn't like using people, but figured they'd both gotten something from their slightly-more-than-casual relationship.

Veils

Secrecy was Heller's trump card. According to her source, he was suspected of killing at least a half dozen people, and he was likely responsible for more. Her mission, to hunt him down and hopefully *put him down*, had begun when he killed her father. She missed him dearly, as did his many friends, family members, and students. A gentle man, he'd nonetheless taken a loud, vocal stand against corruption, especially when it involved elected officials and bureaucrats, though he focused on one man in particular. He wrote letters to editors, raged on social media, and made demands of politicians at many levels. In the process, he stepped on one toe too many.

Millie forced herself to focus on something other than memories. Since she didn't know where the killer was staying, she opted to keep an eye on Gianella. She'd seen where he parked his car and managed to grab a space for her own a short distance away. There, she waited, hoping the killer would appear.

When he actually did, she felt a moment of surprise. She got that emotion tucked away quickly and watched as Dak Heller attached something to the undercarriage of Gianella's car. It appeared to be a very small device, so she ruled out an explosive.

GPS, she thought.

She watched as the man straightened up, dusted off his slacks, and sauntered away: innocence on parade, an utterly average guy, a nobody.

What an asshole.

Her every instinct screamed, "Kill him!" But she surprised herself and tamped such thoughts down. It would have been easy to kill him the way he'd killed her father—a bullet to the head, the body left on a side street to be found by someone walking a dog or taking out the trash.

Something put those instincts on hold as she realized the killer didn't intend to kill Gianella. At least, not right away. He was after something else, a bigger target perhaps, or... She couldn't imagine what it might be. But she wanted to find out. As long as Dak Heller remained unaware that his own life would soon end, Millie could continue to follow him. For the moment, however, she simply wanted him out of the way.

She waited until he left the area before she stirred. It hadn't taken her long to decide she'd rather follow Gianella than Heller. Besides, she had a plan that, if it worked, would send the killer on his way into the boondocks.

Slipping quietly toward Gianella's car, Millie stretched out on the soiled concrete and illuminated the underside of the vehicle with a small flashlight. She quickly located Heller's GPS device and tugged it loose. The magnetic fastener had remarkable strength which made it easy to install but tricky to dislodge. She replaced his device with one of her own, smiling all the while.

With the killer's GPS in hand, she began looking for a vehicle with an out of state license plate. Alaska or Hawaii would have been nice,

Finland or Azerbaijan would have been ideal, but there were very few non-Georgia plates in the area.

Eventually she found an aging Ford pickup truck which hailed from Missouri. After a quick look around to make sure she was still alone, Millie knelt down and attached Heller's GPS locater to the underside of the truck.

She gave a silent prayer that Heller would continue to track the wrong person all the way to St. Louis or beyond. She knew the subterfuge wouldn't last long; the man wasn't stupid, and he'd know someone was messing with him. It might even be enough to deter him from continuing with his contract. If not, she vowed to keep an eye on Gianella, at least for a few more days. She had found Heller once; she could do it again. And then she'd put him down for good.

Chapter 5

"We've had cloning in the South for years. It's called cousins." – Robin Williams

"Have you ever been down this way?" Lenny asked glancing at their rural, south Alabama surroundings.

"Sure." Sam tapped the front of her lightweight top, which displayed Auburn's Tiger mascot. "My family has always been Auburn football fans." She cleared her throat before voicing a hearty, "War Eagle!"

"I've never understood the eagle thing," he said. "Y'all have two mascots?"

She gave him a look of mild scorn. "You say you're a Southerner, and you don't know the difference between a mascot and a war cry?"

"Actually, I'm more into soccer than football. Getting knocked on my ass never appealed to me."

"Hm."

"What?"

"It's weird, that's all. C'mon, Lenny! Football is a Southern institution."

"Well, yeah," he conceded. "Okay, so, the eagle thing?"

"According to my Daddy," she began, "it started in the 1890s. Auburn was playing their first ever game against the University of Georgia. Daddy says folks called it Athens back then instead of Georgia. I guess Auburn and Clemson stuck with their geographic names. Anyway, late in the game an eagle began to circle the football field, and as it did, the Auburn fans pointed at it and started shouting 'War Eagle.' And just like that the Tigers marched down the field and scored the winning touchdown. Auburn fans have been greeting each other that way ever since."

"What happened to the bird?"

"The eagle?"

"Yeah."

"I have no idea."

He grinned and said, "Someone probably stuffed it."

She punched his shoulder, but not hard. Just enough to let him know where she stood on the issue. "Anyway," she went on, "Auburn's not real far from Camp Hill." She rattled her printed instruction sheet at him. "Just keep going the way we're headed. I'll tell you when you need to make a turn."

Suddenly, the steering wheel wrenched sideways and left him barely hanging on.

Sam yelled something—not words, not even a curse. He didn't pay much attention since his focus was on the route the car had suddenly decided to take. It veered across the oncoming lane, headed in a direction that didn't include pavement.

Somehow, he kept most of the car from going into a deep ditch which ran beside the road. His leg cramped from the pressure he'd put on the brake pedal. Sam had both arms extended, her hands all but embedded in the dashboard. But at last they came to a stop.

"What the hell, Lenny? You tryin' to kill us?"

"No! Lord, no. We must've had a blow-out. I'll go look."

"Hang on," she said as she checked to make sure Ebby hadn't been hurt. "I'm comin' too." She told the dog to stay, then pushed her door open.

The car had a distinct lean. He suspected both wheels on his side were in or dangling over the roadside drainage channel, so he climbed over the Toyota's console and got out on Sam's side.

Walking quickly to the front of the car, they both surveyed the situation. The left front tire was mangled, and both it and the rear wheel were, as he feared, hovered over the ditch. The undercarriage was resting on the lightly graveled shoulder of the road. The car looked ready to slide down into the murky sludge at the bottom of the trench.

"Not much room for a jack, is there?" Sam's words were more statement than question. She had her mouth twisted to one side, and while he couldn't help but be concerned about the teetering automobile they'd been riding in, he also couldn't help but notice how cute she looked, even when clearly worried.

He gazed down at the bottom of the ditch and tried to guess how deep the muddy water might be. Sam stood beside him.

"You thinkin' what I'm thinking?" she asked.

He shrugged.

She exhaled. "Should we be worried about snakes and gators?"

"Probably," he said.

"Then you can't go down into that ditch and try to set up a tire jack."

"You're right. God only knows what's crawling or swimming around down in that muck. I'm just not sure what other choices we have." He tried not to look overly concerned and smiled at her. "How far is it to Camp Hill?"

She went back to the car's open door, reached in and grabbed her paperwork, then studied it briefly. "I think we're about halfway between La Fayette and Camp Hill. So, eight miles, give or take."

It wasn't what he was hoping to hear.

"Have you got Triple A?" she asked.

"I can't even afford single A."

She looked at him sideways. "Is that even a thing?"

"Nah. Just me being stupid. Looks like we'll have to hoof it. I sure hope we can find somebody with a tow truck."

"Or a tractor," she said. "There's a good bit of farm land around here. Maybe somebody could at least drag the car out far enough for us to use a jack." She gave him a sidelong look. "You do have a spare, doncha?"

"Of course!" he said, though he wasn't sure there was any air in it.

He looked up at the rumble of an approaching vehicle. The sound came from a mud-crusted pickup truck with a missing headlight and a fully stocked gunrack. It pulled to a stop on the other side of the road amid a cloud of gray exhaust fumes.

Two men clambered out. At least, he thought they were men. Their DNA most likely leaned toward Neanderthals, if not lowland gorillas.

~*~

Dak Heller relaxed as he casually tracked Leonardo Gianella's crappy little Toyota via the screen of his small laptop. The car appeared as a flashing dot which maneuvered through various Atlanta streets on the digital map. Dak had no intention of letting himself be spotted, so he stayed a block or two behind his quarry. When the dot merged with traffic headed north on I-75, Dak sped up a little so the car wouldn't go beyond the range of his tracking device. He'd been told distance didn't matter; GPS would pinpoint the car anywhere in the world. Lacking technical savvy, he wasn't so sure.

Gianella couldn't possibly know that anyone was following him, so Dak maintained a leisurely pursuit. When Gianella exited the Interstate, Dak felt a moment of trepidation, but it quickly subsided when he realized Gianella was merely stopping for gas. Unfortunately, he'd chosen to stop at Plucky's, one in a chain of huge gas station/discount stores. Acres of parking and a hundred gas pumps surrounded an enormous, single-story retail business which marketed clothing, grilled meat, recreational furniture, and everything in between.

Dak circled the pumps but didn't see Gianella's car and assumed he had parked and gone inside for food or to avail himself of the enormous restroom facilities. A normally patient man, Dak chose to get some food to go, fill his gas tank, and resume tracking Gianella whenever he continued on his way.

Though he had no idea where Gianella intended to go, Dak remained committed to following him, hopefully straight to the camper his employers were so eager to get their hands on. Where Gianella's dead aunt had left it parked didn't matter. All Dak wanted from her nephew was the location—and the keys.

According to his GPS tracker, Gianella soon

went back on the road. So did Dak, and neither of them stopped until dusk when Dak's target pulled off the highway just south of Nashville, Tennessee and drove into the parking lot of a roadside motel.

Dak zipped into the same lot a minute or two later and began looking for the Toyota. He found two that were similar to Gianella's, but neither was a match. Counting on his little PC screen, he drove slowly through the lot until he reached a pickup truck at which point the beeper on his laptop reached a crescendo. Dak shut it off and pulled in one space away from the truck.

There were no other cars nearby and no Toyotas within fifty feet of it, maybe more. Either the GPS was defective, or someone had removed it from Gianella's car and attached it to the damn truck.

Dak squinted at the truck while his ears heated up, and his pulse quickened. His grip on the steering wheel grew painfully tight, and he allowed himself a growl which ended in a frustrated groan.

What the hell is going on?

Who's messing with me?

Has my mysterious employer hired someone else? Has my quest *suddenly become a* competition?

Gianella couldn't have been aware of the tracker; he had no idea anyone was following him. He couldn't have been the one to move it. The notion that someone had followed Dak put him thoroughly on edge.

Veils

What's the point? To make me work faster? Or is it something more sinister? Do they intend to follow me to the target and then kill me to save themselves the money they owe me?

Dak pounded on the steering wheel with both hands. He was tempted to call the number he'd been given to report when he'd finished the job and ask what was going on, but he knew it would invalidate his contract. It would certainly end his working relationship, and would likely result in his own death. Terminations in his line of work were permanent. Rules could never be broken. Questions beyond the scope of an assignment were forbidden.

A single thought penetrated his rage and froze him in place. *Are they watching me now? Have I been followed here? Would I even hear the gunshot that kills me?*

He dropped sideways, below the windows of his car, and pulled a Glock 9mm from beneath the seat. Rolling onto his back, he looked up, expecting at any moment to see whoever had been sent to put a bullet in his head.

When no one showed up immediately, he raised his leg and used his toes to adjust the rearview mirror over the dash so he could see if anyone approached his car from behind. He held his breath when a tall, slender man approached. His hands slippery with sweat, Dak ignored the temptation to wipe them on his slacks; the shooter was too close; there was no time.

At any moment the man by the truck would

turn on him, a weapon at the ready. Dak had to be ready himself. Instead of waiting for the man to make the first move, Dak raised the Glock in both hands and sighted on the back of the man's head. Any aggressive move—*any quick movement at all*—would cause Dak to shoot.

But the man never turned. He seemed focused on unlocking the cab of his truck. Once open, he extracted a large, wheeled suitcase which he set on the ground and then hauled toward the motel office.

Dak exhaled, surprised to realize he'd been holding his breath. His hands still shook.

Unless the driver of the truck was merely a decoy, the danger had passed. Still, he was reluctant to sit up enough to look out the window and survey the area. A shooter might still be waiting, might still be set to kill him.

An intense hour passed. During that time, Dak heard two cars enter the lot. Children's voices marked the travelers as innocents.

Another hour passed. Dak had to pee. Edging up on one elbow, he looked out the passenger side window. Not a soul in sight.

Still breathing heavily, Dak slid behind the wheel, cranked the engine, slipped the car in gear, and drove away. Ignoring traffic signs, lights, and arrows painted on the asphalt, he raced off into the night in search of safety. He'd find a place to hole up somewhere. Whoever was after him wouldn't know where he was.

Unless….

He jammed on the brakes, screeched to a halt on the shoulder of the road, and shut the engine off. A quick search of the glove box produced a small, but very bright flashlight.

Dak rolled out of the car and lay flat on the ground. The light proved more than adequate as he searched for a GPS tracker beneath his own vehicle. When he failed to find one, he searched his trunk and the engine compartment. He looked under the seats in front and back. He examined every possible hiding place.

And came up empty.

Ignoring any late-night traffic, he relieved himself on the side of the road.

Clearly, the time had come to re-evaluate his circumstances. It would begin with Gianella, assuming he could find him. That, he figured, shouldn't be too hard. After all, he had the guy's address. And in the process of tracking Gianella down, he hoped to determine just who was playing games with him.

He didn't like games. At all.

Chapter 6

"Nothing makes us more vulnerable than loneliness,
except greed." – Thomas Harris

Frustrated and angry at herself for allowing something to get in the way of her mission, Millie spent much of the night awake. In her car. Again. In order to stretch her soon-to-be-meager funds, she limited how often she stayed in motels. Meals were likewise skimped on, if not skipped altogether. Doing her laundry was a necessity, but she usually tackled it in the washroom of a rest area beside an Interstate highway, the sort of place she often sought for a night in her car. Wet clothes dried fairly quickly hanging from a wire stretched above the back seat, especially when the windows were rolled down and the car was moving. It was summertime after all.

Rest areas weren't the safest places to spend the night, so she slept with a loaded Glock 21 handy.

She had practiced enough to be comfortable with the weapon. If only she could draw a bead on Dak Heller's head; she'd put an end to both her mission and him. The world would instantly become a better place.

She couldn't help but wonder where he was. She could find the Gianella kid easily, or at least his car, since she installed the tracker on it. Her cell phone's locater app told her exactly where he was. She also had his address, so if he wasn't in the car, he would most likely be at home or at work, assuming he had a job.

Pinpointing Heller's whereabouts was more involved but ultimately much easier. It required a phone call to her brother, Tyrone.

Millie speed-dialed his number and blurted out, "Where is he?" the moment he answered. She stared at her phone and waited for an answer.

"Aw, geez," said her brother. "This isn't right, and you know it."

"Please don't start that crap again, Ty. Not now. I'm not— I don't want to go there."

"You've gotta get over your obsession with this Heller clown."

Millie forced herself to relax her grip on the phone. *How many times must we have this stupid conversation?* "He killed Dad, remember?"

"*Maybe* he killed Dad," Tyrone said. "We really don't know that for sure."

"*Seriously?* You think maybe he just happened to wander along after someone else committed the murder and then decided to help himself to Dad's fancy watch?"

"The cops—"

"The cops haven't done shit," Millie said, making no effort to disguise her disgust. "Somebody higher up, some bigwig somewhere, told them to shut the investigation down."

"Listen—"

"Please, Ty, just tell me where he is right now." She pictured him shaking his head. All he had to do was look at the program on their father's phone which constantly tracked the whereabouts of the watch. No wonder it had cost so damned much.

"All you've got is a name, Mills. That's it. And I don't even know how you conned a cop into giving it to you."

"We've gone over this," she said. "I tracked the guy who stole dad's watch, and I got a picture of him."

"Which you shared with some cop—"

"He's a detective."

"—whatever. And out of the goodness of his heart he ran the picture through some kinda facial recognition program, came up with a name, and gave it to you."

"Yeah, more or less. So?"

"Just what did you give him?"

"That's none of your damned business! I got the name. That's what's important."

"Dad would be so proud."

She pictured him doing a tsk-tsk. "Will you just tell me where he is? Please?" On top of everything else, she was getting a headache. She hated arguing.

"Hang on," he said. "Gimme a sec."

Though he was only gone a few moments, Millie's patience reached the boiling point. It would've been so much easier if he'd just given her their father's phone. Instead, he insisted on keeping it, claiming it was the only way he could be sure she'd stay in touch.

"He's a little bit south of Nashville," Ty said.

"Is he moving?"

"Nah."

She did a quick, mental calculation. It would take Heller a good four hours to drive back to Atlanta, unless he got stuck in Chattanooga. That thought made her smile. No one deserved to get stuck on the Interstate in Chattanooga. Except maybe Dak Heller. One could always hope.

"Thanks, Ty," she said, shunting her anger and impatience aside. "I didn't mean to get testy."

"It's okay; I'm used to it. But seriously, you need to see somebody about this obsession of yours."

"Oh, I intend to," she assured him just before she disconnected. "I'm going to see Dak Heller. Dead."

~*~

Samantha stood slightly behind Lenny as the two big men exited their pickup truck and sauntered forward. She stayed there and rooted around in her purse until she found the little spray can Myra had given her. She palmed the sprayer and watched as the two men approached. They left the truck's engine running and a loud country tune blaring on the radio. It took a moment before she recognized it and groaned.

"It's 'Hicktown,'" she said, tugging at Lenny's sleeve.

He nodded. "No shit."

"I meant the music. The song. It's called 'Hicktown.'"

"Of course, it is," he said, his voice constricted, whispery.

The taller of the two new arrivals, dressed in grey overalls and sporting a beard that reached his chest, called to them. "Y'all okay? Looks like you got yourselves in a bit of a fix."

"We're cool," Lenny said. "Tow truck's on the way."

"Really?" The bearded man's companion looked skeptical. "From where, 'zackly?"

Lenny waved his arm toward their destination. "Oh, you know, Camp Hill. It's just down the road."

The two men looked at each other and laughed. The bearded one got himself under control first. "There aren't any tow trucks in Camp Hill. I 'spect the closest one's in Auburn. There's several down that way."

"I— I wasn't sure," stammered Lenny. "I just made the phone call, y'know and— And they told us to wait here while they sent somebody."

"How d'ya know they didn't send *us*?" the

second man asked.

"Well…" began Lenny, "They, uh." He stopped and pointed at their vehicle. "That's the wrong kinda truck."

"And who's that pretty young thing hidin' behind yer back?" asked the bearded man's companion.

"That's my, uhm, physical trainer." Lenny turned toward her just briefly, then looked back at the two big men. "She also teaches karate and y'know… self-defense."

"And *that's* why she's hidin' behind ya?"

With that, Sam stepped up next to Lenny. Hoping to appear unintimidated, she warned the approaching strangers. "Just so you know, we've got a guard dog in the car. The window's down, and if I call her, she knows what to do."

"'A guard dog,' she says. You hear that?" the bearded man asked.

"I can see the dog," the second man said. "But it don't look all that mean to me, Olin. Shoot, my dogs'd be eatin' their way outta the car to git aholt of anybody messin' with me."

The conversation did nothing to slow the two men down as they closed the distance between the truck and the car.

"Easy, girl," Sam said, pretending to calm Ebby who was furiously wagging her tail.

"We just stopped to offer a little roadside assistance," Olin said, stroking his beard. He paused beside the car for a better look through the back window. "Whoa, whoa, whoa! That's Miz Gee-uh-nelly's dog, Ebenezer. I'd recognize her anywhere."

"Yer kiddin," said his partner.

"I wish." Olin turned his attention back to Sam and Lenny. He looked deeply suspicious. "What are you doing with Miz G's dog? Where is she? What's going on?"

"You *knew* Edna Gianella?" Lenny said, shock in his voice.

Sam cleared her throat and explained. "You're right; that's Ebby. Uh, Ebenezer. Mrs. Gianella passed away, and now Ebby lives with me."

"And him?" Olin aimed a thumb at Lenny.

"He didn't want the dog," she said.

"Hey!" bristled Lenny. "That's not exactly—"

"Doesn't matter," Olin said, twisting back toward the dog. "Can you let her out? It's not like there's a whole lot of traffic around here. She won't get run over."

"Sure," Sam said. She opened the car door

and let Ebby squirm out. The dog immediately went to the big, bearded man, tail flapping like a windshield wiper. Sam felt a small wave of relief but hung onto Myra's pepper spray just in case.

Olin knelt down to receive the dog's greeting. He didn't flinch or back away when Ebby slurped his face.

"How did you know my aunt?" Lenny asked.

"Your *aunt?* Well, that answers one question. Miz Gianella helped me out, see? It was a while ago, but I never forgot. Sent her a snapshot of myself in front of the class and a check once the dust settled. Best investment I ever made."

Lenny looked at Sam, totally confused. He held his hands out, palms up, and shrugged. "I don't understand. I had no idea she ran some sort of business."

Olin stood up, brushed the dog hair from his overalls, and squinted at Lenny. "If you really are her nephew—"

"He's her *only* living relative," interjected Sam.

"—how come you don't know what she did for a living?"

"Wait. You're blaming *me* because of something *she* didn't tell me about?" Lenny shook his head. "On what planet does that make sense? And, for that matter, what gives you the right to even ask me a question like that?"

"Okay, sorry. You've got a point. It was… illogical. Anyway, she definitely had a business; but it wasn't the sort of thing just anyone could do. It sure as hell wasn't a franchise!"

"Actually," Lenny said, "we're trying to figure some of that out. Aunt Edna had a post office box in Camp Hill. We're hoping there'll be something in there to point us in the right direction."

"Or," Sam said, "maybe somebody who works there could give us a clue." She gave him a disarming smile. "Or maybe you could."

While Olin considered Sam's remark, Lenny continued. "You said the money you gave her was an investment. So, you bought stocks or bonds? Insurance?"

"Nah. Nothin' like that. She sorta got me a job."

"She ran an employment agency?" Sam asked.

"No. It's what she did that made it possible for me to get a job," Olin said.

Lenny made a face. "She *trained* you in something?"

Olin shook his head. "What she does— Well, what she did, is hard to explain, and to be honest, I don't know how she pulled it off. She did something to me; she made it so job interviewers would see me for what I can do, and not just for what I look like."

Olin's friend then chimed in. "He looks like a redneck, don't he? Me, too, for that matter, but that's what I am, and proud of it. Olin here, he's different."

"How so?" asked Sam.

"He teaches math."

Lenny appeared more than doubtful. "In a cornfield?"

"At Auburn University," Olin said. "I do mostly freshman algebra, but now that I've finally got my PhD, I'm scheduled to do a class in theoretical physics next term."

Lenny burst out laughing until Sam caught him in the ribs with her elbow.

"That's what I mean," Olin said. "You can't see past my beard or my clothes. You made an assumption based solely on my appearance."

"Which suggests that Aunt Edna's treatment, or whatever it was, has worn off," Lenny said.

Olin's companion tugged his sleeve. "C'mon. Let's go. These two don't need or want our help." He nodded toward Lenny. 'Specially that yahoo."

"Wait!" Sam exclaimed. "We do need your help. Is there any way you could pull the car back onto the pavement?" She looked back down at the ditch. "We can't get a jack under it to change the tire."

Olin shrugged. "I s'pose we could do that."

"Hang on a sec," Lenny said. "Lemme make sure the spare's okay."

Sam accompanied Lenny and watched while he opened the trunk and rooted through a collection of junk to get to the hatch covering his spare tire. Pulling it open, he exhaled in disgust.

"What's the matter now?" she asked.

"Let's put it this way," he said. "The spare is in way better shape than the tire that blew out, but it's got roughly the same amount of air inside."

Chapter 7

"The wussiest thing a guy can do is drive a clean truck.
Dents, scratches, and mud—that's manly." – Blake Shelton

Dak Heller motored back to Atlanta without incident, and though he'd spent much of the driving time trying to plan his next move, he had few options. Without the tracker in place on Gianella's car, he had no idea where the man had gone. Nor had he figured out who could have moved it and sent him so far off course. All he had to go on was Gianella's home address. According to the dead woman's lawyer, Gianella was out of work, so he could play around as long as his money held out, which Dak surmised, probably wouldn't take long.

After stopping for a brief rest and a bite to eat, the hired gun made his way to the high-rise condominium where Gianella lived. Though clearly an upper-class address, there was no doorman to slow him down. Getting into the locked building required a bit of acting, which he managed by feigning a phone conversation while following a resident into the building.

Breaking into Gianella's condo proved no more difficult than it had when he snuck into a dozen other places illegally. He hoped the guy was home. If so, he intended to extract whatever information he had on the old lady's camper. Unfortunately, Gianella wasn't there.

Dak expected to find the usual semi-messy domain of a single twenty-something. That's not what he found. Gianella's home was actually fairly neat. The only thing that looked out of place was a stack of flat cardboard boxes. One box sat open on the living room floor; he found a second one in what appeared to be the unit's master bedroom. The boxes were fairly full. But if Gianella planned to move, he had a good way to go before he finished.

All in all, Gianella's moving came as a good sign. It suggested one of two possibilities: either he was moving up in the world, or he could no longer afford the place he had. If he was moving up, it likely meant he had inherited something valuable that formerly belonged to his dead aunt, even though the attorney claimed otherwise. On the other hand, Gianella could just be looking for a cheaper place since he'd lost his job. Dak hoped it was the former rather than the latter since it suggested a better outcome for his current mission.

Slipping on a pair of latex gloves, Dak began picking through Gianella's belongings, starting with the items stashed in the cardboard packing boxes. When those ran out, he searched cabinet shelves, drawers, and closets. Still finding nothing, he removed wall decorations to look for hidden documents. When that turned up nothing, he checked the freezer and toilet tanks to see if anything had been wrapped in plastic and hidden there.

The search, which he considered thorough, turned up nothing of value—no clues about a camper or anything which suggested Gianella even knew the dead woman. In fact, the search confirmed what the lawyer had told him: Gianella had no connection to the woman save a link on their family tree.

As he took one last look around the condo, he saw a notepad on the floor. He would have ignored it except that something had been scribbled on it. The handwriting was even worse than Dak's own, but he finally deciphered it.

The message read: "P.O. Box 204, Camp Hill, AL"

Dak tore the note from the pad and stuffed it in his pocket as he made his way out.

~*~

Sitting in the back of Olin's pickup truck with Ebby, Lenny tried not to be annoyed. He had little success. At least he had fresh air, though it did nothing to lower the temperature. The sun bore down on south Alabama relentlessly.

While Lenny, the dog, and the flat spare tire bounced around in the bed of the truck, Sam sat between the two rednecks up front. The only price she had to pay was listening to the country music booming from the radio, a punishment he, too, had to endure. A window in the back of the cab allowed the hillbilly fare to escape, and that only darkened his mood.

When directed to climb into the back of the truck, he had asked if there were any laws against traveling that way.

"Not here in the Yellowhammer state," Olin said. "As long as you're over fifteen, you're free to ride back there."

"*Yellowhammer?*"

"It's the state bird." Olin looked impatient. "You gettin' in or not? You can always walk. We'll drop your girlfriend off at the post office. If you hurry, you can get there before it closes."

Lenny abandoned caution at that point and climbed up and into the truck bed. Ebby greeted him with a single sniff, then occupied herself watching for intruders, free roaming cattle, and anything else bark-worthy that might suddenly appear. Lenny settled as far from the tailgate as he could get and faced toward the rear.

According to Olin, the nearest tire repair shop was in Auburn, a good half hour's drive away. Though the big bearded man, who claimed to be a physicist, offered to take them to and from the tire place, Lenny guessed they'd never get to the post office in Camp Hill before it closed. He had no idea if the two men would expect some sort of payment or not, and he prayed Sam wouldn't reveal the deal he'd agreed to with her. He needed *another* partner like he needed another mortgage or a splinter up his butt.

While he pondered the immediate future, he heard Sam singing along with the two country clowns in the truck. That pissed him off even more. If he and Sam had any chance at a future together, she would have to widen her taste in music to include something other than steel guitars, banjos, and vocal twang. If so, he'd be willing to listen to some of Nashville's finest, preferably while drinking some of Kentucky's.

~*~

Samantha had no intention of riding in the truck with the two men. Though she felt better about them, she still didn't feel safe, and when she asked to sit in the back with Lenny and her dog, they insisted she ride up front with them.

"It would be more comfortable," they said, but they didn't say for whom.

At least, she reasoned, the music wasn't bad, and after a short while her favorite tune, Zach Brown's "Chicken Fried," came on. She hummed along until the chorus began at which point both Olin and his pal, JG chimed in. Their voices, surprisingly, weren't bad, and she relaxed enough to sing along with them.

They drove on for a quarter hour or so, went

through a small, nearly deserted town she assumed was Camp Hill, and kept going. She wasn't the least bit familiar with the roads they traveled and kept looking for some indication that they were approaching Auburn. But for all she knew, they could have been heading in the opposite direction.

When the music switched from country rock to something a bit more romantic, JG put his hand on her bare leg.

She pushed it away.

"C'mon now," he said. "Don't be like that."

Wishing she wore overalls like Olin and JG instead of skimpy, cut-off jeans, she tried to make her voice sound stern. "Please keep your hands to yourself."

"Here we are tryin' to do you a good deed, and yer actin' all standoffish?" JG put his hand back on her leg and inched it slowly along her thigh.

"Stop it!" she said.

"And if'n I don't?" He slipped two fingers up inside the hem of her shorts.

Sam whipped out the pepper spray and delivered a quick spritz to his face.

His scream was instant and uncontrolled as he threw himself toward the door of the truck and clawed at his face with both hands.

Too amped up to do much other than shake, she eventually turned toward Olin. "You want some of this, too?"

"Oh, hell no," he said, waving at the persistent mist from the potent spray. "You gotta understand, JG may be a total idiot, but I wouldn't let him hurt you, I swear. In fact... Just... Just hold on, okay?"

He slowed the truck, pulled onto the narrow shoulder of the road, and parked. "I'll be right back," he told her, then got out of the truck and hurried around the front of it to the passenger side and yanked the door open.

Sam fanned the fumes from her face and slid across the seat to the driver side door and got out.

JG was still rocking in his seat, moaning, cursing, and rubbing his eyes.

"Get out," Olin said.

JG squinted at him through red, swollen eyes. "Who, me?"

"Yes, you. Get outta the damn truck!"

"Bu- But why?" he blubbered.

"'Cause you're a total dumbass, and you've embarrassed the hell outta me," Olin said. "Now drag yourself out, before I do it for you."

JG slithered off the seat and out of the truck. He stood on the gravel shoulder but quickly shifted and leaned back against the vehicle. "So, what now?" he asked while continuing to rub his eyes.

"It's not that far from here to your place," Olin said. "You can walk the rest of the way."

"Yer just gonna leave me here? Geez, Olin, I'm damn near blind after what that bitch—"

"Shut up and start walking," Olin said. "I'm tired of hearing you whine. And as for what that young lady did, you deserved it."

Olin held the passenger side door open for Sam to get back in, but she refused. "I'd rather ride in the back with Lenny and my dog. The fumes..." She waved her hand in front of her face again.

"And you expect me to drive with that stink in there?"

"Damn right. You can stick your head out the window. You'll have 'em both wide open anyway. It'll air out faster that way."

He appeared dubious.

"It was your pal who made this happen." She gently rolled the small spray can back and forth in her palm.

JG stood by and alternately groused at them or cursed but made no threatening gestures. Meanwhile, Lenny and the dog made room for her in the back of the truck. Ebby must have liked the residual scent of pepper spray on Sam since she wasted little time in curling up next to her. Lenny didn't say a thing until they got back under way.

"I see you got to test out your pepper spray." He chuckled. "What'd that asshole do to earn it?"

"He touched me when I told him not to," Sam said, her voice flat.

"Good to know," Lenny said. "Really, really good to know."

She stroked Ebby's big head and glanced at Lenny. He wore a grin that rivaled the Cheshire Cat's.

~*~

On the road again, this time more or less in pursuit of Leonard Gianella, Millie stayed far behind. She didn't need to see what he was up to unless it provided an opportunity for her real prey, Dak Heller, to put in an appearance.

Still deeply curious about why the Gianella kid had become a target, she knew she had to concentrate on Heller. Putting him down would not only give her some closure after the murder of her father, but it might save Gianella's life in the process.

She noted with more than a little concern that the young man's car had stopped in the middle of nowhere. It took her a while to reach the spot, but by the time she got there, no one remained.

A quick examination of the car, which was off the road and facing in the wrong direction, revealed the devastated tire. The car trunk was closed, and there were several different sizes of footprints in the dirt and gravel shoulder of the road. She assumed Gianella had either walked away in search of help, or someone had picked him up.

Since she hadn't seen him walking toward her, she assumed he had continued west. She hopped back in her car and continued on her way.

With any luck, she'd see him walking, if not hitchhiking. It would have helped a great deal if she knew his destination.

Alas, she didn't.

And unless he returned to his vehicle, the tracker she'd placed in it was utterly useless.

Chapter 8

"Writers who aren't from rural states in the Midwest or the West often treat such people as if they were the Waltons or the Beverly Hillbillies."–Kent Haruf

Dak Heller listened to his car radio and occasionally grunted a lyric or two, though he was more likely to make up the words instead. These sometimes made him laugh, but only because he considered himself witty. He could not have cared less what anyone else thought.

It shouldn't have been a long drive from Atlanta to Camp Hill, but the scenery bored him and made it seem longer. Traffic was light, so he stayed on the Interstate as far as possible. When he reached Auburn, he headed north. Somewhere—out there in the desolate boondocks of southern Alabama—he would locate the tiny, dying town of Camp Hill.

What a stupid name for a town, he thought. *There isn't a hill in sight anywhere! But then, it is Alabama after all, and that alone explains a lot.*

Veils

He reached the town and spent a few minutes driving around in search of the post office. Small and utterly indistinct, the building sat at the outskirts of a town mainly composed of unoccupied buildings, no traffic lights, and damned few people.

It was mid-afternoon, and the temperature had risen to somewhere between miserable and melt-down. Leaving the comfort of the air conditioner in his car, he strolled to the puny post office and went inside. It was blissfully cool there. A double row of post office boxes adorned one wall which gave him a slight lift. Maybe he'd learn something. He wandered closer and located the box number for the Gianella woman. A quick peek through the glass window revealed a thick stack of envelopes inside.

Turning away, he spotted a lone clerk sitting on a stool behind a counter, reading. He worked up a smile as he approached. Her name tag identified her simply as Olivia. Thin and bored, the aging dark-skinned woman appeared reluctant to acknowledge his presence. Eventually she looked up from whatever had held her attention and said, "Help ya?"

Dak smiled. "I hope so. My name is Leonardo Gianella. My late aunt had a mailbox here." He pointed to the double row of lockboxes.

The clerk fixed him with one clear eye. "Yeah. So?"

"So, I've come to clear it out."

"You got an ID?"

He'd worried someone might ask him for that and had rehearsed an answer. "Actually, no. My wallet was stolen, and—"

"That's too bad. The law says I can't give out someone else's mail."

"Even to a relative?"

"Well, maybe. But you ain't proved to me yer related. Come back when ya can."

Dak thought briefly about shooting the woman, but that would have undoubtedly caused him grief he didn't need. It was bad enough worrying that his employer might have sent someone after him; being tracked by the police and the FBI would further complicate matters.

"What happens if nobody collects her mail?" he asked. "Does it go in a dead letter box somewhere?"

"Ain't called it that for years," the woman said. She cleared her throat. "Today, all that goes to the Mail Recovery Center in Atlanta. Once it gets there I don't know what they do with it. Burn it, prob'ly."

"Thanks," he said. "You've been most helpful."

"Any time." She gave him a look that was part smirk and part frown.

He waved as he left the building then walked back to his car, cranked the engine, and basked in the air conditioning.

Veils

His long shot hadn't paid off, but he wasn't ready to give up hope, especially since he didn't have any other leads. He decided to stay right where he was and keep an eye on the little post office and the smarmy clerk who ruled it. If the Gianella kid showed up, he'd follow him wherever he went.

~*~

Though he had not been involved in Sam's encounter with JG, Lenny felt quite proud of her. JG was considerably larger than Sam but obviously far less resourceful. Also to the good, Olin seemed genuinely sorry for the actions of his buddy and promised to help them get the tire repaired and remounted as a way to make up for it. Lenny eagerly agreed.

True to his word, Olin drove straight to Auburn and stopped at the first opportunity, a place specializing in tires, batteries, and accessories. After taking Ebby for a short walk, he and Sam returned her to the truck and went inside the franchise tire store.

When the attendant got a look at Sam and her shirt, he flashed his class ring and gave her a hearty, "War Eagle! What can I do for you today?"

Lenny explained about the tire, and Sam added that they were a little pressed for time. Her smile provided a sympathy-inducing emphasis, and the attendant summoned a tire mechanic.

"We need to help this young lady," he explained, his smile boulevard wide. Then, looking

79

straight at Sam, he waved to some seats in front of a wall-mounted TV screen. "It shouldn't take long."

Sam popped some kind of gum in her mouth and tried to get interested in a daytime soap opera with Olin. Meanwhile, Lenny checked his wallet. He had a few dollars and a credit card he knew was nearly maxed out. He doubted he could stretch Olin's good will far enough to cover the tire repair.

He touched Sam lightly to get her attention and whispered to her about his financial fears. She nodded but didn't say anything, as if that solved the problem. Lenny continued to worry. *What could the store do? Keep the damned tire?*

A short while later, the attendant announced that the repair was complete. Still dreading the bill, Lenny followed Sam to the counter.

"That'll be twenty-two dollars and twenty-four cents," the attendant said, looking directly at Sam. "We guarantee the repair for ninety days, but just between you and me nobody's ever taken us up on that. At least, not since I've been working here."

Sam looked distressed. "I didn't think it'd be that much. It was just a patch, right?"

The attendant pursed his lips but remained silent.

"I'm on a really, really tight budget," Sam said. "You know, with tuition and books and all. So, anything you can do to... you know... Maybe gimme a little bit of a discount?" She winked, which struck Lenny as a bit over the top, but it seemed to work.

"Tell you what," said the attendant, "since you're a Tiger fan, I'll just mark this up as a warranty claim. But there's just one thing."

"What's that?" Sam asked, flashing a full smile.

He grinned, his eyes roaming from side to side. "Next time you come in, don't bring your boyfriend and his dad." He then scratched through a few lines on the bill, scribbled "Warranty" on it, then turned it around for a signature.

"You are now my official hero," Sam said as she scrawled her name on the document. "And I'd be very pleased to drop by—alone—next time."

When she winked again, Lenny felt a bubble of jealousy but kept his emotions under wraps.

Within an hour, Olin had them back at their disabled car. He chained the vehicle to his truck and pulled it out far enough for Lenny to change the tire.

Olin pulled a rag from the truck's glove box and wiped the sweat from his face and neck. He sniffed the rag, then tossed it in the bed of the truck. After apologizing yet again for JG, he rubbed Ebby's ears, climbed back into his truck, and left.

Lenny checked his watch, then looked at Sam. "Do you have any idea how late post offices stay open?"

She just shook her head.

"Okay, then," he said, "let's find out."

~*~

Millie cruised into Camp Hill without seeing anyone other than one weary looking redneck walking slowly along the road. His disheveled appearance, shabby bib overalls, and crusty work boots kept her from offering him a ride even though he appeared to have been weeping. Once she'd gone past him, she glanced in the rearview mirror. He didn't even look up.

Poor schmuck's probably mourning the loss of his beloved coonhound.

She quickly lost interest in the rural pedestrian and drove on to Camp Hill. Knowing the Gianella kid's car was stuck a few miles away, Millie cruised around the dreary little town to kill some time. But then she spotted a familiar sedan parked near the post office. She squinted at the driver as she rolled by. The shock of recognition hit her a split second later.

It's Heller! The asshole's just sitting there!

She kept moving as her heart rate spiked. *What's he doing here? And where is Gianella?*

The next thought she entertained was a great deal more specific. Where could she find a solid vantage point from which she could draw a bead on Heller and blow his head off?

Her getaway had to be clear. She hadn't seen a cop or a state patrol car since leaving Georgia. That didn't mean they didn't exist or they weren't close by, but Camp Hill seemed all but deserted. She doubted there were any police on the town's payroll.

That would help. It would also help, in case she failed to kill him outright, that he had no idea who she was. He wouldn't be able to assist the authorities if they tried to find her.

It seemed like an absolutely perfect opportunity. She made another pass by the parked car to assure herself that it really was Dak Heller and not some unfortunate look-alike.

It was definitely him, and she had no intention of missing her chance. But she had to be smart about it. Though she hadn't seen anyone else when she made her second pass, she couldn't leave anything to chance.

She parked her car out of sight. Lacking a screwdriver with which to remove her license tag, she dug around in the back seat until she found an old towel. This she carefully wrapped around her license plate, tucking the edges in firmly. It was far from permanent, and might even draw attention, but it would have to do.

She got back behind the wheel, continued on around the block, and pulled to a stop directly opposite his car. He paid no attention to her as she rolled down her window. She tried to force herself to be calm, but failed. Taking a deep breath instead, she took aim, and fired.

The single round shattered the driver side window of his car, and he jerked sideways.

A hit!

And hopefully, she thought, a kill. If not, she'd ignore her rapidly beating heart and the ringing in her ears, move a little closer, and finish the job. But as she opened her car door for the final assault, a tall, slender black woman came hurrying out of the post office. Her attention was clearly rivetted on Heller who remained motionless and slumped sideways.

She must've heard the shot, damn it.

Millie pulled her door shut and hit the gas, praying the sole witness hadn't gotten a good look at her.

~*~

Sam hugged Ebby who had endured their brief separation in the truck while Lenny's tire was repaired. She kept her arm around the dog all during the drive back to Lenny's car. With the reinflated spare finally mounted, and their goodbyes said to Olin, they were able to proceed to Camp Hill.

"What time is it?" Lenny asked. "I'm worried we won't get to the post office before they close."

"A little before five, so we'd better get goin'."

Which they did, rolling into Camp Hill with two minutes to spare. They found the post office with little trouble since the town was so small. But they noted some commotion outside the building. A pair of state troopers were talking on their phones, and a handful of people had gathered around a tall, black woman wearing a post office uniform.

"Wonder what that's all about," Lenny said.

Sam shrugged, but it was obvious they wouldn't be getting inside the post office anytime soon. They parked the car in a rare spot of shade and left Ebby in it with the windows down. The sad-eyed dog watched them approach the small crowd.

"What's going on?" Sam asked a heavy-set woman who had been talking to the police.

"Somebody done got shot. Right here!"

Sam and Lenny looked around, but neither could see any signs of violence. "Here?" Sam asked.

"Yeah! Some Eye-talian guy, or maybe he could've bin Eye-raynian. Don't matter. He was in his car and somebody shot him."

"Is he all right?" Lenny asked.

"S'pose so," the woman said. "He drove off before the cops came. I heard he was bleedin' sumpthin awful. All down his face." She then pointed to a tall woman in postal service clothing. "Livie saw it all. Well, maybe not everything. She came runnin' when she heard the gun go off. She checked on the fella in the car and called for help."

"And then the guy drove away?" Lenny snapped his fingers. "Just like that?"

"Uh, no, not right off. Livie thought he was dead when she got to him, but he was just knocked out. He looked bad though, real bad. So much blood. Blood all over him, Livie said." The woman shook her head. "We don't go 'round shootin' folks here in

Camp Hill. No sir, we don't."

Sam and Lenny watched as the state patrolmen got in their cars and left. Two older gents ambled toward Livie and accompanied her away from the scene. The woman Sam and Lenny had been talking to joined the men walking with the postal worker.

"Looks like we got here too late after all," Lenny said.

Sam felt despondent. "Now what're we gonna do?"

"Unless you wanna drive all the way back to Atlanta, we're gonna need to find a place to spend the night."

Sam frowned. "*Together?*"

"You got a better idea?"

Chapter 9

*"Thus, the metric system did not really catch on in the
States, unless you count the increasing popularity of the
nine-millimeter bullet." –Dave Barry*

The woman's words rolled over and over in
Dak's mind: "You damn lucky, you know that? If that
bullet had gone an inch or so further away from the
windshield, you'd be dead. Stone dead."

Drowsing in his car while listening to the
radio, he hadn't seen anyone. Hadn't seen a car or a
truck, no one even walking a dog. Nobody. He'd
never been so bored. *No wonder I couldn't stay
awake. And then somebody comes by and shoots me?
Geez!*

His head throbbed, and blood leaked down
his face from a gash the bullet had carved just above
his thick eyebrows. He'd taken a quick look at
himself in the rearview mirror, but the face that
peered back couldn't have been his. *Shouldn't* have
been his.

The woman from the post office had leaned into his car, and hers was the first face he saw when he regained consciousness.

"I called for help," she said. "But I don't know how long it'll be before anybody gets here."

"That's okay," he said. "I'll be fine. I need... I just need to get my shit together." He swiped at the blood dripping from the end of his nose.

"It don't have nuthin' to do with getting your shit together, son. You need a doctor! Like I said; you damn lucky to be alive. A doctor can help you stay that way."

"I can't stick around here," he said. "The co— I mean, the *shooter* might come back."

"What the hell did you do to make somebody wanna shoot ya?"

"I haven't got a clue." But he felt fairly certain he knew who was responsible. He just didn't want to believe it. He had to remain anonymous, and there was only one possible explanation: his employer wanted him dead.

"All the same," said the woman, "you need to relax. Stay right here. The popo gonna come soon enough, and they'll wanna talk to you."

Dak pretended to be interested in the time. He glanced at his watch and mumbled something about needing to be somewhere.

"Well, leastwise wipe the blood off your face. Anybody sees you the way you are, you'll scare the crap outta them. You hear me?"

"I do," he said, then stripped off his blood-stained golf shirt. He balled it up and wiped off his face as best he could while avoiding the open wound in his forehead. *I'm gonna need one helluva band-aid. What I don't need is cops.*

"I've gotta go," he said.

"Don't be stupid, son. You need to wait!"

"Sorry. Can't."

He drove off without looking back.

"Here's the situation," Lenny said as he and Sam sat in the car outside the post office in Camp Hill. "We can't get inside until tomorrow. So, we either drive all the way back to Atlanta, and then turn around and drive all the way back here, or we find a place to spend the night."

Sam swallowed and put her arm around the dog. "Can't say I like either option."

"Besides," Lenny said, "I don't think I can afford the gas for a round trip to Atlanta, and unless we find a really cheap motel, I might not be able to afford that, either."

"So, what're you suggesting? We sleep in the car?"

Lenny clamped his jaws together. It wasn't a great solution, but they were young; it wouldn't kill them. "Well, yeah. I suppose that's an option."

Sam remained silent for what felt like an awfully long time. "It's just...."

"What? Are you still worried I'll try something stupid? I'm not like that moron, JG, or JP, whatever his initials were. I'd *never* try anything like that. I promise!"

She crossed her arms. "I'm not spending the night in a car. Not this one, anyway. Do the seats even recline?"

"Sort of," he said. "They go back part way."

Sam shook her head. "I've got a few dollars tucked away. It's my emergency fund. I might be able to pay for a room somewhere. That'd take care of me and Ebby, anyway."

"Seriously? You expect me to sleep in the car while you and the dog sleep in a bed? How's that fair? If I'm willing to share whatever's in my aunt's safe deposit box, you ought to be willing to kick something, too. So far, I've paid for everything."

"Like what, the tire repair?"

"How 'bout the gas we used just to get here? That's worth something. Right?"

"I suppose," she said, crossing her arms on her chest. "Okay. *If* we can find a place cheap enough, and *if* they'll allow us to keep Ebby in the room, then I'll pay for it."

Lenny gave a sigh of relief. "Thanks."

"But," she added, "you'll have to figure out

how to pay for dinner."

Lenny scanned the nearly deserted town. "Around here?"

She shrugged. "Anything in Auburn will cost more than some place out here in the sticks."

"I remember seeing a little place when we drove back out here in Olin's truck."

"Do you also remember how to get there?"

"Shouldn't be too hard. There's only one road between here and Auburn."

Twenty minutes later they pulled into the Cotton Gin Inn, a hotel that might have enjoyed its heyday in the 19th century. Just across the road stood a small, shabby building that once housed a gas station. An old Gulf Oil sign lay in the weeds nearby, the orange and blue logo nearly rusted into oblivion. The current occupant advertised fresh barbecue which they smelled when they got out of the car.

Sam gave the barbecue place a skeptical look, but Lenny grinned. "Two birds, one stone!"

"This will have to do, I guess," Sam said, popping a gum bubble. She flipped the little canister of pepper spray up and down in her hand. "Just so you know, I'm sleeping with this under my pillow."

~*~

Though eager to put as much distance as possible between herself and Heller's corpse, assuming he was well and truly dead, Millie stopped long enough to unwrap the towel she'd used to cover her license tag. She tossed it into the back seat with her laundry and sped toward the university town of Auburn, Alabama.

Never a college sports fan, she was unfamiliar with the school that bore the town's name. She knew that schools usually held their football games in the fall, but she'd never been to one, or even watched an entire game on TV, despite her brother's crazy love for the sport. He followed his alma mater's games as if his life goals were somehow coupled with the win/loss record of Bemidji State University.

"Oh, yeah. Go Beavers," she muttered. Try as she might, she would never fully understand Tyrone.

On the other hand, Ty probably wouldn't have been surprised to hear that Auburn University would be conducting something called the A-Day game, a spring football match composed entirely of Auburn players. That didn't make much sense to her, but it quickly became obvious that the Auburn faithful were keen on it. They'd come to town in droves. There wasn't a hotel or motel room available anywhere near the school. The parking lot at the stadium was crowded with campers, grills, and fans eager to watch the totally pointless game.

A sympathetic motel clerk said she'd be unlikely to find a place to stay anywhere close to Interstate 85, which ran just south of town.

It seemed like a good time to find another Interstate rest area.

Veils

~*~

The lobby of the urgent care facility in Auburn was empty when Dak arrived. He entered the building, still holding his heavily bloodstained golf shirt against his forehead. The trip from Camp Hill had been miserable, but blessedly short. His ability to drive had definitely suffered. Between the pain in his head, on-again/off-again dizziness, and a desperate need to find a hiding place, it was all he could do to avoid panic and not veer into oncoming traffic.

He approached a small table under a "Check In" sign to get some help. Previous visitors had listed their names and arrival time on a sheet of paper attached to a clipboard. Dak dripped blood on it when he leaned over to add his name. A quick glance at the watch he'd liberated from one of his kills provided the time: half-past five.

Jumbled thoughts careened from one side of his skull to the other. *Is there anyone here who can help me? Would they recognize my injury as a gunshot wound, or will they fall for my story about running into something? Would the cops find out I was there? Would my employer? Have I just dripped DNA on the damned sign-in sheet?*

"Hello," said a cheery voice. It came from a woman in nurse garb. "How can we help— Oh, my!"

Dak didn't say a word.

"Come right this way," the nurse said. "We need to take a look at your forehead."

She took his arm and walked him through a doorway to a treatment room. "How're you feeling?" she asked as he leaned against a gurney.

"Not great," he mumbled. "A little dizzy."

She pulled his hand and the bloody shirt from his forehead. "What in the world happened?"

"It was stupid. *I'm stupid*," he said. "I walked behind a truck with lumber sticking out the back. I was on my cell phone and wasn't paying attention. I grazed my forehead on a board."

The nurse appeared skeptical, but remained silent as she examined the wound. "A board you say? Like a two-by-four?"

"I dunno." He didn't like her suspicion. "It was sharp. Hard. Hurt like hell."

"You said you feel dizzy?"

"Yeah."

She checked his pulse and blood pressure. "You're sure that's how this happened? You scraped your head on a piece of wood?"

He nodded and adjusted his grip on the gurney in hopes the room would spin a little less.

"I don't think a bandage is going to do you much good," she said. "You need to see a doctor. You definitely need stitches; it's a pretty deep gash. It looks more like..." She paused, pursed her lips, blotted up more blood, and took another look. "I don't know. A bullet wound?"

She took a deep breath and whispered, "Did someone *shoot* you?"

"I— What? No! 'Course not. I already told you—" Dak closed his eyes. "I just banged my skull. I swear." He wanted to shake his head but knew it would hurt too much. "Can't you do the stitches?"

"I can try, but with foreheads there's not a lot of extra skin to work with. You really ought to see a plastic surgeon. There's an excellent one in Opelika, only a few miles away. But I don't think you need to be driving. I can get an ambulance or—"

"No, please. Just do your best. If you can't stitch it, then slap a bandage on it, anything to tide me over until I can get to a hospital."

"Seriously. You need to see a specialist. And even then, you're likely to have a pretty nasty scar."

Dak shrugged. "It's no big deal. Scars I can live with."

"If this really is a gunshot wound," she said, "I'm required by law to report it to the authorities. So, be honest with me. Did someone shoot you?"

"No! I swear."

Her eyes suddenly went wide. "Did you shoot yourself? That happens from time to time. It's nothing to be ashamed of. You don't want to put off treatment just because—"

"I already told you what happened. I don't care if you believe me or not. Now, if you're not going to help me, I'm leaving. Before I bleed out."

"Relax," she said. "Let me clean it up. If I can stitch it, I will. But honestly—"

"I know. I know. See a specialist. I will. First thing tomorrow. Geez. All I want now is to find a place to spend the night."

"Forget about finding a room in town for this evening," she said. "Everything's full 'cause of the A-Day game tomorrow. Your best bet is to head north. There's a motel up that way that'll probably have rooms left. It's not pretty, but it's cheap, and it'd beat sleeping in your car."

After she applied antiseptic, stitches, and a bandage, Dak paid her and left. He was too rattled to give much thought to accommodations and took her advice. A fairly short drive back the way he'd come ended when he saw a sign for a shabby motel called the Cotton Gin Inn. All he wanted to do was lie down and sleep. Hopefully, that would help with the pain.

He parked near an aging Toyota in dire need of detailing. His head hurt so much he almost didn't give it a second look. But then he realized it seemed familiar, and went back to double-check.

Well, I'll be damned.

It only took a moment to review his notes and verify the car's license plate.

Maybe I should go back to the clinic and give that nurse a tip! But then he grimaced at the thought of going anywhere other than bed. *I'll catch up with him later.*

Chapter 10

"Fear is the mother of foresight." –Thomas Hardy

On the way back to the post office in Camp Hill, Samantha couldn't help but think about the odd night she'd just spent with Lenny. And Ebby. They all occupied a bed designed for one person—one *small* person.

True to his word, Lenny hadn't tried anything, and they both slept fully clothed, or tried to. Still, she couldn't shake the image of how her parents would react if they ever discovered she'd been "in bed" with someone, no matter how innocent the circumstances. When she called to tell them she'd be staying with friends and might go to the A-Day game, they sounded doubtful. But, damn it, she was an adult. If she wanted to stay out all night, that was her prerogative. Telling herself that, over and over, didn't help her sleep either.

She was still thinking it through when they reached their destination, and she offered to wait outside with Ebby. Instead, Lenny insisted she come with him. "Leave Ebby in the car. Crack the windows; she'll be all right. We won't be gone long."

With the dog safely inside Lenny's grubby Toyota sedan, they entered the post office. They passed an interior wall sporting a double row of antique brass mailboxes with glass doors. Sam couldn't remember the box number off-hand or she would have stopped to look through the door's little window.

When they reached the service counter, they met the tall black woman they'd seen from a distance the day before. Sam squinted at her name tag: Olivia.

"Good morning," Lenny said to the woman. "I hope you can help me. Well, us, actually."

"I can try." She looked from one to the other, her expression unreadable.

"I'm hoping to access my late aunt's mailbox."

His words seemed to strike a nerve in the woman. She squinted at him and put her hands on her hips. "Yeah? What's your auntie's name?"

"Edna Gianella," he said. "She married my dad's brother. I'm her nephew, Lenny."

Olivia stepped back from the counter. "Now, that's kinda odd. 'Cuz there was a man in here yesterday who said the same thing. I asked him for an ID, and he said he lost it."

"I've got my identification right here." Lenny

fished his wallet from a back pocket, extracted his Georgia Driver's License, and handed it to her.

Sam nudged his arm. "She might want to see the death certificate, too."

"Oh, right." He dug a folded copy of the document from his wallet and handed it to the postal worker.

Olivia examined both and returned them. She shook her head and said, "I ain't never seen anything like what happened yesterday. Somebody shot the man who claimed he was you. Durn bullet opened up his forehead like a zipper, but it didn't kill him." She suddenly appeared apprehensive, her eyes wide. "That wasn't you doin' the shootin', was it?"

"Good God, no!" protested Lenny. "We got here afterwards. In fact, a friend of yours told us about it. I didn't get her name, but she said you helped the guy. Or tried to."

Samantha's mouth suddenly went dry. *What if whoever did the shooting is really coming after us? Is it the same nut case who caused Mr. Putzkin's death? And who in the world would try to impersonate Lenny?*

She nudged him again, harder this time, and whispered, "This is crazy! We should get out of here and go home. Now!"

Olivia's face continued to register alarm, but Lenny held up both his hands. "I don't own a gun. Haven't fired one since— I dunno, high school. All I want is whatever's in my aunt's post office box. Once

I've got that, we'll leave, and you'll never see us again."

"And what if I get more mail in her box?"

"I'll give you a forwarding address, mine. But honestly, how likely is it that she'd get any more mail? The poor woman's dead."

"Stay right there," Olivia said as she sidled away. "I'll get her stuff for ya."

"I'm scared," Samantha said. "This is all just too weird. I didn't sign up for gettin' shot. If there's something you haven't told me—"

"There's not," he said. "I have no idea who's using my name or trying to get their hands on Aunt Edna's stuff. Am I worried by it? Absolutely. Is it enough to make me stop trying to find her safe deposit box? Hell, no!" He put his hand on her shoulder and gave her a gentle squeeze. "Do you seriously want to give up and go home? There must be something really valuable in there if someone else wants it so bad."

Before Sam could answer, Olivia returned. "I'm actually kinda glad you're here to collect all this. There wasn't much room left in there," she said, sliding a pile of envelopes across the counter toward them. "One of 'em looks like a tax bill."

Lenny thanked her, and the pair left. Once inside the car, Ebby parked her upper body between the seats and alternately sniffed and licked them both. It definitely lightened the mood, though Samantha remained concerned.

"What should I open first?" Lenny asked.

"The letters, of course! Anything addressed by hand."

He stared at the pile of envelopes in his lap, then shook his head. "This could take a while."

"Then let me help." Sam reached toward the pile and grabbed half of it.

They began opening the letters and reading them. At first they read them out loud, but as they continued to work through them, they found the majority were requests for help. A small number contained checks and photos. The only official-looking envelope, other than the tax bill, hailed from some political campaign committee. Those two envelopes were set aside while they resumed working on the letters.

Sam paused when she found a check for five hundred dollars. It was accompanied by a photo of a middle-aged couple standing arm-in-arm before a church. Flipping it over, she saw a handwritten note and read it out loud: "'Thanks for everything.' It's signed Francine, but there's no last name."

Lenny just stared at the check.

"What d'ya think?" Sam asked. "Can we cash it?"

"I sure hope so," he said. "I brought a copy of the will. That should prove I'm entitled to what's in her estate. This oughta be part of it."

Sam felt her eyebrow dip. *"You brought the*

will? I didn't see it."

"It's in the trunk in a big envelope, along with all the snapshots Mr. Putzkin gave me."

"That makes you a teensy bit more prepared than I expected." She smiled. "Have you ever looked at those photos?"

He nodded. "I glanced through a few. Didn't see anybody I knew."

"Okay, but were there any messages written on them?" She pointed at the photo in his hand. "Like on the back of that one."

"Maybe. I didn't think to look."

"Well, I'd like to look through them, even if you don't," she said.

"Working through all these letters isn't enough?"

"They make me feel kinda guilty. All these people asking your aunt to help them with their problems. The stories are sad. Most of them are from lonely people, or folks who can't get a job, or are completely misunderstood. I can't help but wonder how they knew to write her, and why they thought she could do something for them."

Lenny pursed his lips and looked at the stack of letters they had opened, then at those they had not yet handled. "I'm guessing it's a word-of-mouth thing. If people are paying her for counseling—"

Sam vigorously shook her head. "I doubt it

has anything to do with counseling. I mean, listening to Olin—"

"The redneck physicist?"

"Yeah. He made what she did sound sort of mysterious. We should have asked him for more details."

Lenny found another check and held it up. "Here's *another* five hundred bucks!" He glanced at the back of the photo that came with it. "It just says, 'Bless you!'"

They finished going through the regular mail, and Sam insisted they group the letters by request.

"Why?" asked Lenny. "It's not like we're going to be able to do anything about them."

"Maybe not, but we're just beginning to get a feel for what your aunt did. Who knows what else we'll find? Now, what about the last two letters—the campaign committee and the tax bill?"

Lenny grimaced as he held the letter from The Patriots for Progress Political Action Committee. "I'll bet it's just a request for a donation, but I can't believe my aunt got herself involved in politics. Based on what I've seen in these letters, I'm guessing she operated from the shadows. And that's also why my dad had so little respect for her.

"Go ahead and open it," Sam said. "We don't have to actually do anything with it."

Lenny extracted a typed sheet and read the short message out loud.

Veils

Mrs. Gianella,

We have been patient, and we understand that you are experiencing some health issues. That is unfortunate, and we would like to offer help. If you'll simply agree to the terms of our previous offer, we will provide more than enough money to cover any medical costs you incur while working to restore your health.

Unfortunately, we cannot be of any help if you choose to continue to ignore our proposals and requests. One simple meeting will resolve this issue for good.

Please contact me at the above number as soon as possible.

"The letter is signed, Clement Bessemer, Special Assistant to United States Senator Terrence Grovemont."

"Grovemont's a bigwig," Sam said. "My dad's mentioned him often enough. He's not a fan, can't stand the man, actually. I try not to get too worked up about politics. But that Grovemont guy? He's a jerk."

"I'm not big on politics either." Lenny stuffed the letter back into the envelope and reached for the tax bill. He opened that and scanned the contents. "Evidently, Aunt Edna owned some land near a place called Beulah."

"Never heard of it," Sam said.

"Ditto. But the county didn't bill her very

much, so I doubt there's a house on it or anything. It's probably just vacant land."

Sam exhaled; glad the fear she'd felt earlier had dissipated. "So, what's next?"

"We look for a place to cash these checks so we can afford breakfast!"

~*~

After another night in a rest area, her companions all 18-wheelers, Millie began the day in a foul mood. She needed Heller's location to determine if he had survived her attempt on his life, and the only person who could supply that data was her brother, Tyrone. The last thing she needed was an argument with him. When she called and told him as much, he relented and told her Heller was on the move.

When she asked Ty to stay on the line until she caught up with Heller, he adamantly refused.

"I'm not doing this," he said. "I'm not getting any further involved in your insane manhunt."

Millie chewed her lip for a moment to let some of the steam out of her response. She desperately needed to sound reasonable. "Y'know what? That's okay. I understand. If you don't want to help me, that's fine. But, I'll make you a deal. I've already downloaded the phone app Dad set up to track his watch. So, if you'll send me an invitation to link up with the same program on the phone you have, I won't have to keep bugging you. Fair enough?"

"Maybe," he said.

"Maybe? Maybe what? If I kill the bastard and then get caught, are you afraid I'll tell them who helped me track him down?"

Tyrone sighed. "The thought had crossed my mind."

What a jerk! "Why the hell would I do that?"

"How should I know? It's obvious you've already gone off the deep end. What's to keep you from implicating me when you get caught? And, by the way, you *will* get caught."

"Would you rather I keep calling you? Five times a day? Ten? The guy keeps moving, for cryin' out loud. If you'd just—"

"Stop!" he yelled. "Enough already. I'll send you the invite. You get one shot. Set it up, but then I'm erasing the stupid thing. If you don't get it right, you're outta luck. You can call me all you want, but I won't have a damn thing to share with you. Got it?"

"Yes," she said, weary of the back and forth, and even more weary of tracking the Gianella kid in hopes of finding Heller.

"All right," Tyrone muttered. "As soon as we're done with this call, I'll send it."

"No," Millie said. "Send it now, while we're still connected."

"I don't—"

"Figure it out! You've used that phone ever

since Dad died. That's been over a year. You're not a moron; you don't need a manual. Just do it. Send me the damned invitation."

There followed a good deal of muttering, some clicks, an occasional curse, and finally, "There. It's done."

It was Millie's turn to sigh. "Thanks."

chapter 11

"If you owe the bank $100, that's your problem. If you owe the bank $100 million, that's the bank's problem."
–J. Paul Getty

Dak began the day by taking aspirin. It didn't help much, and he began to wonder where he might get something stronger. He didn't dare see a doctor; they would likely recognize the type of wound he had and would immediately tell the cops.

He should have been able to sleep like the dead after using what little energy he had left to scour his rented room for the presence of bed bugs, a source of nightmares going back to his childhood. Thankfully, he hadn't found any.

With a mental slap on the back of his head, he realized where he was—The Cotton Gin Inn. The Gianella kid was somewhere in the same crappy motel. Maybe even next door.

Unless he's already left!

Frustration and anger collided as Dak rushed

to the window. Shoving the seedy curtains apart, he spied their two cars, still side-by-side. Relief left him even more light-headed.

Dressing quickly in case his quarry left before he was ready, Dak went downstairs, paid his bill, and then waited in his car. The lull allowed him to focus on his two most immediate problems: the pain in his head for which he had no remedy, and the idea that his employer wanted him dead, though he still couldn't understand why that might be. What else could explain someone trying to kill him?

It makes no friggin' sense!

A call to his employer might square things. But if done, he had to project confidence. He had to assure them he was fully on top of his assignment, even though his grip on it had only just resurfaced in the parking lot where he sat.

~*~

Having had no luck finding an open bank in Camp Hill, Lenny and Sam looked further afield.

Despite his Aunt Edna's assurances, Lenny had serious doubts about Ebenezer's ability to identify any bank, much less a *particular* one. Assuming Edna had done her financial business in Alabama, that reduced the choices to just over a hundred, if the Internet could be believed.

But, since the dear departed owned property in Lee County, and the Camp Hill post office just happened to be in Lee County, he figured that would be the best place to start looking. Another Internet search provided addresses for three dozen banks in Auburn and Opelika, towns that more than a few folks referred to as Lee County's "twin cities." Since Auburn had two-thirds of those addresses, Lenny suggested they begin their Ebby-assisted search in the smaller of the two towns. Sam concurred, and they made their way to Opelika.

As they approached the city limits, Sam giggled.

"What's got you tickled?" he asked.

"I remember the first time my folks brought me down this way. We were going to a football game, and I was pretty little. Dad told me the name of the town, and I thought he said it was 'Hope-ya-like-it.'"

"Cute."

"Yeah. I guess." She looked at their surroundings and spotted the first bank. "Should we park in front? Or do a drive-by?"

"I haven't got a clue. Auntie Edna didn't bother to leave any instructions. I suspect she thought Ebby and Einstein shared some DNA."

Sam ignored the remark and rolled Ebby's window completely down. "Let's try a slow drive-by to begin with and see if Ebby has any reaction at all."

After cruising past three banks at a speed low enough to thoroughly annoy the drivers behind them, Lenny pulled into a parking space in front of a fourth possibility, a savings and loan on a corner.

Sam leashed Ebby, and all three got out of the car.

Ebby wasn't in the least bit interested in the corner location, so they wandered close by each of the first three target buildings just in case. Fortunately, they were within easy walking distance. Ebby ignored them all.

"I feel like a complete idiot doing this," Lenny said as they piled back in his car. "I think our time would be better spent trying to cash the checks we have. The gas gauge is sitting on empty, and so is my wallet."

"We can't give up now. We just started."

"Then let's see if we can find the oldest one in town," Lenny suggested. "I don't know how long Aunt Edna really played her gypsy games, but I suspect she did it for a long time. If a bank gave her good service, she wouldn't have any reason to switch."

Sam started tapping furiously on her cell phone. Lenny merely eased back in his seat and enjoyed the show. The girl had definitely grown on him, and he hoped it would turn into something more.

"Got it!" she exclaimed.

"What?"

"How's this sound: the Yellowhammer Savings and Loan."

"You're kidding. What's a yellowhammer?"

"The state bird. Here, look." She held the phone in front of him, then clicked on the icon for a map.

"It's pretty close," he said.

"Let's give it a shot!"

With that, they were on their way. Ebby stuck her head out the rear window on Sam's side; in the side mirror, Lenny could see her big ears flapping in the wind. It made him smile. If Sam and Ebby were a package deal, he could easily see himself being part of it.

The Yellowhammer Savings and Loan occupied a building that had likely seen its best years during the Hoover administration. It wasn't exactly rundown, but it definitely needed some cosmetics—mostly paint and plaster work.

They parked in a minuscule side lot while Ebby pranced on the back seat. Sam couldn't help but notice and gave Lenny a huge, delightfully dimpled smile.

"Could this be it?" he asked.

Sam was halfway out the door when she replied, "Keep your fingers crossed!"

~*~

The call from Senator Grovemont went straight to the phone in Clement Bessemer's Richmond, Virginia office.

"Clem, damn it all, what's the status on that

Gianella woman? Is she still even alive? Do we have her camper?"

Clement clenched his teeth and once again castigated himself for agreeing to serve the loudmouth Senator on the Political Action Committee that the alleged "public servant" had formed.

"There's been no official word, sir," Clement said. "But we've confirmed that Mrs. Gianella is definitely deceased."

"That's good. Has anyone contacted the heirs? Surely they won't want to ignore a substantial cash offer."

"Apparently there's only one, but there's been some difficulty in—"

"I don't want to hear about 'difficulty,' Clem! We're running out of time. If we can get our hands on that woman's trailer, or whatever it is, it could make a huge difference in my campaign. And all the others the PAC supports, too, of course."

"I understand, sir, and based on your recommendation, we've made a significant contact. I understand the people they assign don't always operate in the open. There's one in particular—"

"Not another word, you idiot! What's the matter with you? I can't be implicated in anything... Uhm, shady."

"I'm sorry, sir. I didn't mean—"

"Just get it done. That's your job. Get ahold of

the woman's camper, wherever it is, and get it back here as soon as you can. Don't share any details with me about how we get it or where it came from. We have people onboard who can figure out everything we need to know. Just get it! Is that clear?"

"Crystal clear, sir," Clement said. He couldn't help but wonder how he might be able to fully implicate Grovemont if and when the whole insane plot went wrong.

~*~

Dak had watched as Gianella and a young woman left the motel. Neither looked rested, a condition he completely understood. Even without the pain in his forehead, he doubted he would have gotten much sleep either, because of his obsession with bedbugs. Getting over that would likely require a great deal of time spent with a shrink, something he could never see himself doing.

He shook off all such thoughts. He had a mission.

Well aware of the pitfalls involved in following a target too closely, Dak took what few precautions he could to keep from being seen. He followed Gianella's shabby little Toyota from the shabby little motel into Opelika, which he assumed would be a shabby little town. To his surprise, it had a good deal going for it. The place seemed calm and colorful; he could even imagine living there once he'd earned enough money and could retire. Sure, he was good at killing people, but he didn't want to do it for the rest of his life.

For now, he just needed to keep an eye on his target. Sooner or later, Gianella would lead him to the old lady's camper. Unfortunately, he and the girl seemed far more interested in Opelika's financial institutions. Dak wondered if they were up to something criminal, though they hardly looked like bank robbers.

When they finally reached the Yellowhammer Savings and Loan, Gianella pulled into the only available parking place in the bank's tiny lot. Dak parked across the street and watched as they unloaded a huge dog that dragged them from the car to the front door.

Why in the world are they taking a great big mutt—a frantic one at that—into a bank? He had to stick around anyway, so maybe he'd find out. Noting the time on his watch, Dak settled in to wait.

~*~

With the tracking program finally working on her phone, Millie relaxed for the first time in a long time. Assuming Dak Heller continued to wear her father's timepiece, she would be able to find him no matter where he went. She was puzzled at first when he drove out of Auburn and stopped for the night in the boondocks north of town, but he didn't go any great distance. This also proved true when he continued on the next day into Opelika.

Millie debated whether she should follow him and maybe put him down for good. Ultimately, she decided against it. After the first attempt on his life, he would be wary. She resolved to give him enough time to get comfortable and perhaps even write off the shooting incident as some sort of mistake.

Personally, she would never have fallen for something like that, but she doubted Heller was savvy enough to think it through. Not that it mattered. She could track him down at her convenience now.

"Thanks, Ty," she muttered out loud. "It won't be long before I finally nail that son of a bitch."

Samantha struggled to hold onto the leash as Ebby strained to get into the bank. "C'mon, Lenny! Gimme a hand," she grumbled.

Lenny joined her, but his efforts to slow the dog down failed utterly. They both hung on as the dog dragged them forward. Between them, they finally got Ebby under control, which meant they arrived at the front door of the Yellowhammer Savings and Loan two or three seconds later than Ebby intended.

Once at the front door, she sat with her tail wagging furiously, and waited to be admitted.

Ebby's handlers, also relieved to have finally arrived at their destination, chuckled at their good fortune. "Do you realize," Sam said, "that we've managed to avoid driving by another hundred banks?"

"Maybe." Lenny didn't look too confident. "Should we put Ebby in the car?"

Sam laughed. "Do you think she'd stay there? Or, at least, stay there without tearing up your car? I doubt it. C'mon."

Lenny opened the bank's door and waved Sam and Ebby through.

A teller who had been walking across the main lobby stopped and stared at the prancing dog, then broke into a huge smile. "Ebby!" she cried. "Look, y'all—it's Ebenezer!"

For a short while, it seemed everyone in the building forgot about bank business and focused their attention on Ebby, and belatedly, on the two humans she'd brought with her. Before long the commotion subsided, so Lenny and Sam approached one of the managers and explained their mission.

As they'd hoped, the death certificate, the copy of Edna Gianella's will, and Lenny's driver's license provided everything the bank needed for them to be ushered into the vault. Meanwhile, a teller and a security guard fawned over Ebby. "She'll be right here, safe and sound, when y'all come out," the teller advised.

The vault wasn't a large room, and Sam was glad she didn't suffer claustrophobia. Three of the four gray walls held lock boxes; a plain wooden table filled much of the interior. There were no chairs.

Lenny produced his key, the bank manager produced its mate, and they unlocked the door to the cubby hole in which Edna's box lay. The bank employee slid the box out and set it gently on the table. "I'll leave y'all alone. If you need anything, just pop your head out and holler for one of us."

Lenny thanked him, and the man left. When the two were alone, Lenny took a deep breath, then gazed at Sam. "You ready?"

"Of course, I'm ready. Open it!"

"All right then. Here goes." Without another word, he lifted the lid from the long, rectangular box.

chapter 12

"Hell hath no fury like a bureaucrat scorned."
–Milton Friedman

Clement Bessemer dialed the number he'd been given supposedly by a "friend" of Senator Grovemont's PAC, Patriot's For Progress. Whoever answered would have no name, and Clement knew their location would also remain a secret.

The phone rang several times before a male answered it with a curt, "Yes?"

"I need to speak with our operative," Clement said, putting his efforts into making himself sound far more confident than he felt.

"Impossible."

"Might I remind you who your employer is?" Clement asked.

"Doesn't matter." The voice carried so little emotion it sounded mechanical.

"The people who hired you—"

Veils

"I wasn't involved in that. I have no knowledge—"

"Are you familiar with the FBI?"

"Of course."

"They can find you," Clement said. "I imagine someone in that organization already knows who you are and where you are."

"Nonsense."

"Care to find out?" Clement knew it was a bluff; he hoped whoever he was talking to wouldn't think so. "The people I work for are... important. Powerful. They can have anyone who is deemed a threat to the United States eliminated."

"So?"

"That includes you."

"Bullshit. I—"

"You sell murder. You hire people to kill other people. That makes you the worst kind of criminal, and next to the Russians and Chinese, the worst kind of threat to the republic."

"I— That's not—"

"*Fair?*" Clement actually laughed. "You, of all people, want to talk about fair? Okay then, how fair is this: either you connect me with your operative, or my boss will have a Special Forces team pay you a visit. They don't give a shit where in the world you are. They'll grab your ass and stash you away in a place nobody's ever heard of, a place you'll never

111

leave. Got that?"

For a long, long moment, there was silence, then, "I will give you his phone number, but only on one condition."

"That being?"

"You pay the full amount of the contract to us—"

"No problem."

"—and you also pay the operative when the job is done. I... No, *we* will no longer be involved."

"I need a number *and* a name," Clement said. "Give me that, and you have a deal."

"I need an hour or so, then I'll call you back."

"Fine," Clement said, but he was talking to himself. The connection was dead.

~*~

Dak checked his watch for what must have been the tenth time. As far as he could tell, there was absolutely nothing going on in the stupid bank into which Gianella, the girl, and their hound had disappeared.

The sun had risen higher as had the temperature. Dak glared at the remains of the windows on either side of his car. Squarish bits of glass littered the passenger seat and the floor. Both side windows had been destroyed by the bullet that grazed his forehead. Now, when he desperately needed to run the air conditioner, he had no choice but to do it with both windows wide open and hot air coming in from both sides.

How the hell would he be able to get the windows replaced without losing sight of his target? He'd used the last of his GPS trackers; it was probably on its way to Missouri under a truck he'd last seen outside of Nashville. After a few minutes thought, he exited his car and opened the trunk where he stashed a collection of gadgets and weaponry. This included a selection of tools for opening a locked car without a key—and without damaging the vehicle.

Dak tucked the "Unlock-It" kit under his arm and jogged across the street to the bank's puny parking area. As he had most fervently prayed, Gianella's cell phone sat on the console between the front seats. In moments he had the car door open and the phone in his pocket.

Leaving the car unlocked, he returned to his own vehicle and pulled out the slim file he had on Leonardo Gianella. It included his home address, phone number, date of birth, and little else. Dak hoped it was enough.

He brought Gianella's phone to life and was presented with a screen for entering a code to unlock the device. After trying and failing with zeros, number series one through nine and the reverse, he tried entering Gianella's birthday, May 2, 1999. That translated to 5299, which did the trick.

Dak quickly downloaded and installed a free locater function intended for parents needing to track the whereabouts of their children. He then entered Gianella's phone number in the matching app on his own phone.

Gotcha now!

After returning the phone to Gianella's car and locking it, Dak drove away in search of a company that could replace the windows in his car. With any luck, he could get a tinted version.

~*~

Lenny took a deep breath and a quick look at Sam before focusing on the contents of Edna Gianella's safe deposit box. With no expectations about what he might find, he began to remove items from it one-by-one and spread them out on the table.

The first thing he pulled from the narrow metal box appeared to be a clear glass spray bottle of cologne.

"Oh ho! What's this?" Sam reached past him, grasped the delicate atomizer, and held it up to the light. She sniffed it and smiled, then gently sprayed a bit on the inside of her wrist and held it close to Lenny's face for his opinion.

"It's nice," he said, "and, thank God, it's not overpowering."

Sam proceeded to spray a little on either side of her neck. "I like it," she said and gave him a light spritz, too.

Lenny feigned a frightened reaction and then

got back to business. "C'mon, you goof. We've got some stuff to look through. Put the stink-um away."

"Okay," she muttered and slipped it into a pocket of her cut-offs. Her voice carried a note of disappointment, but he spotted the dimples which always appeared when she smiled.

The next item of interest was a fat, business-size envelope. It wasn't sealed; instead, the flap was merely folded over the contents. Lenny flipped it open with his thumb and felt an instant shock of recognition when he realized the contents amounted to a thick wad of cash.

"Holy Mother of God," he breathed.

"Lemme see," Sam said as she crowded close.

Lenny could feel the heat of her body through her thin T-shirt as she pressed up against him. He prayed she wouldn't move away anytime soon.

"Count it!" she whispered, pressing even closer.

Lenny split the bills like a deck of cards and handed half to her.

She wasted no time examining the stack. "Good Lord, Len, they're all hundreds!"

Lenny's hand seemed to have developed a slight tremor as he fanned out the bills he had. They, too, were all hundreds. "There's a small fortune here," he said, his voice tight.

Sam giggled. "Think we can afford lunch

now? I don't know about you, but I'm starved." She paused, stood on her tiptoes and gave him a quick kiss on his cheek. "It's buried treasure, Lenny. And it's ours!"

In light of the promise she'd extracted from him, he expected his reaction to be anger or disappointment at having to share the money. Instead, he only felt relief. For now, anyway, his money worries had been diminished. Unemployment no longer hung over him like the blade of a guillotine. Besides, he had an amazing young woman at his side, and she seemed to like being exactly where she was—with him.

"Oh, dear," Sam said. "I forgot about poor Ebby. She hasn't had a thing to eat since we left Atlanta."

"I gave her some of my barbeque last night," Lenny said, as if the morsel he'd shared with her was somehow significant.

"C'mon," she said, pulling on his arm. "We need to take care of her."

"I know; I know, but we're not done here." He pointed at the table. "We haven't even looked at those."

The object of his gesture was a pair of books, one apparently ancient, the other a spiral-bound notebook with a sticky note on top bearing a short message: Read me first!

"Grab 'em," Sam said. "We'll check them out over lunch." She drew as close as before and added,

"You weren't planning to leave anything behind, were you?"

He shook his head, no, and took a last look in the box. Tucked away in the far corner was a key fob for some sort of vehicle. His Toyota hadn't come with one; it wasn't new enough, but he'd seen them before and recognized what it was.

"I wonder what that goes to," he said, extracting the fob from the now empty metal box.

"Who knows?" Sam picked up the two books and waved them at him. "But I'll bet the explanation is in here."

Lenny felt like he was missing something, but he couldn't imagine what it was. "Okay," he said. "Let's go." Between them, they gathered up everything that had been in the box, slipped it all into the grocery bag, and left.

As they exited the vault, the teller in the lobby released Ebby, who raced over to them as if they'd been separated for months.

With Ebby's leash in hand, Sam slipped her arm around Lenny's waist while he wrapped his arm around her back and rested it on her shoulder. They left the bank as if joined at the hip. When Lenny gave her shoulder a gentle bit of pressure, she responded by lowering her hand to his butt and giving one cheek a quick but definite squeeze.

~*~

By mid-afternoon, Millie thoroughly

regretted her decision to give Dak Heller enough time to think he was safe.

What's the point? He doesn't know me. He wouldn't recognize me and think, "Oh, shit. Here comes the woman who wants to kill me."

Besides that, she was bored silly. Sitting in her car, waiting, listening to the radio, and/or fiddling with her phone proved ridiculous. The only way she'd make any progress was to track the bastard down and shoot him.

Dead.

"Most *sincerely* dead," she told herself as she conjured a mental image of a Munchkin in the "Wizard of Oz" movie.

It was time to find Heller again. Happy with her decision, she slipped her car into reverse, took a split-second glance at the rearview mirror, and gave it some gas. The sudden crunch of her bumper into whoever was backing out of the space directly behind her came as a complete surprise.

She pulled forward, parked, and got out of the car. A tall man did the same, exiting his vehicle and walking toward her like she imagined some huge, brainless football player might. He wasn't smiling.

"I'm sorry," she said. "I didn't see you backing up."

He didn't respond.

"Let's see how bad it is." She stepped away

and inspected her rear bumper, pleased to see it was merely dented.

Millie then turned and walked toward him as he knelt to get a better look at his own bumper.

"Is yours okay?" she asked.

"Yeah."

"That's a relief. You looked pretty uhm… You know… Upset."

"That's 'cause it's not my car." He stood up and shoved his hands in his pockets. "I'd just as soon not get into the whole insurance, registration, and driver's license thing," he said. "Rather than have the owner see that the bumper's got a little scratch, I'll pay to have it fixed."

"That doesn't seem right. I mean, I backed into you," she said, hoping he'd stick with what he'd just said.

"Really?" He screwed up his face on one side; it looked pretty funny. "It appears to me that *I backed into you*. Do you want *my* info?"

She shook her head no. "I— It isn't necessary. There's barely a mark on my bumper. Just a little dent. I was more worried about yours."

He started to laugh.

"What?" she asked.

"This is all kinda dumb, isn't it?" He stuck out his hand. "My name's Mel. I'm on my way to New Orleans, but I've been in that stupid car since before sunup, and I'm just about wiped out. Not thinkin' straight; otherwise, I wouldn't have tried to occupy the same space as you."

Millie shook his hand; she tried to match his firm grip. "It's *Mel?* Really?"

"Yeah. It's short for... Well, something else," he said.

"My name's Millie, and it's short for something else, too." She couldn't help but smile, and when he returned it with his own, she realized he didn't look anything like the football-playing gorilla she'd presumed him to be. In fact, he looked quite pleasant, even handsome.

"Seems we've got lots in common."

She agreed.

"Maybe we could discuss the finer details somewhere else." He looked at the buildings that made up the rest stop. "Somewhere other than here."

"Like over an adult beverage?" she asked, her pulse quickening. "I could use one about now."

"Me, too. I'd like that. But I'm not from around here. I don't really know the area."

"I haven't been here long, either," she said. "But I saw a place near the university. If a college town doesn't have a decent bar, it's not much of a college town."

"I'll follow you, then," he said.

"Deal."

And as she merged with traffic on the Interstate headed back to Auburn, she couldn't help but think about how easily she'd given up on her original plan—to track down Heller. She glanced at her phone and called up the wristwatch tracker. Heller hadn't moved since the last time she'd checked on him. That had been three hours ago.

Don't get too comfy, you bastard. I haven't forgotten about you!

Chapter 13

"Painting is an illusion, a piece of magic, so what you see is not what you see." –Philip Guston

The trip from Opelika to Auburn had been thankfully short, and they had no trouble finding a place to eat. They even found a parking spot in the shade, so Ebby would be comfortable while they were gone.

Once inside, Samantha sank her teeth into a cheeseburger, closed her eyes, and savored the delicious mix of textures and flavors—a lush tomato slice, tart pickle, crisp lettuce, and thick, cheddar cheese. They all conspired to be the best thing she'd ever tasted, at least since the sticky bun she had back in Atlanta.

She grinned at Lenny, sitting across from her and munching on a burger of his own. And yet, he seemed more interested in her than the food. And, she admitted to herself, she'd been seeing him in a different way as well, a very complimentary way.

She had to ask, "What're you thinking?"

He chuckled and shook his head. "We—Uhm... Y'know, I'd rather not say. I wouldn't want to embarrass myself. Or you."

She didn't want to tell him she'd been having some pretty randy thoughts of her own, the kind that should have made her blush from the tip of her chin to the part in her hair. A crowded burger joint in a college town clearly wasn't the best venue for taking such thoughts to another level. So, she pushed her curiosity in a different direction.

Tapping the pile of stuff they found in the safe deposit box, Sam said, "We really need to look at the notebook. It's what your aunt intended."

Lenny swallowed and chased his bite of burger with a gulp of imported lager. He then covered his mouth to conceal a burp. "Why don't you slip around to this side of the table so we can both read it at the same time?"

She made the shift in record time, pressing up against him in the booth they'd secured in a corner of the War Eagle Bar and Grill. Most of the other patrons watched a live stream broadcast of the A-Day game, and many of them noisily shared their thoughts. Combined with the venue's supply of pulsating rock music and the general hubbub, the noise level made it difficult to communicate.

Samantha leaned close to Lenny's ear. "Let's get the party started!"

Lenny opened the notebook. The inside front

cover provided a pocket containing yet another business size envelope.

More money? Geez! She held her breath.

Instead of cash, Lenny extracted an invoice stamped PAID in red ink. The address in the header proclaimed it came from Happy Times Ten RV Acres in Montgomery, Alabama.

The invoice described the services provided. They included a major tune-up, replacement of all fluids, detailing, and "preferred" storage of a Class C recreational vehicle. A note near the bottom of the invoice explained that whoever picked up the vehicle was entitled to a free course covering driving and maintenance.

Lenny scratched his temple. "Well, I guess we know what the fob is for."

"I know what an RV is," Sam said, "my uncle had one. But what does Class C mean? C for cheap or—" she thought for a moment "—classy?"

"Who knows?" He looked at her and grinned. "But Montgomery's only an hour or so away from here. Let's go find out."

"You're on," Sam said. "As soon as I finish my lunch."

Lenny put the invoice back in the notebook then found a slip of paper clipped to the back of the first page. The handwriting was tiny and hard to read; the ink wasn't very dark, and the letters were made by an unsteady hand, unlike the rest of the notebook's contents.

"Listen to this," he said, then began to read the note out loud. "It says—"

"I can't hear you in here," Samantha cried. She tried to read it herself but couldn't. She watched as he traced a sentence with his finger, squinting at the words made even more difficult to read in the subdued light of the restaurant.

"Uh-oh," he said.

Sam squeezed closer, but she still couldn't read the message. "What? What's 'uh-oh?'"

Lenny closed the cover of the notebook and set it aside. "We need to finish up here and get going."

"To Montgomery?"

"Yeah. You can read the note yourself when we're on the way."

"Gimme a hint, Len. Is it real bad? Or just sorta bad? Or even *maybe* bad?"

"I'll need to think about it for a while before I can answer that. And who knows? Once you've read the note, you might not feel the same way."

Sam had to make a trip to the bathroom, but attacked her burger with renewed vigor when she returned. Anything either of them had left over would go to Ebby along with a beef patty sans bun they'd bought for her earlier.

Still, Lenny's cryptic comment played over

and over in her head: "Uh-oh." *Uh-oh? What the hell is that all about?*

~*~

Dak had spent far more time in the waiting area of the auto glass shop than he'd anticipated. Whoever was working on his car had to have been doing it in slow motion. It hadn't helped that the tinted windows he wanted had to be brought in from somewhere else. Considering how long it took to deliver them, he assumed they'd come from the West Coast or maybe Indonesia. All of which meant he was in a thoroughly rotten mood when his phone rang.

He glanced at the screen on his cell phone, but the caller's number had been blocked. That usually meant either a spam call or one from his employer. He answered them all, though he only cared about those from the people he worked for.

"H'lo," he muttered, prepared to hang up when some idiot made a pitch for a warranty extension or some other stupid come-on.

"I'm your new contact," said the voice on the phone.

He didn't sound anything like the monotone of his usual contact. "Go on."

"We need an update, a progress report."

"About what?"

"About your... assignment."

Veils

Dak stared at the phone in his hand then put it back to his ear. "Hold on." He walked out of the shop to avoid being overheard. "Okay," he said. "Who the hell are you, and how did you get this number?"

"I told you. I'm your new contact. I—"

Dak hung up. His employer didn't change contacts. It might've been possible if, for instance, his usual contact was suddenly dead. He doubted there was much chance of that.

His phone rang again, and he answered it with an irritated, "What?"

"Don't ever hang up on me again."

"Or what?"

"Or... Or—"

Dak hit the "End Call" button and smiled. *Take that, asshole.*

The phone rang again, and Dak answered it without saying a word.

"You there?" the voice asked.

"Yeah."

"Before you hang up on me again, just know that I can have you killed anytime I want."

"You haven't answered my questions," Dak said. "Who are you, and how did you get this number?"

"Okay! Okay. My name's Clement, and we

bought your contract. You work for us now."

"Who's us?"

"That's not impor—"

Dak hung up on him again, smirking this time while he waited for the idiot to call him back. When he did, Dak said, "Listen Clementine; it's not *your* ass out here in the boondocks. You aren't the one dealing with local yokels. And it sure as hell ain't you getting shot at."

He took a breath. "So, here's the deal: you tell me what happened to my usual contact and explain *exactly* why I should give a damn about anything you say. Because if you make me hang up again, I'll chuck this phone in a dumpster and take a nice long vacation where you'll never find me. Got that, asshole?"

"I— Uh, yes. Sorry we got off on the wrong foot."

"I don't give a shit about apologies. I want answers."

"Okay, okay. I work for a political action committee."

"Which one?"

"Is that really important?"

Dak paused just briefly. "Do you really want me to hang up? My God, you're a slow learner."

"It's called Pa— Patriots for Progress, not that it matters."

"All right, Clementine, and what's your last name?"

"It's Bessemer. *Clement* Bessemer. We bought your contract, and you're no longer obligated to your former employer."

"Why?" Dak asked.

"Why what?"

"Why'd you buy my contract? Has anything changed? Who am I supposed to kill?"

"*Kill?*" Bessemer's voice went shrill. "You're not supposed to kill anyone! That wasn't part of your previous contract, was it?"

"I was told to take out anyone who got in the way. Has that changed?"

"Hell yes! We don't want you 'taking out' anyone. Understood? We want the camper and its contents, that's all. Have you located it yet?"

"No."

"Why not?"

Stunned by the stupidity of the question, Dak took a moment to stare at the phone in his hand before responding. "Because it's hidden, dumbass. The old lady who owned it didn't want anyone to find it, except maybe her nephew."

"Why aren't you following him?"

"I *am* following him! And who the fuck are you to be asking me about it? Geez. When I find the friggin' camper, I'll let you know."

It was Bessemer's turn to pause. Dak could hear him breathing. "That's... Uhm... Fine. It's just... There are people I have to answer to. So, please, do your best to find it. And when you do, be prepared to deliver it."

"Where?"

"I'll find a place that's near you, or near wherever you find it, if possible. In the meantime, I want updates on your progress."

"Updates?"

"Yeah."

"We'll see," Dak said, and ended the call. "In your dreams, Clementine."

~*~

It seemed to Millie that every bar and restaurant in town was crowded. Finding a parking place proved difficult, and she worried that Mel would think she was trying to elude him when in reality she just wanted to find spaces for their cars.

Am I crazy to do this? I don't know anything about this guy. He could be a serial rapist. Or a killer!

But he didn't seem in the least bit threatening, and he didn't object to meeting her in a public place. She decided to put her Glock in her handbag and take it with her wherever they might go. Satisfied with her preparations, she located two spots at the edge of town with only a few cars in-between. She rolled her window down, gave him a thumbs up sign, and parked her car.

Veils

A quick look in the mirror dampened her spirits a notch. She quickly fussed with her hair and planned a quick visit to the Ladies Room as soon as they were seated in the restaurant. When she got out of her car, Mel was standing on the sidewalk waiting.

"You hungry or thirsty?" he asked.

She grinned. "Both."

Their brisk walk ended at a trendy bar and grill sporting a huge orange and blue eagle over the door. They had to get on a waiting list, but Millie figured that would be the case no matter where they went.

"I'll be back in a minute," she said. "I've gotta make a trip to the loo."

He looked around briefly then waved her toward a hallway featuring a large cartoon tiger perched on a toilet. "They must train their wildlife well around here."

She laughed all the way into the restroom then stopped and leaned against the closed door. *I'm really doing this! I'm actually—*

She paused in mid-thought, her mind shifting to more practical matters. *Get it together, girl. Hair. Eyeliner? Nah. Lipstick, definitely.*

Two of the three sinks were in use by other patrons, one of whom looked familiar, though she couldn't quite place her. Easily ten years younger, the girl appeared to be a college student. Her T-shirt and cutoff shorts fit her well and accentuated her slim figure.

Millie stepped up next to her and began applying her lipstick.

The girl beside her pulled a dainty perfume atomizer from her pocket and applied a gentle spritz of it to her throat.

"That's a wonderful fragrance," Millie said to her. "What's it called?"

"I honestly don't know," the girl said. "I only got it today. A little while ago, actually. Would you like to try some?"

Knowing how long it had been since her last shower, Millie eagerly agreed.

"Help yourself," the girl said. "It's not terribly strong. I used some a while ago, and I can't smell it at all now."

"Thank you," Millie said. "You're a lifesaver."

The girl then slipped from the room. Millie still couldn't quite place her, but she remained convinced she'd seen her before.

Chapter 14

"It is impossible to imagine a more complete fusion with nature than that of the gypsy." –Franz Liszt

Once they were in the car, Sam wasted no time reaching for the notebook. "I can't believe you left me hanging back there in the restaurant."

"Sorry about that, but it was dark and noisy, so—"

"Hush!" she said and swatted him lightly on the shoulder.

Lenny bit his lip and kept quiet while Sam struggled to read Edna's note. She soon inhaled in shock. "It's— The perfume thingy... It's—"

He tried desperately not to smile.

"It's an... Uhm... You know. Kinda like a love potion."

"Is it working?" he asked.

Her voice came out constricted. "Why would I

admit that?"

"'Cause it's definitely had an effect on me."

"I hadn't... uh... noticed."

"Yeah, well I've done my best to hide it."

Sam suddenly went rigid. "Oh, geez."

"What is it?"

"There was a woman in the restroom with me. I let her use some of the perfume."

Lenny couldn't keep from laughing. "Well, somebody could be in for a big surprise." He looked at her and smiled. "I've never seen you blush like that."

Sam put her hands on either side of his face and turned his head toward the street. "Drive. Now. Concentrate on the road."

"Yes'm."

Still chuckling, Lenny pulled out and maneuvered through traffic as thousands of football fans from Auburn University's massive Jordan-Hare stadium filled the streets of the college town. Many skipped the local sights and began their journeys home. Fortunately, he had a decent head start and reached the Interstate before most of them.

During the drive to Montgomery, Sam read sections of the notebook and commented on them out loud. "Your Aunt Edna referred to the stuff in the perfume bottle as an attractant, not a love potion or an aphrodisiac."

"That would explain why I haven't been kissin' everything in sight like it says in the song."

Sam appeared mystified. "What song?"

"'Love Potion Number Nine.' It's a classic."

"Never heard of it," she said. "I'm more into country than classical."

Lenny guffawed. "It's a rock tune. Came out in the 60s, I think. It's about a guy who gets a secret potion from a gypsy and goes nuts because of it. I think it's pretty funny, and the tune is catchy."

"If you say so. Now, according to your Aunt Edna, there are several variations of the stuff. One of them she calls a 'repellant.' I'm glad she didn't leave *that* one in the safe deposit box. Evidently the attractant is the most popular version. She claims to have sold a lot of it."

"Oh. My. Gawd. My Aunt Edna was a gypsy!"

"Maybe, maybe not. Did you look at the other book? The old one with the raggedy leather cover?"

"I glanced at it, but it's in some weird foreign script—strange symbols with only a few letters I recognized. I couldn't make out a word of it."

"Apparently, Edna figured a good bit of it out. A lot of it, actually, according to what she wrote in here. These are her translations." Sam closed the notebook and gently set it down. "This could be incredibly valuable. If it's true, I can see how she made a living selling the stuff."

"But only via word of mouth," Lenny said. "Can you imagine what the federal government would do if they found out? The people in the Food and Drug Administration would have a collective stroke."

"They wouldn't be the only ones. How 'bout the Infernal Revenue Service?"

"Infern— Oh. Yeah. I get it. You're right. Just 'cause something may not be legal doesn't mean it won't be taxed. Al Capone learned that the hard way."

Sam shaded her eyes against the late afternoon sun. "Is that the camper place up ahead?"

"Yep," said Lenny. "I sure hope it's open. We should've called first."

~*~

"Got anything new on the Gianella woman's damned trailer?"

The voice on the phone belonged to Senator Grovemont, the absolute last person Clement Bessemer wanted to deal with. "Yessir," he said. "We're narrowing the search. In fact, I was on the phone earlier today with—"

"No details! For the love of God, Clem, you know I can't be privy to anything specific. Use your head."

"Sorry sir. I didn't mean—"

"Just let me know when we can send a team

to get the camper. The primaries aren't that far off. We're on a very tight timeline here."

"I'm aware of that, Senator."

"Sometimes I wonder. Just get it done. And the sooner the better."

"Yessir," said Clement into a phone already gone dead.

And that pompous ass thinks people will vote him into the White House? Who'd be that stupid?

Unfortunately, he had yet another pompous ass to deal with. Clement did not relish the thought of calling Dak Heller, the man who'd hung up on him a half dozen times in their only conversation—the same man who'd asked him who the PAC wanted him to kill. But Clement had no choice.

Using the untraceable cellphone he'd been given by some nameless, faceless go-between on Senator Grovemont's staff, he dialed the hitman's number and quickly got an answer.

"Yeah?"

"This is—"

"I know who it is. What d'you want?"

"An update," Clement said.

Heller exhaled dramatically before answering. "I'm following the old lady's nephew. He stopped just outside Montgomery. According to the map on my phone, he's at an RV place."

"A campground?"

"No. I dunno. Maybe. All it says on the screen is Happy Times Ten RV Acres. Could be a campground; could be a dealership. I can't tell."

"How long will it take you to get there?"

Clearly exasperated, Heller said, "How the hell should I know?"

"Surely you know the distance between you and—"

"I'm stuck in traffic!" Heller yelled. "I haven't moved a goddam inch in the past fifteen minutes. I'm stuck out here in a friggin' wasteland. There's no exits, and traffic is backed up as far as I can see."

"I'm sure that's frustrating. Here in DC—"

"Do you honestly think I give a shit about DC? I'll call you when I know something. Until then, leave me the hell—"

Clement stabbed the End Call button before Heller finished ranting. It provided the only smile Clement had all day.

~*~

Irritated to the point of throwing his phone out the car window, Dak forced himself to calm down. Allowing some gutless, ass-kissing bureaucrat to wind him up did nothing to improve his situation. Having spent far too much of the day waiting for his windows to be replaced, he barely had time to grab something to eat before once again going after Gianella.

Veils

A quick glance at his phone confirmed that his target remained at the RV place, but how long was he liable to stay? Getting there had become urgent, and Clementine, or whatever his name was, had sucked out the last of his patience.

Dak honked his horn at the car in front of him. When the car didn't move, he honked again, longer. The driver flipped him off, but edged forward a few feet, creating enough space for Dak to ease over onto the shoulder. Once he'd maneuvered out of the traffic jam, he accelerated.

Pleased to be moving once again, he ignored the cars and drivers he passed while zipping along on the shoulder. As he reached the midpoint of a long, gentle curve in the highway, he could finally see what had caused the backup, a wreck involving an 18-wheeler. The huge vehicle lay on its side with the back doors open. Dak couldn't tell what had spilled out onto the road, but whatever it was, the state troopers working the scene weren't letting anyone drive through it.

He also spotted an exit ramp a shorter distance away. As he was about to increase his speed, a pickup truck pulled halfway onto the shoulder, blocking his path. The big, commercial truck had dual rear wheels and was considerably wider than a standard pickup.

Dak drove up close and honked. The truck edged further out onto the shoulder, without completely leaving the highway. There it stopped as highway traffic completely ceased to move.

Dak rolled the new driver side window down, stuck his head out and yelled, "Move your damn truck!" He emphasized the command with more honks of his horn. That earned him a middle finger but nothing else.

His anger mounted as he sat, immobilized, agonizingly close to the exit. Did the guy in the truck think he was competing for a Citizen of the Year Award? Did blocking Dak's path give the jerk some sort of thrill? *What a complete ass!*

If the bumper on the bastard's truck wasn't so far above his own, Dak would have given the truck a little bump, maybe two. But that would only damage his own vehicle.

That's when the trucker backed up and tapped Dak's car.

Dak leaned on the horn and didn't let up until people in the cars beside him rolled down their windows and hollered at him. The truck remained where it was.

"I'll show the motherfucker," Dak grumbled as he reached into the glove box and withdrew a compact Glock G43X. After quickly chambering a round, he gave the truck another prolonged blast of his horn, all the while watching for the driver to look back at him, either in his rearview mirror or out the window. Dak didn't care, he'd wave the deadly little handgun to let the truck's driver know he meant business.

The driver in the truck appeared to shake his

head. By then, Dak was ready. He leaned out his window with the gun in his left hand and pretended to take aim. If that didn't get the idiot's attention, nothing would.

And yet the moron didn't do anything.

Dak honked again.

Still nothing.

Though sorely tempted to get out of his car, stroll up to the truck, and stick his gun in the guy's face, Dak forced himself to be calm. The world was full of idiots; killing one wouldn't change much other than briefly making him feel better. Besides, he had no way of knowing if the trucker was armed, too.

He decided to wait.

Moments later, a vehicle with flashing blue lights came roaring up the shoulder of the Interstate. It then decelerated to a stop, pinning Dak's car between the trucker and the trooper.

~*~

It wasn't because Millie was naked. Nor was it because she was in bed. It wasn't even because she barely knew Mel, the naked man lying beside her, or the fact that after one drink each and a handful of salted nuts at the bar, they both felt driven to find a hotel room where they could make love. The kind a band was named after: Hot, Monkey Love. Insanely hot monkey love.

Which happened, repeatedly. Until they were too worn out to do anything but order room service.

The thing that kept bugging her was the sudden, practically explosive desire she felt for Mel. She hadn't even bothered to ask his last name, where he came from, or if he was married. None of that seemed to matter. She'd looked for a wedding ring or a telltale band of pale skin on his ring finger, but found neither. It didn't change her attitude. It just didn't matter.

And the attraction, she felt sure, was entirely mutual. If Cupid actually existed, the little imp must've emptied his entire quiver of arrows into them, and then gone home to reload.

It wasn't just the sex; she'd had her share of lovers, and Mel ranked with the best of them. No, it was the sheer, raw *need* she felt for him. It drove her as harshly as a trail hand with a bullwhip.

And even if there had been the sting of a whip, it wouldn't have mattered. If that was the price of desire, then so be it. She'd take it and keep on keepin' on.

When Mel threw on some clothes and answered whoever brought their food, Millie recalled one of what her brother called "observations;" she thought of them as complaints. "You're too damned impulsive," he'd exclaim and then add, "Nobody else in the family acts that way."

For once, the recollection didn't make her mad. She just smiled. She had desire, and it had been fulfilled. She felt ready for whatever came next.

Chapter 15

"Love is a strange emotion. It is ever evolving. Lust is transient. With time, one realizes that love and togetherness are two different things. Very few people are lucky enough to experience the two emotions simultaneously." –Randeep Hooda

A salesman emerged from the offices of Happy Times Ten RV Acres and smiled as he introduced himself and offered to let Sam and Lenny in on what he considered the "greatest deal ever on a brand-new recreational vehicle." Sam stifled a groan.

"Actually," Lenny said, "we're here about this." He handed the man the paid receipt they'd found in Edna's notebook.

After a quick glance at the document, the look on the salesman's face changed from friendly to forlorn. "Oh," he muttered. "You already have one." Then he brightened. "But, this might still be your lucky day 'cause no matter how nice your class C rig is, it's no match for the class A models. You sure don't need a dinky class B; they're just vans with beds. C'mon, follow me. I'll show ya an *amazing* A."

Lenny stood still and shook his head. He pointed at the receipt in the man's hand. "We're here about that. We want to see the camper, inside and out. After that, we'll decide what comes next."

The salesman reviewed the name on the paper and eyed Lenny with suspicion. "You don't look like an Edna."

"She was my aunt," Lenny said. He then showed the man his driver's license. "She passed away and left everything to me. I've got the documents to prove it."

With a gesture of dismissal, the man said, "So, think you might want to sell it?"

"Who knows?" Sam said, stepping close to Lenny. She stood on tiptoe, her lips brushing lightly against his ear and whispered, "I'm pretty sure Ebby needs to pee." She tipped her head in the direction of a thin strip of grass. "You go on; I'll catch up. We'll be over there," she said as Ebby pulled at the leash to begin her search for the perfect spot.

Lenny extracted the key fob for the RV from his pocket and asked the salesman to take him to the camper.

"Quickest way to find it is to click the alarm button," the salesman said.

Lenny complied, and the two men took off toward the clamor of a car alarm.

Veils

Sam watched Lenny and the salesman stroll toward a sea of boxy vehicles. Happy Times Ten RV Acres *did* stretch for acres, most of which were covered with campers. She was surprised to see such an astonishing array of sizes. She had to nudge Ebby away from one that appeared a good bit larger than a city bus parked next to a trailer small enough to be pulled by a motorcycle.

When Ebby finally finished, Samantha had to jog to catch up with Lenny who stood beside a medium-sized RV. He appeared frustrated in his efforts to be rid of the salesman.

Impatient for a little more alone time with Lenny, Sam butted into the conversation. "Can't we just go in?"

"Oh, yes. Sure," the salesman said. "Let's."

Lenny frowned. "My... uhm... partner and I need some time alone in there." He gestured at the camper. "Edna was my beloved aunt, and frankly, I'd rather not share this... Uh—"

"Moment," Sam said. She put her arm around Lenny's waist and pulled him close. "We need some time to reflect, to think about dear Edna, and to try and connect with her past."

"Of course. Of course," the salesman said. "I didn't mean to intrude."

Lenny nodded. "No problem."

"It's just that we close in about twenty minutes. The gate to the lots will be shut and locked.

If you're still in the RV, you'll be locked in, too."

Samantha glanced at the gate. Though stout, it wasn't solid, and there was plenty of open space below the main crossbar. "It's okay. We can always crawl out and get back to the car. The main entrance isn't gated."

"You're right, I suppose, but—"

"Great!" she said and shouldered Lenny toward the vehicle as she pulled on Ebby's leash. "C'mon, girl. We're going inside."

Lenny opened the door, Samantha dropped the leash, and Ebby raced up the steps. Samantha wondered briefly if the poor dog hoped to find her original owner inside.

"After you," Lenny said and waved her into the camper ahead of him.

Once inside, Sam hugged Lenny. "I didn't think that guy would ever take the hint." She then turned and surveyed the interior of the RV. "It's a lot bigger than I imagined."

The central area felt spacious. Decorated in soothing tones of beige and navy, it had surprisingly contemporary furniture. The walls held several framed photos of Ebby along with two much older ones of Edna and Lenny's uncle. The couple looked extraordinarily happy.

"It's a helluva lot nicer than I expected." Lenny turned toward the entrance at the sound of a knock.

Veils

The salesman opened the door and stuck his head in. "There's nobody here right now who can go over the maintenance plan or give you any driving instructions. That'll have to wait until tomorrow."

"Good to know," Lenny said.

The salesman continued, "Are you sure—"

Samantha cut him off with a wave of her hand and a cheery, "G'bye!" When he closed the door, she made sure it and the driver-side door were both locked.

She breathed a sigh. "Finally. Maybe now we can check this place out."

Standing side-by-side, they held hands and slowly surveyed the interior.

"It's really nice in here," Lenny said as he guided her to a sofa on one side of the motorcoach. "It's modern. Look at all the appliances and cabinets. The fridge is nicer than the one in my condo. So's the TV."

He pressed a button on the wall behind them labeled "Table." Immediately, the floor in front of them unfolded, and a table rose from somewhere below until it reached meal height.

"Way cool," Sam breathed. "I wonder what other kinds of stuff are hidden away in here." She stood and walked to the back where a door opened onto a room filled nearly wall-to-wall by a double bed. It offered just enough space to walk beside it on either side. Next to an ordinary light switch on the inside wall, she located a button like the one which disgorged the table. When she pressed it, the room expanded in one direction, pulling the bed with it. It stopped after three or four feet, enough to provide walking space at the foot of the mattress.

On the far side of the little room, a low, round doggie bed had been revealed. Ebby ran to it, circled on top three times, then plunked herself down, chin on paws and eyes closed.

"She looks comfy," Lenny said as he stepped beside Sam and slipped his arm around her waist. She nestled her head on his shoulder. But instead of feeling relaxed, she felt an air of tension.

"Y'know," Lenny began, "we really ought to go through Edna's notebook."

"Later, maybe," Sam said. "Not right now." She put a hand on his chest and ever so lightly traced little circles with her index finger.

Lenny cleared his throat. "Uhm... Actually... There's a good chance we're still under the influence of that spray."

"Ya think?" she whispered.

"It's just... Well, since we know about it, and since we're aware of it, maybe it won't be as effective."

"Hmm," Samantha purred.

He chuckled. "C'mon now. I'm tryin' to be realistic."

"I know."

"Well, maybe we should leave."

"Are you serious?" She raised her head. "Leave *this?* Would you rather go back to that crummy motel we stayed in last night?"

"Of course not. But— Well, for one thing, we don't have any food."

"Food is not what I'm hungry for."

"See? That's what I'm saying." A tiny note of desperation crept into his voice. "It's that spray—the whatchamacallit—the attractant, the love stuff. We don't know if what we're feeling is real."

"So, what're you suggesting?" Once again, she drew little circles on his chest.

"Maybe we should, you know, chill out, find a distraction."

She laughed. "Like what? Twenty questions?"

"Actually, that's not a bad idea."

Her eyes went wide. *"Twenty questions? Now?"*

"Not necessarily that, but maybe we could play a game of some kind. Know what? I saw a deck of cards in a basket on the kitchen counter. Do you know how to play gin rummy?"

"No."

He pulled her into the main room. "How 'bout poker?"

"You're serious."

"Yeah." He grabbed the deck from the basket and guided her toward the table. "Sit. Relax. I'll deal."

Sam settled into the soft cushions on the sofa. "We don't have anything to bet with."

"There's all that cash in the car," he said. "I could run get it."

She shook her head. "I meant chips or change. It's no fun if we can't bet anything."

He looked perplexed.

She perked up. "Wait! I've got it."

"You do?"

"How about strip poker?"

Lenny appeared to have received a few thousand volts of undiluted electricity in a part of his anatomy not designed for the charge. "What? *Here? Now?* I—"

"Yeah! C'mon. Don't tell me you're chicken."

"No! It's just—"

"Then shut up and deal."

She couldn't stop grinning while Lenny carefully shuffled the cards and dealt two hands.

"It's five-card draw," he said, splitting the hands between them. He waited while she arranged her cards, then asked. "So, how many do you want? If you've got an ace, you can get four."

"I'm good," she said, staring at her cards. "I like these."

He took two. "To be honest, I've never actually played strip poker. How do we bet? Do we each ante up a shoe or something?"

"Nah. Nothing that involved. We just compare hands. The best one wins." She gave him the wickedest smile she could conjure. "I've got a pair."

He blinked and then chuckled. "Me, too."

Samantha took two cards from her hand and dropped them, face up, on the table. "A queen of hearts and a king of diamonds," she said. "Beat that!"

"But that's not a pair!"

"Looks like a perfect match to me."

"No, no. The cards have to be the same. Like these." He put two sevens on the table. "*That's* a pair."

She gave him an innocent blink. "So, you mean... I lose?"

"'Fraid so."

"Well, just darn." She slipped slowly out from the table and stood up while Lenny watched. Once on her feet, she headed for the bedroom as she pulled her T-shirt over her head.

"Where are you going?"

"To the bedroom. I'll finish stripping in there."

"I— Uhm. That's not— I mean...."

"Are you going to join me or not?"

~*~

When the burner phone rang on Clement Bessemer's desk, it took him by surprise. He hadn't expected a call from Dak Heller, but no one else knew the number. And, if asked, he'd have said the chances of Heller calling with a status report were remote at best. And yet the phone had rung.

Clement answered without identifying himself. "Update?"

"Sort of," said Heller. "We have a little problem here in paradise."

"Go on."

"I've been arrested."

Oh, God! He's killed someone. Clement sat back in his chair, shaking his head. "For what?"

"Assault."

Not murder after all. He relaxed a bit. "What did you do?"

"I got stuck in traffic on my way to Montgomery. An idiot in front of me wouldn't let me pass."

"So?"

"So, I tried to get his attention and convince him to get out of the way."

Clement's tension returned. "You were

arrested for assault because you *yelled* at him? What the hell did you say?"

"Nothing! Not a damned word. I waved a gun at him. But I didn't shoot!"

"Oh, for the love of—"

"Problem is, the guy's connected. His wife works for the government, and he's a big deal in the party. Or, I dunno. Maybe it's the other way around, maybe she's connected and—"

Clement swallowed. "Which party?"

"Hell if I know. That's all the cops told me."

"Do you know the name of the person you assaulted?"

"I never *touched* the guy! I swear."

"That'd be battery, you moron. A threat is an assault, and you threatened him with a gun. It doesn't get much worse."

"I—"

"Shut up. I'm thinking." Clement's thoughts swirled at tornado speeds. *Had the gun been used in another crime? Should I even tell the Senator? When would be the best time to ditch my burner phone and cut off all ties to Heller? But then, how would I find the damned camper?*

Clement forced himself calm. "I'll ask you again. What's the name of the guy you threatened?"

Heller paused. "Nichols, maybe? Michaels? Something like that."

Clement pulled up a map of Alabama on his computer. "Where are you now?"

"In the fucking jail!"

"But which one? Montgomery County? Elmore? Macon? It depends on where you got arrested."

"I don't know. I'm on an old wall phone; people have scribbled shit all over the wall next to it, but nothing useful."

Heller's voice no longer bore the bravado it had during their earlier calls. Clement took more than a little pleasure from that. "Then just ask someone!"

He heard several voices in the background before Heller came back on the line. "Montgomery County."

"Okay. That helps."

"Get me outta here," Heller said. "If you want that damned camper anytime soon, you've gotta get me out."

"We'll see," Clement said. "We'll see."

Chapter 16

"There are some people who live in a dream world, and there are some who face reality, and then there are those who turn one into the other." –Desiderius Erasmus

Lenny had never felt so fulfilled and yet so puzzled at the same time. The afternoon and evening he'd spent with Samantha, mostly in bed, topped any date with any female in any scenario he could imagine. Simply put, she captivated him, utterly, and he found himself willing to do anything for her—anytime, anywhere.

And she seemed to feel about him in exactly the same way.

But there was a problem—a big one. He didn't know if they were reacting to Edna's crazy potion or to each other. And it was driving him to distraction. He wanted their affection for each other to be real, but he couldn't escape the possibility that it had all evolved from a couple squirts of whatever Edna had put in her damned spray bottle.

"We need to talk," he said when Sam joined him at the pop-up table in the RV's main room.

"That sounds ominous."

"I didn't mean it to be."

"Good." She snuggled close to him and breathed in his ear. "I had a wonderful night."

"Oh, me, too," he said. "The most—"

She put a finger to his lips. "No superlatives, okay? I'd like to think we're just getting started."

"I know, me, too! But is it real? Doesn't it bother you that we could be infatuated with each other simply because of Edna's potion?"

Sam smiled. "Does it matter? I'm quite happy with things as they are. Aren't you?"

"Well, yes. And... Actually, no. I want this thing we have to be real. I've been in relationships before—okay, maybe just a couple—but they didn't feel anywhere near this intense, this... I dunno, complete."

"And you're worried those feelings will fade as soon as Edna's stuff wears off?"

He felt himself frown. "Yeah."

"What does she say about it in her notes? Anything?"

His frown dissolved into a chuckle. "We seem to have put all our efforts into... You know."

"Sex?"

"Yeah."

"It's not a dirty word, y'know."

"No! Of course not. I know that. I just meant—"

"Shut up, Len. You're overthinking this. Why can't you just enjoy it, whatever it is? Call it life. Call it... Love!" She paused long enough to plant a doubt-withering smile on him. "Just don't let your overactive gray matter call it quits."

"Can I be honest?" he asked.

She twisted her lips, and her eyes seemed focused on the ceiling. "I guess."

"Do you remember when we were in the tire shop, and the guy at the counter was flirting with you?"

"Yeah."

"Well, I... Uhm...."

"What?"

"It made me a little jealous."

"Really?"

"Yeah. 'Cause you were—"

"Leading him on?" She laughed. "Of course I was. And it worked, didn't it? He didn't charge us for the repair."

"I know. But still—"

"Shouldn't *that* tell you something? There

was no Edna stuff involved. You felt something, something in your heart. And you know what? If our roles had been reversed, I'm certain I'd have felt the same way."

"You're right, I think. At least, I hope you're right. I want you to be right. I—"

"So, dig out the damned notebook, *Leonardo*. Let's see what Auntie Edna said about it."

~*~

Despite being a career criminal, Dak had never had to spend a minute in jail. He'd never been caught for the crimes he'd committed. He felt quite sure his efforts to eliminate evidence of his participation made that possible. *So why did I let my guard down? Why did I let my impatience cost me when nothing else had?*

The only good thing he could think of was the fact he no longer worked for a nameless, faceless assassination broker. Instead, he now worked for a bunch of politicians. And they had pull. They had connections. They could make things happen.

They could get him sprung.

Or they could abandon me and hire someone else to do their dirty work, the bastards. If only Clementine had been more positive. If only—

"Hey, you. Meathead."

Dak turned in his cell to face the speaker through the bars. "What?"

"You're in deep, deep shit, ya know that?"

The man wore a deputy's uniform stretched to the limit by his muscular physique. He had a shaved head and a five o'clock shadow that would likely become a full beard by midnight. Tall, massive, and grumpy, he looked more like a professional wrestler than a guard.

Sometimes bravado worked. Dak prayed it would this time. "Deep shit, huh? How deep?"

"You messed with the wrong people."

"So I heard. Guy named Nickels, right?"

"McMichael. *Mister* McMichael."

"Okay, so? I'm in jail. What more does he want?"

"He wants you to set things right."

Dak chuckled. "He wants me to apologize? No problem. I can do that."

It was the guard's turn to laugh. "You want a beatdown?"

"Of course not."

"Then it's gonna cost ya."

"How much?"

The guard appeared to be doing a calculation in his head, something he clearly wasn't designed to do. "Ten grand ought to cover it."

"And what if I don't happen to have that much?"

"Then you'll only have to cover the cost of a doctor and stitches."

Dak had some cash in reserve, carefully hidden in his car. Assuming the Montgomery County police hadn't dismantled his vehicle, the money should still be there. But it was woefully short of the ten-thousand-dollar mark. At last count, he had less than half that much.

Before Dak could respond, the guard asked, "You got insurance?"

"No."

"So, ya wanna buy some?"

Dak eyed the brute with suspicion. "What'll that cost?"

"Ten grand. Like I said." The guard smiled. "Thing is, you gotta pay it before they haul you in for your arraignment. This needs to be pre-arranged."

"You don't suppose anyone will notice I've been beaten up on account of a traffic offense?"

"Buddy, you already look beat up. With two black eyes and that row of stitches in your forehead, you look more like a raccoon than a human. Or maybe a wimpy version of Frankenstein." He chuckled. "We took pictures when we booked ya, and honestly, you looked like shit. You don't look any better now."

"You think I won't rat you and this McMichael character out?" Dak said. "You don't think the DA will be interested in what I have to say?"

"You mean District Attorney McMichael?"

Shit. "Okay, okay. I just need to make another phone call."

~*~

Mel looked at Millie and said, "I've gotta get goin'."

"Why?"

He grinned. "'Cause I've got a job. I have work to do in New Orleans. But believe me, I'd much rather stay here with you and continue doing what we've been doing."

"So, it was okay for you?"

"Way beyond just 'okay.'"

"When will you be back?"

He shrugged. "If you'd asked me that yesterday morning, I'd have said in a week. But if there's a chance you'll be hanging around here for a while, I'm sure I could shorten the trip by a day or two."

The comment caused her to stop thinking about their time in bed and focus instead on the sole reason she was in Alabama—Dak Heller. It wasn't a pleasant thought.

"Hold on," she said and dug her cell phone from her purse. She clicked on the tracking app linked to her father's stolen watch and made a shocking discovery. The watch was in Montgomery, an hour's drive away. She expanded the view of the map until she could determine exactly where Heller was and made another shocking discovery. *The watch is in the Montgomery County jail—Heller's been arrested!*

Now what? Sit here and hope I hear something? Maybe wait and see if Heller gets out on bail so I can hunt him down and shoot him? Or bail him out myself? And then *shoot him?*

She glanced up at Mel. "I— Uhm... I doubt I'll be going anywhere. Though I sure can't afford to stay here."

"Okay," he said. "How 'bout I give you a call when I'm on my way back?"

"I guess that'd work." She looked around the room. "It's just—"

"Or," he said, "you could come with me. My boss bought a house in the French Quarter. He said it needed some work, and he's paying me to check it out and make sure it's done well. I'll be living there, so no hotel bills. Food's on me. Well, on him; he gave me a credit card."

She stared at him, unable to contain her surprise. "You really mean it?"

"Damn right I do."

Her smile made him laugh. "Well?" he asked.

"Give me a minute, okay? I've got to make one quick phone call."

"Sure! Just don't leave me hanging too long."

Veils

Millie hurried out onto the room's balcony and closed the sliding door behind her. She found a phone number for the Montgomery County Jail and dialed. After short conversations with three different employees, her suspicions were confirmed. Dak Heller was definitely in the slammer, and no one was willing to tell her if he'd be out any time soon.

When she returned to the room, Mel hadn't moved. "Got it figured out?" he asked.

Why the hell not? Heller isn't going anywhere. And I get free food? A shower? Great sex? And besides, I've never been to New Orleans!

She grinned at him. "When do we leave?"

Samantha didn't bother waiting for Lenny to dig out Edna's notebook. In their previous attempts to glean information from the journal, they'd focused on the sprays which generated the extremes of desirability. Edna referred to them collectively as veils. Neither Sam nor Lenny had given much thought to the other options Edna's veils seemed to provide, one of which supposedly created an air of respectability that allowed the user to appear "normal" in the eyes of the beholder. The redneck physics professor they'd met immediately came to mind.

The formulas did not appear complicated, but they required very exacting measurements. The recipe for one result called for a tiny difference in a single ingredient, and that in turn could alter the second product in a dramatic fashion. If, for instance, one's dream was to be a rock star, the potion for the veil of respectability wouldn't do. But a tiny change, a mere dash of something different, would generate a veil suggesting immense talent.

The problem, and it related to every recipe Samantha studied, applied to the breakdown of the veil. With the passage of time, the effects wore off. If the user lacked the innate skills the veil suggested, then there would be an inevitable return to the status quo. The veils didn't generate ability, but many allowed it to be discovered.

The same issue applied to the attraction and repellant sprays. Each of them generated a veil that temporarily inhibited the appearance of negatives or positives. Feelings were amplified in both users and those immediately connected. Thus, lovers fell more deeply in love, while ignoble elements rose to the fore in those doused in repellants.

Sam boiled it down for Lenny. "If we don't love each other, the potion won't make us fall in love. The affection has to be there before it begins."

"And the repellant?"

"It works the same way. If you didn't really like someone when you first met them, the spray is only going to make you dislike them more. When it wears off, they won't be switching places with any true friends."

"So, we really are in love?" he asked.

"It sure seems like it."

"And we'll still love each other when the stuff wears off?"

"According to your Aunt Edna, yes."

Lenny seemed to levitate off the sofa and float toward her. She opened her arms wide to accommodate him, and they hugged each other for what she deemed a ridiculous length of time. Not that she cared to end the embrace any sooner than he did.

"Y'know, Len...."

"Yeah?"

"I hate to change the subject."

"But?"

"I haven't changed my clothes in forever. I don't have anything else to wear!"

"Neither do I," he said.

"Don't you think we oughta do something about that?"

He nodded. "How 'bout right after we get the lessons on how to drive this rig?"

"And maintain it?"

"Bingo."

"Where's that grungy little sales guy when we need him?"

Chapter 17

"A professional politician is a professionally dishonorable man. In order to get anywhere near high office, he has to make so many compromises and submit to so many humiliations, that he becomes indistinguishable from a streetwalker." –H.L. Mencken

Clement had vacillated over what to do about Dak Heller's arrest. He had no intention of taking over the hunt for the Gianella woman's elusive camper, nor could he take the problem to Senator Grovemont. Clement could easily imagine the reaction Grovemont would have if he gave him details the Senator couldn't deny knowing about later. The old bastard was all about plausible deniability. No, he reasoned, solving this problem was entirely his responsibility, and once he'd settled on a plan, things would be just fine.

As long as nothing went wrong.

Hoping for the best, he dug into the PAC's records and located the name of a U.S. Congressional candidate from Montgomery, Alabama: Adrian

McMichael. After receiving feedback from a handful of carefully worded inquiries, Clement felt satisfied that he'd found a win-win solution for his problem. Despite lacking any specifics he could hold over McMichael's head, PAC staff swore the man would do almost anything to build his campaign fund.

McMichael's secretary fielded Clement's call, but when he told her Senator Grovemont's PAC wished to speak to her boss, she quickly put the call through.

"McMichael here," said the Montgomery County District Attorney. "What can I do for you?"

Clement introduced himself, then launched into the reason for his call. "You have someone in custody who works for us," he said. "It is vital that he complete his mission as soon as possible."

"What's the charge against him?"

"Assault."

"Hmm."

"Apparently, he was provoked by a driver who wouldn't allow him to pass."

"Happens all the time," McMichael said. "What was the basis for the assault charge?"

"Our operative claims he merely waved a pistol, but he never—"

"Hold the hell on," grumbled the attorney. "When did this happen?"

"Late yesterday afternoon."

"On I-85?"

"Maybe, I don't have many details."

"What is this asshole's name?"

Clement cleared his throat. "May I remind you that this individual is in the employ of Senator Grovemont's PAC? He—"

"What's his name?"

"It's Heller. Dak Heller."

After a brief silence, McMichael's voice dropped low. "Unbe-fucking-lievable. He waved a damn gun at my wife!"

"Your wife?" *Oh shit!* "I'm sure he didn't intend to use it."

"Oh, really? Were you there?"

"Of course not. And I completely understand your feelings. But there has to be a way—"

"No."

Clement's worst fears about the incident felt imminent. "I can't— Please. Listen. There's got to be a way we can resolve this to our mutual... satisfaction."

"I doubt it," McMichael said. "My wife won't be happy until that idiot is in prison for the next decade. And I assure you, I can make that happen."

"She wasn't injured, was she?"

"No."

"And Heller didn't fire the weapon, did he?"

"No."

"Have you spoken to him?"

McMichael was slow to respond but eventually said, "Not directly."

"I don't know what that means."

"A subordinate has been in touch with him."

"I see."

"That's unlikely."

Clement shifted gears and dropped any ideas he had about not offering a *quid pro quo*—campaign contributions in exchange for Heller's release. "I understand you're running for a Congressional seat."

"That's true."

"And you realize that Heller works for us, the Patriots for Progress Committee." He paused for a breath. "From what I hear, you're a patriot."

"Obviously."

"Then it seems like we should be able—"

"He's going to pay a price," McMichael said. "He's not getting off scot free."

"He can't do time. We need him in the field. Now."

"All right," the attorney said at last, "I'm keeping him locked up for a while, long enough for him to understand the gravity of his offense."

"One night? Two?"

"A week at the very least. Maybe two, my court calendar is pretty crowded right now. His arraignment is already scheduled, and under ordinary circumstances, taking him to trial could take months."

Grovemont will have a coronary! "Please," Clement said, trying not to sound like he was begging. "Two weeks is not— We just can't do without him for that long. You have no idea how important he is."

"Then perhaps you need to rethink your PAC's obligations. Either that, or get yourselves a new operative."

"Five days," Clement said. "After that, we've gotta have him back out in the field."

"If you'll send me something official that outlines any donations the Patriots for Progress Committee will make, I'll see what I can do for Mr. Heller."

"Excellent! I'll draft something immediately."

"By the way," McMichael added, "I understand your man looks pretty rough."

"I don't know anything about his appearance," Clement said. "I've spoken with him on the phone, but we've never met in person."

"By 'rough' I didn't mean he looked like a derelict. I'm told he appears to have been shot, grazed by a bullet and possibly beaten up."

What? "That's—" Clement swallowed. "That's news to me. Is he all right? Has he been seen by a doctor?"

"He's got some stitches," McMichael said. "Now you know as much as I do."

"I need to speak with him."

"I'll set it up," the attorney said, "as soon as I get that document we discussed."

~*~

Their early bedtime did not result in an early wake-up, since neither slept much during the night. What did rouse them was a firm rap on the door of the camper and a voice they recognized as that of the salesman they'd met the day before.

Lenny stumbled halfway to the door, then yelled, "We'll be out in a little while."

"Don't wait around too long," the man said. "Our instructor is a busy man. He's got a lot to do besides show you the ropes on this rig."

"Gotcha," Lenny shouted, then added, "Give us ten" before returning to the vehicle's bedroom.

He watched Sam reach for her T-shirt, hold it close to her nose, sniff, and make a face that told him everything he needed to know about her conclusion.

"Shopping," he said. "Right after class. Okay?"

"I've got a better idea," she responded, her voice slightly muffled as she pulled the tainted garment over her head. "Why don't you find out how to operate this thing, while I run out and get a few things I— No, make that things *we* need. Toothbrushes, toothpaste, soap, deodorant—"

"Food?"

"And at least one change of clothing."

"I don't have any idea how long the owner/operator lesson will take," he said.

"I'll try not to be away too long. Maybe you can grab a cup of coffee in the sales office." She brightened. "They might even have doughnuts."

She slipped into her cut-off jeans and faced him with her hand out, palm up. "Car keys, please."

"Are you at least gonna give me a goodbye kiss before you leave me?"

Her lips twisted into a dimpled smile. "Hm. I guess one little kiss wouldn't hurt." She pecked him on the cheek. "Be sure to take Ebby out before you do anything else."

"Like get dressed?"

"Okay," she said with a giggle. "That might be a good idea."

Lenny watched her go and felt suddenly alone. He shook his head, got dressed, took Ebby outside, and wondered if he'd just been given a look at his future.

~*~

The muscle-bound jailer Dak had encountered the day before returned to his cell bearing a food tray. "Got yer breakfast," he said as he slid the tray and its contents through a horizontal gap in the bars. "Eat up. Yer gonna need your strength."

"I doubt it'll take too much muscle power to make a phone call and arrange to get your money."

The guard looked disappointed. "Unfortunately, that's been taken care of. It's too bad. I was looking forward to beating the crap outta you."

Dak squinted at him. "It's paid? Seriously?"

"Yeah. But, see, here's the thing. You still gotta stay locked up for a few days."

"Why?"

"'Cause you threatened the DA's wife, dumbass."

"I had no idea a woman was driving that truck."

"Would it have made a difference?"

"Probably not." Dak stared down at the food on the tray. "What's this?"

"Grits, bacon, and toast."

It neither looked nor smelled like anything the guard mentioned. "I think I'll pass."

"Suit yerself. Just leave that stuff where it is. Someone'll come along and collect it once you're in your new cell." He chuckled. "Yer gonna love it, I'm sure."

"What're you talking about?"

"I've been ordered to take you down to the old wing of the jail. Bottom floor, in fact."

"Yeah? So what?"

"There's a couple cells down there we don't use much anymore. My orders are to make sure you're locked up in one of 'em." The guard crossed his arms, pulled his shoulders up around his ears, and pretended to shiver. "I hope you like little crawly things."

~*~

Clement Bessemer had given serious thought to calling in sick, but he knew that even if he did, someone—most likely Senator Grovemont—would dial him up anyway. If you weren't in surgery or on your death bed, the PAC considered you available, no matter where you were.

Resigned to the inevitable, he felt no surprise at all when his secretary told him he had a call from his boss. "Good morning, Senator," Clement said.

"Who the hell is Adrian McMichael, and why on Earth is the PAC putting twenty fucking grand into his campaign?"

I'm just fine, Senator. And you? Clement rubbed his brow in anticipation of another politician-induced migraine. "I'll be happy to fill you in on the details, Senator, but I was under the impression you didn't want to know anything specific about—"

"Stop right there."

"Yessir."

"Does this have anything to do with our efforts to locate a certain recreational vehicle?"

"It does." Clement muffled a cough with his fist.

"As I feared. One of my aides says this McMichael character is a district attorney."

"That's correct."

"You've spoken with him?"

"Yessir. It seems our operative—"

Grovemont cleared his throat with such volume that Clement jerked the phone away from his ear. *Right. Message received.*

"Are we looking at potential delays in the effort to... You know."

"Five days," Clement said. "Counting yesterday."

The Senator went quiet for an overlong stretch. Eventually he spoke. "That is simply not acceptable. We don't have time for bullshit delays."

"I understand, sir, but—"

"You have no idea how important this is."

"Evidently not."

"We've got to make some changes, starting with this idiot in Alabama."

Clement winced. "McMichael? The DA?"

"No! Of course not. With the idiot in jail."

"You know about him? About Heller?"

"I didn't know his name," Grovemont said, "until now." He paused again; Clement assumed he was trying to figure out how to admit his knowledge without actually doing so, something only politicians and pathological liars could do. "Okay. From now on, this is just between us. No one else. Got it?"

"Uh, sure," said Clement, utterly unsure about what he'd just agreed to.

"We need to cut any and all ties with the moron in jail. Tell him he's done. We've paid for his release, but that's it."

"You want *me* to tell him?"

"It's just you and me, remember? Nobody else knows about this, right?"

"I— Uhm...."

"Get the file we gave him and any information he has on the location of the camper."

"Hang on a sec," Clement said. "I've gotta ask. What's so special about the camper? Why not just buy one and—"

"It's what's in it that matters," Grovemont said. "That's what we need to get our hands on. And damned soon. The primaries are almost upon us."

Clement's mind spun with thoughts about what might be hidden in an old lady's camper. *Could it be an incriminating recording or photos of something the Senator wanted to keep buried? Could he and the old lady have... No!*

"From now on, you're my point man. You have my trust, Clem. It's all on you."

It was Clement's turn to remain silent.

"Are we good?" Grovemont asked.

"This feels like the sort of thing that's... you know. Above my pay grade."

The Senator laughed. "Get me what's in that damned camper, and I'll make sure you're set up for life. Fair enough?"

"I— Uh—"

"Good."

<Click>

Chapter 18

"The only thing that saves us from the bureaucracy is its inefficiency." –Milton Friedman

Samantha shopped as quickly as she could and not simply because that's what she'd told Lenny she would do. She just missed him, missed being with him, and missed the connection they'd so suddenly discovered.

A nearby pharmacy provided the essentials for their hygiene, but she had to search a bit further before she found a big retailer with affordable clothing. But instead of cruising aisle after aisle and searching rack after rack for outfits, she grabbed the simplest, quickest solutions for her needs: underwear, four tops, and two pairs of shorts. But just before checking out, she wandered through the lingerie department where she found an absolutely scandalous negligée on sale. Based on the very physical nature of the time they'd recently shared together, it seemed unlikely that Lenny's desire for her might fade.

But it made sense to be prepared just in case, so she slipped the silky bit of sex cloth into her shopping cart and cruised on to the check-out lane. There she spotted a rack filled with candy and gum. She spotted her favorite chew, a strawberry flavor that lasted longer than most, and added it to her other selections.

On the way back to Happy Times Ten RV Acres, she stopped at a fast-food place for breakfast goodies. While waiting for her order she thought back to the time she and Lenny spent reading the mail they'd collected from his aunt's post office box.

Many of the letters had been plaintive in their requests. People with little hope of solving their problems had reached out to Edna Gianella, who no longer existed. But the solutions she could have offered certainly did still exist, assuming she and Lenny found the ingredients and followed the directions.

It quickly became all too clear that while they didn't have jobs, they certainly had work to do. When her food arrived, she packed it up and hurried back to Lenny.

~*~

Dak's fears grew as the hulking jailer pushed him toward his new quarters in the basement of a much older building. Though they only went down a single flight of stairs, their passage into the dank lower level had him perspiring. The guard noticed.

"You sweatin' already?"

Dak remained silent.

"You ain't even seen the best part yet."

Fluorescent lighting blinked occasionally, just often enough to suggest an imminent blackout.

Bedbugs love the dark.

The guard opened a steel door and hustled Dak through to a space with four cells, two on either side of a wide corridor. None of the cells held prisoners.

"Take yer pick," the guard said as if the selection mattered. The units were identical.

Dak strained to look at the grubby blanket on the thin mattress of the nearest cell. Bedbugs were tiny, invisible except up close. Seeing any from several feet away was impossible.

"Quit stallin'," the guard grumbled. "Get in one of these near the door." He shoved Dak toward on open cell then told him to stop. After removing the handcuffs from Dak's wrists, he shoved him again, then closed and locked the door.

"It stinks in here," Dak said.

Gorilla-man grunted. "Prob'ly the mold."

Dak's heartbeat clicked up an additional notch. "You can't seriously expect me to stay down here."

"I sure do. DA's orders. Mr. McMichael says you'll be a guest in here for the next few days."

"It's filthy in here! Smells like a sewer."

Veils

"What'd you expect? It's a jail cell. It's where lowlifes like you go. You've got a bed, a crapper, and three free meals a day. What're you bitchin' about?"

"There's not even a window!"

The guard chuckled. "Can't get anything past you."

Dak glared at him.

"Oh, and just so you know, it's lights out at nine o'clock. So, if you're gonna do any readin', you'd best get it done before then."

Dak glanced around at the empty cell. "Reading? I don't—"

"Pays to plan ahead, don't it?" The guard made a show of rattling the keys to the cell doors.

"And since I won't be on duty tonight, I'll just share with you what my momma always told me when she tucked me in." He cleared his throat and adopted a higher pitch. "Nighty-night. Sleep tight. Don't let the bedbugs—"

"Fuck you!" Dak screamed.

The guard laughed all the way through the main door which he closed and locked behind himself.

~*~

Millie couldn't remember a time during her adult life when she felt so utterly relaxed. Mel had lived up to his word about the house in New Orleans as well as his willingness to spring for food.

Though she wasn't quite sure exactly what he did for his employer, it couldn't have been too difficult and certainly wasn't terribly time consuming. She doubted he left her alone for more than a few hours at a time, and she used the opportunity to explore the French Quarter.

She would occasionally check on the whereabouts of Dak Heller, but nothing changed. He either remained in jail or, if he'd been released, he must've pawned her father's watch or left it somewhere. Neither of the latter two possibilities seemed likely.

The release of built-up tension gave her added flexibility in almost everything. Her attitude improved; she tended to look at new things without suspicion, something she'd struggled with since the day of her father's murder.

Her intense feelings for Mel had mellowed somewhat, but she still enjoyed being with him, and he seemed to feel the same way.

The newfound sense of freedom prompted a new set of questions. *Can I maintain my relationship with Mel if I continue to hunt Heller? Can I even tell him what I've been up to, even if I promised to give it up?*

She never intended to live the life of a vigilante. If someone with political pull hadn't ended the official search for her father's killer, she'd never have given a thought to finding him herself. Everything in her life had been twisted and contorted because some well-connected asshat pulled the plug on the investigation. Her laissez faire attitude about life had taken a radical turn. Her focus had become one of simple revenge.

Up until she met Mel.

Once they became an item, and an instant one at that, prior to that she'd limited herself to a single life goal: the extinction of Dak Heller.

And now?

Mel would be leaving New Orleans in a day or two, she thought. She prayed she could find the answers to her questions before he dropped her off back in Alabama.

~*~

Lenny didn't find the driving lesson too challenging. His aunt's RV handled nicely, but finding suitable parking spaces for it would be a constant problem. In addition to coaching him on driving the big rig, Lenny's instructor, an affable young black man named Alonzo, also showed him how to care for it. That meant looking after everything from the tires to the toilet. Fortunately, the vehicle came with a pair of heavily indexed maintenance manuals.

When the instruction sessions finally ended, Alonzo congratulated Lenny and shook his hand. "Your aunt was a wonderful person," he said. "If it wasn't for her, I'd never have gotten this job."

"Really? That's wild. I can't believe you knew her!" He paused and scratched his chin, thinking back to all the money they'd found in her safe deposit box. "I hope you won't mind my asking, but how much did she charge you?"

"Charge?" Alonzo's eyebrows dipped. "She didn't charge me anything. But I made it up to her anyway. She asked me if I knew anyone who could make some modifications to the RV."

"Like the table in the floor and the expanding bedroom?"

"Nah. Those were built-ins, by the manufacturer. She wanted what she called 'hidey holes.' You know, secret storage compartments."

Lenny had a pretty good idea what Edna would have hidden, cash for starters. "Did she ever get any secret compartments installed?"

"Oh, sure. My dad and I did the work. He's a genius at stuff like that. He got real sick when I was a kid and couldn't find much work after that. But, he told me what to do every step of the way. Miz Gianella was happy with the work and paid us a pretty penny for it, prob'ly more than we deserved. She was a real angel, I swear."

"It sounds like it," Lenny said. "Sadly, I didn't know her at all. And yet, it sounds like she knew everyone in Camp Hill."

Alonzo laughed. "That's a fact, and she knew folks all over. But I think she got started in Camp Hill. It ain't much of a town. Small, poor, and everybody pretty much knows everybody. Some folks are a lot better off than others. If somebody like that needed her help, I s'pect she'd have charged 'em. But poor folk like me and my dad? Nope. She never mentioned it."

Lenny couldn't help but wonder where Alonzo and his father had installed hiding places in the camper. "Can you show me the hidey holes?"

"Oh, sure! Follow me," Alonzo said, and he promptly headed for the back of the RV where a spare tire sat just above the bumper and shared the back wall with a ladder leading to the roof.

Alonzo pointed at the tire. "There's the first one."

Lenny stared at the round, black wall tire. When nothing appeared odd about it, he felt all around and behind it, but came up bewildered.

"Give up?" Alonzo grinned at him.

Lenny nodded.

"I kinda cheated. There's no latch you can get to back here. It's hidden under the dashboard," Alonzo said. "C'mon, I'll show ya."

They entered the RV, and Lenny quickly learned where the switch activating the rear hidey hole was hidden—behind the fuse box which had been reengineered to swing out of the way.

Lenny tripped the switch, and they both hurried to the rear of the vehicle. The tire was already swinging out of the way when they got there.

"There's something in it," Lenny said, making no effort to hide his excitement. He then abruptly looked at Alonzo. "Have you messed around in there?"

"Not since we rigged it," he said. "Whatever's in there is yours man, not mine."

Lenny reached into a shallow, horizontal bin, and removed a three-foot-wide basket filled with an array of tiny atomizers, each bearing a number.

Alonzo grinned. "Is that cool or what? She gave me a little bottle just like one of those. Told me to spray myself before I went on my first job interview. Stuff worked like magic. I felt confident. Relaxed. I knew I could answer any question they threw my way. Seriously man, the stuff really worked!"

Lenny pulled a pair of bottles from the narrow box and examined them. Other than a number, there was nothing to describe the contents. "Do you remember what number was on the bottle she gave you?"

Alonzo shrugged. "Twenty-something, I think. There wasn't a whole lot in it. Maybe a half dozen squirts. Thank God there was enough to cover both of my interviews!"

"I guess the whole point is, there *was* enough," Lenny said. "But if what you've told me about her is true, she'd have probably given you more if you needed it."

"Like I said, your aunt was a good person.

Maybe better than good. She cared about folks." He looked down at the dozens of tiny bottles filling the box from the hidden compartment. "What're you gonna do with all that?"

"Honestly? I'm not sure yet. But my... partner and I will work something out, I'm sure."

"Your *partner?*" Alonzo gave him a puzzled look.

"Her name's Samantha. We uhm... work together."

"You just work together?"

"Yeah."

"Then why are you blushin' so hard?"

"I am?"

"Dude, don't take this the wrong way, but white folks are easy to read. And you kinda look like a tomato."

Chapter 19

"Fear is our immediate response to uncertainty. There's nothing wrong with experiencing fear. The key is not to get stuck in it." –Gabrielle Bernstein

Clement Bessemer was an office worker; he always had been, and he had no desire to work anywhere other than a cozy space dedicated to him and whatever he'd been hired to do. When the Patriots for Progress PAC offered him a job in upper management, he jumped at the chance. Not only would he have a dedicated space, he'd have a corner suite with windows and a secretary. And all he had to do was put up with one colossal pain in the ass, Senator Terrence Grovemont.

But at the time, he didn't know how much of a pain Grovemont would become.

If he had known what sort of man the senator was and how much he would interfere, Clement wouldn't have taken the job. But it was far too late to do anything about it now. He had an ex-wife and three kids who depended on his alimony and child support payments.

He'd managed to avoid thoughts of his stupid life choices as he prepared for an extended stay in the wilds of rural Alabama searching for a camper with some sort of valuable contraband aboard. It might have helped if the Senator had bothered to reveal exactly why he wanted it, whatever it was.

But no, he sent me on my merry way with a credit card and a half-assed mandate to take over the work previously done by Dak Heller, a man who likely killed people for a living. In other words, a fucking sociopath.

Swell.

Clement figured the drive from Maryland to Montgomery would take 14 hours. With stops, maybe 16. He decided to break the trip in half. If Grovemont didn't like it, he had only himself to blame. Clement wanted to fly in and rent a car, but the Senator wouldn't hear of it. Apparently the paperwork would be too hard to disguise.

Thanks, Senator. You're a real... peach.

~*~

When Samantha returned to the RV lot, Lenny stood outside Edna's camper with a smile spreading his unshaven cheeks. "Welcome back. And man, have I got something to show you!"

"Can it wait until we get all this stuff inside? I'm hungry, and breakfast is right here." She waved a white, paper bag at him and shoved a foam tray bearing two large, insulated cups of coffee into his hands.

"What took so long?"

She gave him a look of disbelief. "*Long?* I've never shopped so fast in my life. I figure I got back here in record time."

"I'm kidding," he said. "It's just... Aw hell. I missed you is all."

She figured he'd earned a kiss and gave him one. "Now, let's eat. I'm starved. You can tell me about your mysterious 'something' over breakfast." She glanced at her watch and added, "Okay, brunch."

While she unwrapped their food, Lenny went into the bedroom and came back holding a long, narrow, low-sided, metal box which he placed across the table, dividing their two meals. Sam couldn't resist examining its contents—tiny atomizers like the one they'd found in the safe deposit box.

"What d'ya think?" he asked.

She gave him a grin. "If all this is the same stuff we sprayed ourselves with before, we'll never, ever, get out of bed again."

"It's not," he said. "At least, I don't think it is. See? Each of the bottles is labeled with a number. There are quite a few duplicates, but the numbers are consecutive. I think each one coincides with whatever the stuff is supposed to do. This could be the whole range of Edna's veils."

Veils

Sam wasn't entirely comfortable with calling the diminutive spray bottles 'veils' even though that's how Lenny's aunt referred to them. The veil was the outcome, not the product, but it seemed to be a distinction without a difference. She gazed at him while chewing on a breakfast burrito that would have tasted much better if it hadn't cooled off. "So, what do we do with 'em?"

"I don't know," he said. "I haven't given it a lot of thought."

"Seriously?"

"Hey! I've been learning how to drive this rig and take care of the eight bazillion things that need to be done to keep it operating. Okay? C'mon."

She giggled. "You look so... wounded."

"Well, yeah. Okay," he said relaxing visibly.

After a swig of coffee, Sam continued, "I've been thinking about all those letters we got from Edna's post office box. Remember? People asking her for help?"

Lenny nodded. "I talked to Alonzo about that."

"Alonzo?"

Lenny waved his arms, pointing at different spots within the RV. "He's the guy who taught me how to drive this thing. He's also the one who told me about Edna's hidey holes."

Sam stopped chewing. "Hidey holes?"

"Secret compartments. There are two of them. This box was in the first."

"What was in the second?"

"Nothing." Lenny frowned. "And that really surprised me. It's built into the mattress in the bedroom. There's a hidden switch that makes a drawer slide out. Ebby's doggie bed is in the way, but moving that is no big deal."

"So, it's just an empty drawer?"

"Yeah," said Lenny, "but it's big, and it's a 'hidden' drawer. A casual observer wouldn't know it was there."

"What d'you suppose she used it for?" She paused long enough to chuckle. "Sex toys?"

"Try to be serious, okay?"

Sam nodded and somehow managed to stifle her laughter.

"Where do we go from here?" he asked.

"We dig into her notebook," Sam said after a deep breath. "We find out what each of those numbers represents, and then we take a long, hard look at the letters we have. If we can match a solution to some of those problems, we're looking at a terrific way to make some money. It could turn into a career!"

It was Lenny's turn to nod his head. "You're something else, ya know that? You can turn me on just by sitting next to me chewing your goofy gum."

"I'm inclined to reward you for that," she said, "but first we need to get you some clean clothes, and I know just where we can get them. And we could both do with a shower."

Lenny grinned wickedly. "Together?"

Why did I even bother to buy that stupid nighty?

~*~

Despite repeatedly telling himself he was the victim of a cruel hoax, and that someone would soon let him out of the dungeon in which they'd put him, no one rescued him. It was the story of Dak's life—no one had ever rescued him.

Why should I expect anything different now?

He could hear the faint sounds of a train; beyond that, nothing. He may as well have been deaf. The bars of his cell bore a coat of rust. That, and various colored blotches and smears on the cement walls were the only things that broke up the drab, depressing gray. He had no desire to inspect his bedding, and the smell from the toilet told him everything he wanted to know about that. He couldn't help but wonder how long he'd be able to abstain from using it.

His overriding concern, however, was something he couldn't hear and could only sometimes smell—bedbugs. Under flickering neon ceiling lights, the damned things were nearly invisible. They lived in clusters and could hide in the narrowest of cracks or even in electrical outlets.

Though not an expert, Dak had spent a fair amount of time studying them after having an allergic reaction to their bites. The little monsters lived on blood, preferably human. And they seemed addicted to his.

Never a patient man, Dak struggled to find a way to pass the time while standing as far from the bed and the toilet as possible. Hoping to get his mind off the bugs and the contents of the commode, he tried counting—first by ones, then threes, and then nines, but when the numbers piled up, he wearied of the effort. There were no bricks to count, nothing with which to write or draw, or mark his time or his presence.

Eventually, however, someone entered the four-cell chamber, and Dak's pulse quickened. *Release! Finally. Someone got the message. Bless you, Clementine!*

The person who entered the chamber struck Dak as the complete opposite of the gorilla-like deputy who locked him in. Short, chubby, and obviously uncomfortable, the guard approached him slowly and slid a white bread sandwich on a paper plate through a slot in the cell door.

"Lunch," he said, his voice barely audible.

Dak accepted the sandwich and gave it a quick glance.

"Baloney and cheese," said the guard. He then reached into a back pocket and produced a small plastic bottle of water.

"No napkin?" snarled Dak as he set the jail delicacy on the floor.

"Nah." The little man turned to go.

Dak gripped the cell doors. "Wait! What time is it?"

"Noon," said the guard. "I guess. Maybe a little later."

"Listen. I don't think I'm supposed to be in here," Dak said. "There's a law against cruel and unusual punishment, right?"

"I ain't a lawyer."

"Doesn't matter. Just look at this hell hole! Making anyone stay in this is inhuman. Whoever had me locked up in here is breaking the law. If you don't let me out, wouldn't that mean you're breaking the law, too?"

"I don't know who you are, mister, but I do know one thing. You must've screwed up pretty bad to end up in there. Mr. McMichael has us put only the worst offenders in this lock-up. You better pray you don't have to spend too many nights in there. The bedbugs—"

Dak frantically waved him to silence. "I need help. I've gotta get outta here. I'm allergic to the damned things. I could die in here!"

The guard chewed his lip for a moment before responding. "Maybe you oughta pray that you don't."

"Pray? You're shitting me! I don't— It's just not something I—"

"Well maybe it's time to start."

Dak stared at him, unable to do anything else.

"I'll be back in a bit," the guard said and strolled out of the cell cluster.

Dak had no idea what the man intended, though he suspected the guy might try to convert him to some weird religious cult. *Just what I need. But if it'll get me outta this shit hole any sooner, I'm all in. Halle-frickin'-luyah.*

As promised, the guard returned and slid a worn, paperback Bible through the same slot in the cell door he'd used to deliver the sandwich.

Dak accepted it in silence.

"Have you spent much time with the Good Book?" asked the guard.

"Not really."

"It ain't never too late."

Dak watched the guard leave and lock the door behind him. The Bible felt heavy in his hands.

He had no desire to read it, but he had nothing else to do.

If it comes to it, I can always use it to swat bugs. The dead ones don't bite.

As he leaned back against the corner angle of his metal cage and slid slowly to the cement floor,

Dak mentally replayed a bit of his conversation with the guard.

McMichael only puts the worst offenders in this lock-up. But McMichael is a district attorney, not a cop. And yet he has the power to say who gets locked up where?

Maybe it was that idiot Clementine. He not only didn't get me out, maybe he was the one who got me thrown into this shitty cell. Maybe he was the one who ordered somebody to take a shot at me.

Dak no longer gave a damn about who his employer might be. All he wanted was revenge, and once he got out, he'd make good use of his time. But first he had to figure out which of the two assholes he'd kill first.

And who knows? Maybe there's more than two.

Chapter 20

"If you want to know who your friends are, get yourself a jail sentence." –Charles Bukowski

With Lenny's car attached to the back of the camper, and Ebby asleep on the sofa, he and Sam belted in and prepared to leave the RV lot and head for Beulah, Alabama. According to Edna's notes, she had a small but well-stocked place there where she mixed, measured, and stored the ingredients that went into the veils.

As Lenny slowly approached the exit, having navigated through a dozen rows of parked campers, he spotted Alonzo sprinting out of the sales office and straight toward them. Lenny applied the brakes and stopped just as the man reached them.

Lenny rolled down the driver side window, stuck his head out, and asked, "What's up?"

Alonzo's voice, thready from his race to the camper, was appreciative. "Thanks for stopping. I'd have hated to chase you down on foot."

"Relax," Lenny said. "We're not in any hurry."

"I just needed to ask you for a favor."

Lenny and Sam exchanged looks. When Sam shrugged and gave him the universal palms up sign, he turned back to Alonzo. "You were awfully patient showing me how to take care of this rig." He waved a hand at the RV. "And you showed me the uhm... hidden extras. So, I think I owe ya."

"Thank you. But this isn't about me, it's for my sister, Fara," Alonzo began. "She got herself mixed up with a seriously bad dude. He was nice to her before he proposed, but ever since she accepted, he's been treating her horribly."

"He's what, rude? I dunno—"

"He beats her if she doesn't do exactly what he tells her to do."

Sam had unbuckled her seat belt and slipped closer to Lenny. She stretched across him and poked her head out the window. "She needs to get away from him. Fast!"

"That's the thing; Fara's afraid he'll track her down and beat her up even worse."

"She should call the police," Lenny said. "And get a restraining order."

Alonzo shrugged. "That's *exactly* what I told her to do. But she doesn't trust the cops around here. And besides, once that asshole gives her another beating, she might not be able to call for help. I'm tellin' ya, Fara's scared out of her mind."

"Hang on," Lenny told him. "Lemme park this thing and—"

"Leave it right where it is," Alonzo said. "If anyone complains, I'll deal with 'em."

Lenny shut the engine off, then turned to Sam. "What d'ya think?"

Sam grimaced. "If it were up to me, I'd give her a gun and some shooting lessons. There are way too many buttheads like the one she's dealing with."

"I agree with you, but assuming that providing the means for her to kill the guy is slightly beyond the scope of the veils, what can we do to help her? Spray her with a repellent?"

The suggestion caused Sam to lighten up. "What if we did that along with a dose of something to make her look like a badass? You know, give her a shot of confidence."

"Is that an option?"

"There are a ton of options. They're all numbered and listed in the notebook. Weirdos like the guy she's dealing with feed on fear; they crave the feeling of dominance and superiority."

Lenny nodded. "I'm feeling more and more like your first suggestion is the best option."

"Teach her how to shoot him?"

"Yeah."

"And bury the body? Are you willing to become an accomplice?" She shook her head.

"C'mon, Len. This is serious. This girl is in trouble, and we need to help her."

"So, you're taking this seriously?"

"Damn right. I had a friend who went through something similar. Only...."

"Only what?"

"She didn't survive."

Sam's words cut to his heart and ignited his compassion. *Fara needed them, desperately.* "Let's check with Alonzo and see what he can set up for us. We need to talk to this gal. There's got to be a way we can help."

Clement Bessemer hated traveling. At least, especially by car, and even more especially when *he* had to drive. Having someone to talk to would have made it almost tolerable, but Grovemont wouldn't hear of it. His was a solo mission. A *secret* solo mission. So secret, Clement didn't know what the hell it was really about.

Other than knowing he had to locate a dead old woman's stupid camper, he was barely in the loop. The whole damned project left him feeling impotent. He'd become a functionary in Grovemont's political shenanigans. He didn't like the feeling. So, when he saw a sign advertising a hotel in the LandSide chain, he quickly changed lanes and headed for the exit. LandSide properties offered three free drinks to adult lodgers during Happy

Hour, a period which stretched daily from five to eight P.M.

He was right on time.

Between drinks he went over his options, the ones involving the jailed killer—his best hope for finding the camper. He drank much faster than he ordinarily did. And when he'd finished his three free cocktails, he bought a double to take to his room.

Unable to find anything worth watching on TV, Clement opted for old reruns of "Gunsmoke."

Miss Kitty didn't look half bad, he thought. His only regret was that he didn't resemble Marshall Dillon. At all.

He fell asleep much earlier than usual and dreamt of romancing the lovely, blonde saloonkeeper when the tall, lanky Marshall passed out from too much cheap whiskey.

~*~

Millie remained undecided about whether to continue her quest to kill Dak Heller or seek happiness with Mel, her newfound love interest. Maybe, she told herself, those two things didn't have to be mutually exclusive. Maybe she could follow her heart with Mel and still get the revenge she'd been seeking for so long.

But what if Mel found out he was in a relationship with a vigilante, or worse, a murderer? She could always tell him why she had such a strong desire for revenge; surely he would understand.

Or not. And that's where her ability to plan completely fell apart.

But there was one thing she could absolutely do, and it was something she had debated about with herself: tell the Gianella kid a killer was tracking him.

A kid? Geez. Okay, so maybe he is too old to be considered a kid, but in any event, he has no idea someone is after him, someone who has no scruples when it comes to killing people.

Unfortunately, that only triggered more questions. *When* should she tell him? She left a GPS tracker on his car, so finding him presented no challenges. But she didn't have a car of her own in New Orleans; she'd ridden there with Mel. Maybe she could borrow his car and drive off without telling him what she was up to?

No. That was crazy. She'd have to explain what she was doing, and this definitely wasn't the time to make any such confessions. So, she reasoned, she'd need to wait until he finished his business here, and they headed back east to Alabama. He would drop her off there and continue on his way to... where? Had he said Virginia? West Virginia? Maryland? DC?

She felt sure he'd told her, but she couldn't remember any details.

And that seemed odd. She recalled that they'd talked sparingly about their backgrounds, but it hadn't seemed odd at the time.

Now it sorta did.

~*~

Sam saw the look on Lenny's face and knew her words had a weighty effect. Rather than drive to the little country town of Beulah to dig further into the mysteries of his Aunt Edna, Lenny postponed the trip and worked with Alonzo to set up a meeting with his sister, Fara.

Though tempted to join the conversation, she knew Lenny would do the right thing, whatever that turned out to be. Instead, she continued reading Edna's oddly organized notes about the veils. Two paragraphs in particular jumped out at her.

> At first, I had no idea my veils could impact anything other than people. They can have an effect when used on buildings, too. Why that came as a surprise is a mystery to me. I also learned that while the veils work on dogs and cats, they don't always work the same way as they do on humans. For one thing, dogs over-react. It first happened when I sprayed attractant on the Yellowhammer Savings and Loan. Ebby smelled it and went crazy! She not only fell in love (if you can call it that) with the building, she craved contact with everyone inside, including customers.
>
> I don't dare use the repellant on anyone while Ebby is around. I fear it would enrage her.

Veils

Sam leaned back in her seat, turned her face toward the ceiling, and smiled. It seemed clear all they had to do was spray repellant on the jerk hurting Fara and then let Ebby loose. God help him when confronted by seventy pounds of pissed off puppy.

When Lenny returned to the RV, Sam told him what she'd learned.

"I guess that explains how Ebby could pick out the bank. And it's obvious the effects don't wear off of real estate."

Sam then related her idea about using Ebby to take care of Fara's fiancé.

Lenny pursed his lips in thought then replied, "What if this meathead hurts her? For all we know, he could be armed."

She had to admit he was right. They didn't know nearly enough about the guy. "We don't even know his name!"

"Alonzo told me his first name is Jamar, but he couldn't remember the jerk's last name." He then flashed her a big smile.

"You find that amusing?"

He chuckled. "No, that's not it. He has a dog, a pit bull."

Sam shrugged. "Some pitties are sweethearts. I hate the way so many people automatically assume they're mean. Mostly, they're just protective."

"This pit bull belongs to Jamar. He bets on him at dog fights—"

Sam inhaled suddenly; her face reflected outrage.

"—but get this; he makes Fara take care of it. If what you told me about how dogs react to veils is true, all we need to do is spray her with attractant and him with repellant. The pit bull will do the rest."

"And," Sam said, "he'll continue to act that way as long as Fara keeps him."

"Seems so," Lenny said. "But I still think she could use a gun of some kind, just in case ol' Jamar shows up while the pit bull's not around."

"We'd best leave that up to Fara and Alonzo." Sam tightened her seatbelt. "Now, let's get going. After we take care of Fara, we're going to need to find somewhere to spend the night."

Lenny waved at the RV. "Why not here?"

She giggled. "I meant we need to find a parking space."

~*~

Dak managed to concentrate during the afternoon and spent most of the time searching for a biblical reference he could use on the jailer who'd given him the worn King James version of the holy book. He had little success and blamed it on his parents for failing to give him a Christian upbringing. Or, he lamented, any sort of real upbringing at all.

When the short, chubby guard appeared with his dinner on another paper plate, Dak was ready for him. "Doesn't the Bible tell us to forgive and forget?"

"Mine doesn't," said the guard. "And neither does the one I gave you."

"But—"

"What it says is..." The jailer closed his eyes in concentration. "It says 'For if you forgive other people when they sin against you, God will also forgive you. But if you don't forgive the sins of others, God won't forgive yours.' Or something like that."

"So, just who the hell am I supposed to forgive?"

"That'd be Mrs. McMichael. She's the one you tried to shoot."

Dak grabbed the bars of his cell in anger. "But I didn't! I didn't shoot anybody or anything."

"You *threatened* to shoot her. I reckon Mr. McMichael reads it the same way. You screwed yerself. Quit blamin' somebody else for your own stupidity." He shoved another white bread sandwich and paper plate through the slot in the cell door. "Eat up. You'll need your strength. And eat yer lunch, too. No sense waitin' for some kinda gourmet stuff."

The jailer left without another word, and Dak cursed himself for not pleading his case, his fear, and his severe allergies to bed bugs.

He found it nearly impossible to sleep. Every

time he dozed off while leaning against the bars, he'd wake up to a new bite. It made the night last a very long time.

Chapter 21

"To exact revenge for yourself or your friends is not only a right, it's an absolute duty." –Stieg Larsson

Clement had an early start; breakfast hours at the motel had ended much earlier than usual. As a result, he crossed the Georgia/Alabama line in what he considered record time and arrived at the Montgomery County Jail just ahead of lunch hour.

After a long, annoying exchange with the man supposedly in charge, a muscular deputy who looked more like a professional wrestler than a professional anything else, Clement got permission to visit Dak Heller. A short, balding, overweight guard led the way into the basement of an older adjoining building.

"Just a short walk more," he said, his voice devoid of emotion. "Your guy didn't eat any of his breakfast."

Clement cringed as the grim state of the underground cells became all too readily apparent.

"You actually keep people locked up down here? This is nothing but a dungeon."

"Nah. That's medieval stuff." The guard gestured for Clement to continue following him. "Just through this last door." It opened with a brief, metal-on-metal squeal.

Clement stepped past the guard and walked into an area containing four decrepit cells. Competing odors of sewerage and sweat assaulted him, and the flash and buzz of blinking tube lights overhead deepened the pervasive gloom.

"This is complete bullshit," Clement groused. "No one deserves to be held in here, no matter what they've done!"

He held his nose and walked toward the only cell with an occupant, a man who lay on the floor pressed up against the bars in a corner. His head rested on a Bible. He didn't move.

Oh, for the love of God, Heller's dead?

"Dak. Dak! You okay?"

When the hitman failed to respond, Clement stepped closer and peered down at him. Heller's skin was puffy, and scores of dark red pustules peppered his exposed flesh. Kneeling, Clement stuck his arm through the bars and felt Dak's throat for a pulse. He had to probe a bit before he detected the unconscious man's weak heartbeat.

Clement stood and snarled at the guard, "Call an ambulance!"

The guard appeared nonchalant. "Why?"

"Because, you idiot, this man will likely die if he isn't seen by a doctor. Now call for a goddam ambulance!"

"But Mr. McMichael—"

"*Adrian McMichael*, the DA?"

"Yessir."

"What the hell does he have to do with it? Unless, of course, DA stands for dumbass." Clement fumbled his cell phone from his pocket and dialed 9-1-1.

"The Sheriff's sister is Mr. McMichael's wife. She was drivin' the Sheriff's truck when that man right there—" he pointed at Heller "—when he threatened to shoot her."

"*9-1-1. What is your emergency?*"

Clement waved the guard to silence, then answered the emergency operator. "I'm calling from the basement of the old county jail. There's a man here on the floor, unconscious, and covered with bites or stings from something."

"Bedbugs," said the guard. "I warned him about 'em."

"Apparently they're bedbug bites, and the victim here is clearly allergic to them. We need an ambulance right away."

"I have an ambulance on the way, sir. Can you clear a path for the EMTs?"

"Definitely," he said, and after identifying himself, ended the call.

"I don't think Mr. McMichael is gonna like this."

Clement turned and stared at the man. "Do I look frightened? I'll deal with the DA when and if I have to. For now, you might want to think about getting yourself a lawyer of your own."

"What for?"

"In case Mr. Heller here survives and accuses you of attempted murder."

With that, the formerly casual guard no longer appeared nonchalant.

~*~

Lenny pulled up to the address Alonzo had given him. The neighborhood looked rundown, and he worried someone might try to rob the camper while he and Sam visited Alonzo's sister, Fara.

"C'mon, Len," Sam said, pulling on the sleeve of his T-shirt, one of three they'd bought the day before. "We're runnin' late."

"No, we're not. Alonzo said she'd be home alone just before lunchtime. It's only half past eleven. I think we're right on time. And besides, I'm not real comfortable leaving Ebby here while we go off and try to help Fara."

Sam nodded. "We may not be late, but we still need to get a move on."

Veils

"Have you got the sprays?"

"All three of 'em," she said.

"*Three?*"

"Yeah. The two we talked about and my pepper spray—the one my friend Myra gave me. She said I should never leave home without it."

Lenny chuckled. "I'm pretty sure that's a slogan for a credit card."

"Whatever. I think it's good advice, and it already came in handy. Remember that redneck in the pickup truck who—"

"Yeah. I remember." He smiled. "That stuff works well."

"If all else fails, I can use it on Fara's fiancé. It'd give us enough time to skedaddle."

"I've heard it's hard to outrun a bullet."

"If the shooter can't see anything, I'm not going to worry," Sam said. "Now, c'mon! Fara's expecting us."

The RV took up half the width of the road, but they had nowhere else to park it. Cars could still get by, and they didn't intend to stay long. Hopefully, Ebby would dissuade any would-be thieves.

Fara met them at the door and ushered them inside. They paused when they heard a growl. "That's just Killa. Don't mind him; he growls at everybody." She gestured toward a worn sofa. "Have a seat."

The pit bull, bearing several scars and a pair of fresh bite marks, stood between them and the couch. He issued a low-pitched rumble and showed his teeth, but when Fara approached him and gestured for him to sit, he complied, though he clearly wasn't happy about it. Lenny and Sam slipped past him and sat down.

Once they'd settled in, and the dog had given them both a good sniffing, Fara thanked them for coming. "I'll be honest with y'all. I don't really believe there's much you can do for me. Jamar, my fiancé, is uhm... call it hot-headed. He gets a notion and won't let go."

Lenny could see bruises on Fara's face, neck, and arms. He gave her a sympathetic smile. "I suspect 'hot-headed' doesn't quite explain things, as I understand it from Alonzo."

"I just don't want to put y'all at risk, too," she said. "Jamar's got a really short fuse. Once it's lit, it only takes a few seconds before he gets crazy."

"We're prepared for that," Sam said. She even smiled, which Lenny knew was utterly unwarranted bravado.

"We have an idea for how to solve the issue," Lenny said. He then explained about two of Edna's veils—the attractant and the repellant. "Here's the thing, though," he added. "Dogs will overreact to this stuff. May I demonstrate with the attractant?"

Fara looked skeptical. "I— I guess. Should I lock up Killa first?"

Lenny shook his head, no. "We need him here, and I think you might enjoy his reaction."

"Or, maybe not if it's like you said, his *overreaction?*"

"Let's find out. We'll be in here with you, and Sam has some pepper spray in case this goes sideways."

Fara swallowed and nodded. "Let's do it."

Sam first applied a very light spritz of the attractant to herself and Lenny, then emptied the rest of the atomizer on Fara. "I don't smell hardly anything," she said as she joined them on the sofa. She sat beside Lenny as all three waited for the dog to respond to the stimulant.

It didn't take long. Killa moved his ponderous head slowly from side to side and sniffed, then stood up and trotted directly toward Fara. She sat motionless, a look of apprehension on her face.

The dog's stubbed tail wagged furiously as he approached her and gently put his head in her lap. He exhaled as if he'd just run a long way.

"Oh. My. God! Oh, my God," Fara whispered over and over. "He's never, and I mean *never*, done anything like this. He's acting all sweet and cuddly. That's never—"

She stopped talking when she heard a car pull into the driveway.

"Oh, shit! Jamar's here early. Y'all gotta get outta here."

"We didn't come here just to run away," Sam said.

Fara's voice dropped to a nervous whisper, "I'll tell him you're old friends. From, you know, like before he and I met."

"That'll work," Lenny said. With the value of Edna's veils fully in evidence—the dog was still snuggling with Fara—he felt confident. If the veils didn't work, Sam's pepper spray would.

Jamar threw open the door and stalked inside. He looked first at Fara and then at her visitors. "That your big-ass rig parked out front?"

"Yes," said Lenny, trying to make his voice sound friendly. He pointed at a window overlooking the driveway where Jamar had parked his car. "I see you got around it okay."

"Yeah, well, it's still a pain in the ass. Blocks traffic. If you don't move it, I'ma call the cops."

"We won't stay long," Sam assured him. "We have a line of unique perfumes and colognes, and we just wanted to offer y'all some free samples."

Jamar looked suspicious. "We don't need no fancy perfume shit."

Sam and Lenny stood and faced him. "Really?" Lenny said. "What we've got can be life-changing, and I'm not exaggerating." He nodded toward Sam. "This young lady is prepared to offer you your choice of two products, a mild cologne, or something you'll simply cry over."

He feigned a whisper. "Me? I'd go with the cologne."

"I don't give a damn what—"

Sam spritzed him with Edna's repellant.

Startled, Jamar's expression turned to one of uncertainty.

"Rub it in," Sam urged. "It works better that way. In fact, you probably need a bit more." She spritzed him again despite his raised palm.

"Stop!" he yelled. "Knock that shit off."

Sam stepped back and swapped the atomizer for the pepper spray. Despite her words, Lenny could see the fear on her face.

"There's no need for hysterics," Lenny said. "It's just—"

"Will you shut the fuck up?" Jamar suddenly turned toward Fara who was still rubbing the sweet spot behind Killa's ears.

"Fara! Goddamn it! What'd you do to my dog?"

"Nothing," she said. "He just likes me. He—"

"Killa!" Jamar said. The command came out as low and guttural as the dog's growl when they first arrived. "C'mere," Jamar said. "Now, damnit!"

The dog slowly raised his head and turned to look at him. He sniffed and promptly snarled, the sound rumbled from deep within his chest.

"Don't you growl at me, asshole." Jamar looked up at Fara. "What'd you do? He's a damn fightin' dog. He don't need no lovey-dovey cra—"

With that, Killa lowered himself, preparing to lunge, his peaceful, loving demeanor gone. Instead, his eyes narrowed and he showed his teeth; saliva drooled on the floor as he prepared to charge. Jamar backed two steps away only to stop and grab a handgun from a shelf in the tiny kitchen.

"Don't shoot him!" Fara screamed as he raised the gun and took aim.

Sam immediately hosed Jamar with pepper spray, to which he reacted as if he'd shot himself. His second scream came a moment later and was significantly louder.

Lenny grimaced as he watched Jamar try to dislodge Killa from his crotch. Fara's fiancé pounded the top of the dog's skull but couldn't shake the animal loose.

Sam's expression remained neutral until she got Lenny's attention. She gave him a dimpled smile. "Y'know, I'd have to give that veil five stars."

"I just hope the dog doesn't kill him," Lenny said through gritted teeth.

"Why? You feel sorry for that dirtbag?"

"It's not that. I'm afraid Animal Control will want to put the dog down."

"Oh! I hadn't thought of—" Sam turned and looked at Fara for the first time since the dog attack began. Like Sam's early reaction, Fara's expression revealed nothing. "You need to call him back."

"Why? Jamal deserves what he's getting."

"I agree. But see, here's the thing." Sam very briefly explained their fears that the authorities would demand that the dog be euthanized.

Fara exhaled her disappointment, but agreed. "Killa," she said. When the dog didn't react, she repeated his name, only louder. "Now, come! Come to Mama."

Killa whined, but eventually let go of Jamar who lay sprawled and groaning on the floor with one hand clutching his groin. He rubbed his eyes with the other.

With the still-foaming dog at her side, Fara nudged Jamar with her toe. "You go on now, git. You hear me? And don't you ever come back. 'Cause next time, I ain't callin' the dog off. For all I care, he can chew on you 'til there's nothin' left."

Sam and Lenny helped Jamar stand and guided him outside and back to his car.

"Did ya hear what that bitch said to me?"

"Yep," said Sam. "And if you've got any brains, you'll do exactly what she told you to do."

"But— But she gots my damn dog!"

"The one that just tried to give you a sex change?" Lenny chuckled. "I'm pretty sure that's her dog now."

Chapter 22

"A man whose life has been dishonorable is not entitled to escape disgrace in death." –Lucius Accius

Dak woke up slowly; he could barely open his eyes. The room was brightly lit, so it definitely wasn't the one he'd passed out in. And he was comfortable, in a bed, and the sheets felt clean; they didn't stink. There seemed to be something antiseptic in the air, the exact opposite of the pungent odor of a backed-up toilet. The stink had gone away.

So had the bars.

So had the gray walls.

And the bugs.

They could still be here—in the bedding!

That thought launched a frantic effort to free himself of the covers, a task made difficult because one of his wrists was handcuffed to a bedrail.

What the hell?

Veils

His hands and arms were swollen; he could barely bend his fingers enough to grasp the sheet and blanket. The sight of his puffy, red flesh oozing out from either side of the steel restraint looked unreal. It couldn't be *his* arm, but he knew it was. Wishing wouldn't make the crimson boils and the swelling go away.

He vowed, once again, to punish the DA. *What the hell is his name? McNickel? McKnuckle? Something like that. I'll find out.*

And he'd give the same treatment to Clementine, whose last name he couldn't quite remember either, but both names would come eventually. He wasn't thinking as clearly as he needed to. But the thought of killing them—*that* was something he could focus on easily. Just like the shackle on his wrist.

"Oh! I see you're awake."

Dak dragged his gaze from his handcuff to the woman who had just spoken, a middle-aged nurse with a lopsided smile.

"Too warm?" she asked.

"What? Uh... no. Bugs. The little bastards are everywhere."

"No," she said, patiently. "They *were* everywhere. On you, anyway. But we got rid of them while you were unconscious. This is a hospital; we can't be having vermin running around out of control."

Hospital. Makes sense. Why didn't I realize it? Geez. "I... Um, that's good. Thank you."

"I wasn't on duty when you were brought in." She pointed at his restraint. "We're not supposed to ask, but this isn't the first time someone's been brought in covered with bug bites. But, I've gotta say, yours look worse than the others I've seen."

Dak waved away the question with his free hand. "I got involved in a traffic thing, and now they're accusing me of all kinds of crazy shit."

"Well, I'd say you're darn lucky that guy saw what shape you were in and insisted you be brought here."

"What guy?" he asked.

"Clement... something. I don't recall his last name, but his first name's the same as my granddaddy. Rest his soul."

Driven by surprise, Dak levered himself up to a sitting position. "And this Clement guy, he got me outta that hell hole?"

"That's my understanding. And I heard he's also trying to get the charges against you dropped. But until that happens, the guard who accompanied you said you have to wear the cuff."

Dak fell back against the bed.

"My name is Lula," the nurse said, her voice cheerful. "I work day shifts, so if you need anything, just punch the little buzzer clipped to the handrail."

Being in contact with a potential ally, Dak tried to make a joke. "So, the buzzer's a jailbird, too?"

She smiled. "Yeah, I guess so."

"Is there any way I can contact him? Mr. Clement Something, I mean. I'd like to... uhm, you know, thank him." *And I'd also like to find out what the hell is going on, before I cut his throat.*

The nurse shrugged. "Like I said, I wasn't here when you were brought in, but it wasn't that long ago. I'll check the nurse's desk and see if anyone knows anything. But don't get your hopes up. We don't usually act as a message service for patients."

"And what about my stuff?"

"What stuff?"

"My clothes, my watch, and my wallet. I had a ring, too. Gold, with an emerald on it."

She walked over to a set of shelves built into a closet. "If there's anything, it'll be right in—" She turned and smiled at him. "Your clothes are here on the top shelf, but from the smell, they need laundering. There's also a sealed envelope with your name on it. There's a note on a big sticker from the county jail."

Dak felt a surge of relief. Now, if he could just find a paper clip or a bobby pin, he might be able to pick the lock on the handcuff and get the hell away.

~*~

223

Millie's day began on a high note. Mel had ordered breakfast from a fancy French cafe. "They'll deliver soon," he said on his way to the shower. "Best croissants you've ever tasted."

As she got the coffee perking, someone knocked on the front door. When Millie answered it, a thin, smiling young man stood facing her. He held a bag of pastries at his side and handed her a receipt, then held out his hand for payment.

"Oops, my bad," she said. "I thought it was prepaid."

"No ma'am," he said. "And I can't take a credit card or a check."

Millie nodded. "Got it. I'll be right back." She looked over the receipt as she opened her purse which was nearly devoid of cash.

Oh, poop.

Mel's wallet lay on the nightstand, so she grabbed it and carried it back to the front door. While the delivery man watched, she plucked a twenty-dollar bill and a ten out of Mel's billfold, enough to cover the meal and a tip.

The delivery guy gave her the food, thanked her, and left. Millie set the bag of fragrant goodies on the kitchen counter and paused before returning to the bedroom to put Mel's wallet back where she'd found it. Driven by curiosity, she reopened the wallet and flipped through the photos in it. She blanched when she discovered one showing Mel, a woman, and three small children. It was taken at

Christmas time, and the family, all dressed in candy cane pajamas, stood in front of a decorated tree.

Millie's lip curled. *You lying, cheating bastard!*

She wanted to throttle him and started toward the shower with the damning photo in hand when she heard Mel shut the water off. She stopped abruptly.

Oh, just farking great. Now I'm supposed to confront a naked man for making love to me while his wife and kiddies sit at home waiting for him? The hell with that! Not while I'm stuck here in Louisiana.

Still angry, Millie retrieved her phone. She hadn't used it since arriving in New Orleans, other than to monitor Dak Heller's location. He'd been in jail, but now she realized he'd moved several miles away from there. As she focused further on his location, she realized it was a hospital.

Had somebody shanked him? That seemed to be the preferred method of dispatching jailbirds. At least, that's the way they did it on TV. She wondered, briefly, if she should stick a knife in Mel, the philandering phony.

Though the thought was tempting, there was no way on Earth she'd ever do something that drastic. But, if nothing else, it ended her fears over what to reveal about her self-declared mission to kill Dak Heller. After what she'd seen in Mel's wallet, she no longer gave a damn what he thought.

Finally, she could focus, guilt-free, on the task that brought her to the South in the first place. Any accusations she might have tossed in Mel's direction could damn well wait until he took her back to her car in Alabama. If he wasn't ready to leave that day, she'd book a flight to Montgomery and leave on her own.

And take the damned croissants with me!

Screw him.

~*~

Sam gazed at the countryside as she and Lenny drove toward Beulah. Hopefully, they'd be able to find the place where Edna prepared her veils. Her thoughts kept drifting back to mental images of the dog attacking Jamar. It was a vicious and violent, but necessary way to end his brutal assaults on a woman who had no way to protect herself.

But Sam's sense of guilt continued to grow, and not because of what she and Lenny had sprung on Jamar. She was fine with that; he got exactly what he deserved. But, she wondered, was it possible for someone to feel guilty because they felt no guilt? It seemed absurd. And yet....

The hell with Jamar. He earned his reward, and I don't need to feel sorry for any of it.

Turning her thoughts to their planned destination in Beulah, Sam reached down toward Ebby who was sprawled awkwardly, but mostly behind, their seats. She scratched the top of the dog's head, pleased to hear Ebby respond with a contented groan.

Veils

While looking at the road in front of them, she asked, "What do you think we'll find in Beulah?"

Lenny shrugged. "I've no idea. It seems like every time we think we've got a handle on what Edna did, we discover there's more. It's... I dunno, tiring."

"But not exhausting. There've been only good things to come out of it so far. And there's no reason to think we can't do more."

"I'm sure you're right," Lenny said, shifting slightly behind the wheel and continually checking the rearview mirrors on both sides of the RV. "It's just—" He paused and took a deep breath. "What if we discover something negative? You know, like maybe the veils break down and whatever good they've done disappears. I've had that thought in the back of my head since this all started."

Sam pursed her lips as she looked at him. "So, you think maybe when the attractant we used wears off, we won't love each other anymore?"

"I can't imagine that happening," he said. "But... Well, what if it does?"

"C'mon, Len, we've been over this before."

"I know. It's just—"

She didn't wait for him to finish whatever nutty thought had wormed its way into his brain. "Do you remember how Ebby reacted to that bank in Opelika?"

"Yeah."

"Well, how long has it been since your aunt hosed it down with attractant? Months ago? A year? Maybe longer ago than that. We don't know how long she was ill before she died."

"So? Dogs have a much stronger sense of smell."

"I'm sure smell has something to do with it, but geez, Len, think. The bank's been rained on hundreds of times. Wouldn't it wash away?"

"I suppose, but—"

"Based on our personal experience and some of Edna's notes, I think the veils are incredibly potent when fresh. And I think the reason their effects linger, is because they trigger something in our brains, something that causes us to accept the feelings we had when we were initially exposed."

"So—"

"So, I think we're in love, and we're gonna stay in love." She paused. "Unless...."

"Oh, Lord," Lenny breathed. "Unless what?"

"Unless you keep worrying about how it's all going to fall apart. That's just crazy talk, so stop it! You hear me?" She gave him a fierce look.

"Yes ma'am," Lenny said, grinning. "I get it."

"Good. Now tell me you're in love with me."

"You know I am!" he said.

"Nope." She sniffed. "Not good enough. Try again."

Veils

Lenny double-checked the rearview mirrors, then eased off the gas, pulled the RV onto the shoulder of the road, and parked. He turned in his seat and faced her. "Samantha Everton, I've been meaning to say this for a while now, but I just... It's, uhm... I wasn't sure how to get started."

"For cryin' out loud, Lenny. Get to the point!"

"The point is," he said, "I love you. No, it's more than that. I'm *crazy* about you! I've never in my life felt this way about anyone. But you— I'm— Geez." He shook his head as if to clear it. "The thing is...."

"What? What is the thing? Just say what you need to say!"

"Will you marry me?"

Sam felt her jaw drop as she inhaled, and quite suddenly she couldn't breathe. She couldn't take in the tiniest whisp of air.

Chapter 23

"There are four kinds of homicide: felonious, excusable, justifiable, and... praiseworthy." –Ambrose Bierce

After pacing back and forth in the outer office of Adrian McMichael, the Montgomery County District Attorney, Clement Bessemer's patience finally gave out. He stomped over to McMichael's secretary, a woman in her thirties, heavily made up and wearing a gray suit a couple of sizes too small.

"I've been waiting for over two hours," Clement said.

"I told you; Mr. McMichael is a busy man. You just wouldn't believe how many meetings he attends. And it seems like he has more and more every day. It's astonishing, really. I think it's—"

"Ridiculous?"

She seemed taken aback. "Uh, that wasn't—"

"Obviously, the man has no idea how to maintain a proper schedule."

"I don't think—"

"You shouldn't *have* to think! It's not your job to supervise his comings and goings. That said, when the hell am I going to get to see him?"

"Actually," she said, with more than a little attitude, "I just got a text message from him. He won't be coming back to the office today."

"Did you tell him I was here, *waiting?*"

"Yessir."

"Did he ask about me, or offer to see me somewhere else?"

"I'm afraid not."

"Is he even aware of the reason for my call? That because of him and the Sheriff, a man is in the hospital fighting for his life?"

"That can't be true. I know them both."

"Oh, really? And are you aware of the dungeon they run in the basement of the old jail?"

She dismissed the idea with a wave of her hand. "That hasn't been used in years."

"Try telling that to the man stuck in there!"

After hastily checking her notes, she asked, "Would that be Mr. Uh... Heller?"

"Yes," Clement hissed.

"Mr. McMichael said Mr. Heller had earned 'special treatment' as a courtesy to someone by the name of Grovemont. Do you know who that is?"

"Only too well."

"Well, according to my notes, Mr. Heller is to remain locked up for a couple more days."

Clement briefly chewed on his upper lip. "In that case, kindly give your boss a message from me. It's important."

"Of course." She produced a note pad and pen, sat up straight, and prepared to take dictation. "All right, fire away."

"The Patriots for Progress PAC expects to have reasonable access to the people we benefit. Your Mr. McMichael's failure to provide that could cost him the donation we have scheduled for his campaign. I will be discussing this with Senator Grovemont in a matter of minutes. If McMichael fails to reach me before then, he can kiss our donation goodbye."

"That's not— I mean, I doubt he had any idea that—"

"Stupidity is not a defense. A good attorney would know that. On the other hand, McMichael may think his campaign is well funded, but it certainly didn't look that way when I investigated it. He might think we're some sort of a gift horse, but believe me honey, this horse can and will kick."

He walked to the door, stopped, and then looked back over his shoulder. He raised his voice to make sure she heard him. "On second thought, tell that jerk not to bother calling me at all."

Still fuming, Clement knew better than to call Grovemont before he regained control of his temper. Instead, he grabbed a bite of fast food and gobbled it down on his way back to the hospital.

He went straight to Heller's room, pleased to see the man awake. Some of his swelling had gone down, and the nasty boils on his arms, neck, and face had subsided somewhat. "You look a lot better," Clement said. "How do you feel?"

Heller blinked. "I think I got shit by a cactus."

"I can only imagine."

"I doubt it," Heller said. "A nurse told me you got me outta the dungeon."

"True."

"And that you're trying to get me released."

Clement pursed his lips. "That's kinda true."

Dak's puffy face made his frown seem worse.

Clement hoped he could make it go away. "I've got a proposition for you."

Dak groaned.

"If you give me everything you have on the old lady's camper, I'll not only help you get out of here, I'll help you file suit against the DA and the Sheriff for attempted murder."

"So, that's your way of telling me I'm fired?"

"I suppose. But you're also free to go on with your life. Thing is, if you don't take the deal, I can't guarantee you won't go right back down into the shithole where I found you."

"And if the bastards hadn't fed me to the bedbugs, what would you have offered me then?"

Clement hiked his shoulders up and down. "I guess I would've appealed to your better nature."

Dak stared at him for a moment and then laughed. "*My* better nature? What makes you think I have one?"

"I think everyone has one. At least, I hope they do."

"Then you're an idiot."

"Maybe so. But who else do you have to lean on right now? A nurse? A deputy?"

"Okay," said Heller. "You get me outta here, and I'll give you everything I've got on the camper."

"Deal," said Clement. "I'm going to make some phone calls. We'll know pretty soon if they work."

"But—"

"Later!" Clement waved on his way out.

~*~

Lenny found himself in full-on panic mode. Sam's face had turned red as she struggled to breathe. Immobilized by fear at first, he finally broke out of his emotional straight-jacket and got moving.

Throwing open the driver side door, he hustled out and over to Sam's side. He tried to open the door, but it wouldn't budge. He pounded on it and yelled, "Unlock it!"

With eyes wide and still unable to breathe, Sam pointed to her throat.

"The door! It's locked!"

She unlocked it, Lenny yanked it open, and held his arms out for her. "C'mon down. Hurry! I'll try the Heimlich thing."

Sam nodded her head vigorously. She tried to talk, but no words came out. Thoroughly flustered, she slipped off her seat and down into Lenny's arms.

Leaning on fragmented memories of lifeguard training he had after finishing high school, Lenny turned Sam so she faced away from him. He'd never performed the Heimlich on a real person; his experience consisted of a limbless, rubber torso. He hoped it was enough.

With his arms around her, Lenny mentally recounted the steps. He began by making a fist which he gripped with his free hand. The fist, he recalled, had to be positioned below the ribs and above the belly button.

"Here goes," he said and pumped his fists into her stomach. When nothing happened, he repeated the process, but with more force.

She still couldn't breathe, and Lenny feared he may have made things worse.

Sam put her hands on top of his and yanked them into her belly. She was unable to fuel the effort with much strength, but it was enough to encourage Lenny to keep trying.

After several more thrusts, a wad of pink chewing gum flew from her mouth. She hung limp in Lenny's arms until she could take in several deep breaths.

"Oh, my God," Lenny said, turning her to face him. "You had me scared to death!"

"I'm okay now," she whispered. "Honest."

"You sure? At first I thought maybe you had a heart attack when I asked you to marry me."

"*What?* No! Of course, I'll marry you! I mean— Geez. You just saved my life! How could I *not* agree to marry you?" She gave him the fiercest hug he'd ever experienced.

"I was afraid that... Well, since we've only known each other for what? A week or so? I mean that's not—"

"It's okay, Len. We're not getting married any time soon. I've gotta tell my folks, and Lord only knows how little I've spoken with them since this whole thing started."

"You're right, of course," Lenny said. "We don't have to do anything in a hurry, except maybe keep going to Edna's hideout in Beulah. After that, maybe we should go back to Atlanta. I've got a lot of loose ends to tie up there. But at least I don't have to worry about finding a new place to live." He patted the RV.

Sam smiled, put her hands on either side of his head, and kissed him. "There's just one thing."

Lenny felt a twinge of apprehension. "What?"

"We won't be officially engaged until you give me a ring."

"No problem," he said. "As soon as we get back to Atlanta—"

"Y'know what? There's an amazing little jewelry shop in Auburn."

He looked at her in surprise. "How would you know that? We barely drove through, and as I recall, we were looking for a place to eat. So, how—"

She patted his chest, still grinning. "Girls know these things. We do. Trust me."

~*~

When Clement returned to Dak's hospital room, and the prisoner told him where to look for the material sent with him from the jail. They went through all the paperwork it contained—mostly handwritten notes copied from the original file given to him weeks earlier. Dak surrendered all of it.

"Now listen," Dak said. "I need to know if you can spring me in the next couple hours. If not, let me know. Call the nurse or something. Whatever. For now, take my car keys and get it out of the impound. I'll need it."

"Wait. If I can't get you sprung, what'll I do with your car? I don't even know what it looks like.

As for the impound—"

"Figure it out! Punch the car alarm, or ask the guard. Whatever. Then I need you to park the car where I can find it. Just text me the location."

"But—"

"I'm getting out of here today, one way or another. If I don't hear from you in a couple hours, I'll get out on my own."

Dak gave him a phone number for text messages and a description of his car.

"Just do me one favor," Clement said. "Don't hurt anyone on your way out."

"We'll see."

"And one last thing. Do you know where the camper is right now?"

"No, but if you give me my phone, I'll tell you where the Gianella kid is. Find him, and you'll find the camper."

Dak's phone was in the envelope which held the notes they'd just gone through. Dak pulled up the GPS tracker he'd put in Gianella's phone. "Looks like he's on the move, headed back into the boondocks west of Columbus."

"Whatever for?"

"The old lady owned some land around there. I checked it out but didn't find anything."

"You know," Clement began, "I think—"

"I think you're wasting time. Now get the hell outta here!"

Clement left the room, muttering. The only word Dak made out was "grumpy."

Yeah, so what?

Alone again, Dak straightened the paper clip he'd removed from the notes he gave to Clement and went to work on the lock mechanism of the handcuff. He made short work of it. Once free he stood up and stretched. His entire body felt tight, no doubt because the swelling hadn't gone completely away.

His skin remained pink and a little puffy, and the now pimple-size bug bites still itched. He hurried to the closet, got his clothes, and dressed. The smell didn't bother him too much. He had a change of clothes in his car, assuming Clementine didn't double-cross him.

None of that mattered. Instead, he focused on how best to kill DA McMichael and his brother-in-law, the Sheriff. The easiest way, of course, would be to simply shoot them. But then, that would be way too easy on them, too. No, he needed something uglier, something slower and a great deal more painful. After what they'd done to him, they deserved nothing less.

Chapter 24

"People who don't have experience setting healthy boundaries have secrets instead." –Jill Soloway

Mel walked into the kitchen after his shower, and passed Millie headed the other way. "Ah, the goodies arrived."

"Yeah," she said from the bedroom. "I took some money from your wallet. I didn't have enough to cover it."

"Sorry. I didn't mean for you to pay," he said.

"It's fine," Millie grumbled.

He frowned. "Whoa. You're in a mood."

She walked out with her travel bag in hand. She'd made no effort to pack it neatly; the only thing on her mind was getting back to her car and her mission.

Mel bit into one of the croissants and chewed, a look of satisfaction on his face. "These are really good. Have you had one yet?"

Veils

She looked at him, barely able to maintain a neutral expression. "We can eat 'em on the road."

"The road?"

"I've got to get back to Alabama."

"I thought—"

"Today. I need to get back today." She crossed her arms on her chest as if daring him to protest.

"I hadn't planned to leave just yet."

"Too bad. I don't have a choice. I've got to get back right away, and since I don't have a car, my options are limited. So, you can either drive me or buy me a plane ticket. What's it going to be."

"What's changed all of a sudden? You're not acting like yourself."

"Let's just say I got some bad news."

His demeanor changed, but not to one of sympathy. "Just because *you* get bad news, I'm supposed to drop everything and drive you somewhere?" He shook his head. "I don't think so. Rent a car or take the bus."

"I hate buses, and I can't afford a rental."

"Bummer."

She pursed her lips before responding. "If you don't do as I ask, I'll be forced to tell your wife about our little love nest here in New Orleans."

"My *what?* I don't have—"

"A wife and kids?" She laughed. "There's a

photo of them in your wallet—a really cute Christmas pic, and you're all wearing the same kind of pajamas. I found it near your driver's license, which I read, so I know where you live."

"That's blackmail!"

"Call it anything you like. Just do what you *said* you'd do; take me back to my car. Do that, and I'll forget all about your family and your address. And I'll forget all about you, too."

His lips twisted into a smirk. "Threatening me won't do you any good. Elaine and I are divorced. She has the kids."

"That'll be easy enough to check," Millie said. "I can talk to your neighbors, and if that doesn't work, there are always public records."

"You're ruthless."

It was her turn to smirk. "You have no idea."

"Throw your crap in the car," he said. "I'll toss on some clothes and meet you in the garage."

Millie nodded and said, "I'll bring the croissants." Which earned her another nasty look.

~*~

Sam had a tough time wrapping her head around everything she'd been through that day—the dog, Lenny's proposal, and the chewing gum fiasco. She had already ditched the rest of the pack with a vow not to buy any more, ever. To get her mind off things, Sam focused on Edna's notebook, and the often-cryptic observations recorded in it. Neither she nor Lenny had any idea what language was used in Edna's other book, the ancient one.

The late afternoon sun perched above the pine trees behind them as they pulled to a stop at what they hoped was Enda's property. All they had to go on was a rural route box number on the property tax bill they'd found in her mail. They saw just a few houses nearby, and most were in sad-to-poor condition.

While driving to the area, they'd seen some nice homes and two well-maintained schools. Edna's property lay well outside of the small, rural town.

Lenny put the RV in Park, sat back in his seat, and gazed at Sam. "Is there anything in Edna's notes about where her workshop is?"

"Not that I found, but she hinted often at the need for secrecy. Maybe Ebby could lead us there. She needs to get out and pee anyway."

They let the dog run free and waited for her to show some familiarity with the area. She explored it for a long while, and Sam worried that she might've gotten lost. But Ebby eventually came back, looking as if she'd been swimming. Still in a playful mood, she briefly chased a squirrel, tried her best to eat a gumball-size bumblebee, and then sprawled out in the shade of an immense oak tree to rest.

"Big help you are," Lenny muttered.

"Be nice." Sam gave his shoulder a soft jab. They sat on the ground beside Ebby and leaned their backs against the big hardwood.

"Kin I help y'all with sumpthin'?"

The voice belonged to an elderly bearded man standing beside their RV. He had his arms crossed and an odd look on his face. Sam couldn't read his expression, but the tenor of his voice suggested he was suspicious.

"Maybe you can," Lenny said, sounding cheery. He pulled Sam to her feet, and they dusted themselves off as they approached him. Ebby raised her head, looked at the old timer, and then raced toward him.

"Ebby!" the man cried. Eager to accept the dog's enthusiastic greeting, he managed to get to his knees just before Ebby plowed into him. "I was afraid I'd never see you again," he said as he massaged the wooly dog's face and neck.

Ebby was still lavishing affection on him when Sam and Lenny reached them.

"You must be Edna's kin," the old man said as he slowly stood up. Sam couldn't tell if the crackling noises she heard came from his hips or his knees.

He held out his hand, first to Lenny and then Sam. "Edna hoped you'd be comin' 'round someday. But I confess, I had my doubts. 'Bout the only strangers we see around these parts work for the quarry company." He spat out an expletive for emphasis. "My name's Robert, but most folks call me Bobby." He sighed. "Or Bubba."

Lenny introduced himself and Samantha then asked what the problem was with the quarry.

"They wanna dig a huge pit and haul out truckload after truckload of granite." He gestured toward the surrounding trees. "Basically, they want to wipe out a big chunk of our woods. They don't give a damn about the people who live here, much less the wildlife."

"How did Edna feel about it?" Sam asked.

"She hated the idea! Not only would it destroy the woodlands, it'd wipe out the natural spring she used for her... uhm... stuff."

"We know about her stuff," Lenny said. "That's why we came here. But we searched all around and couldn't find anything that looked like a cabin or a workshop." He smiled and pointed at the dog. "Ebby might've found the spring, though. We didn't see it, but she went out in the woods and came back all wet."

"Sounds 'bout right," Bobby said. "Edna said somebody'd likely be comin' around lookin' for her kitchen; that's what she called it. Said she cooked up all kinda stuff in there."

"So," Sam said, "do you know where it is?"

Bobby gave them a gap-toothed smile. "Y'know, if y'all hadn't brought ol' Ebby with ya, I wouldn't have trusted you enough to say anything."

"But you do know where it is?" Lenny asked.

Sam thought he sounded too insistent.

"'Course I know where it's at. There's only a few of us left that do."

Lenny beamed. "That's great! Can you please take us to it?"

"Happy to oblige, but you gotta follow me." Bobby grinned. "'Cause it sure ain't on *her* property."

"It's not?"

"Nope. It's on mine."

Sam and Lenny exchanged puzzled looks.

Bobby explained while they accompanied him away from Edna's property. He told them to leave the RV where it was. "She was afraid somebody she didn't know might stumble across it. That became even more of a possibility when the damned quarry people started comin' around a few years back. So some of us got together and worked out a plan. We tore down the shack she'd been using and built one that's underground. Edna paid for the construction, but we turned her down when she offered to pay us, too. We owed her."

Sam had to ask. "What's this about a plan?"

"Oh, that. Yeah, we rigged up a secure entry."

"Like for a bank vault?"

Bobby laughed. "Not *that* secure. None of us had the money for that. What we came up with is sorta like a trap. Ya gotta know the code to get in, otherwise you get a big dose of one of Edna's sprays."

Veils

Lenny dipped an eyebrow and asked, "Which one?"

"I don't exactly 'member what she called it, but that stuff worked like magic. If you got splashed with it, just about anything on four legs would come after you like you was dinner."

"The repellant," Sam and Lenny said.

"Y'all gotta understand," Bobby continued, "we've got lotsa dogs 'round here. Coyotes, too. And more'n a couple bears."

A bit nervous, Sam looked around as they walked. "Has anyone tried to get in who wasn't... expected?"

"Just one." Bobby frowned. "It weren't one of them quarry clowns; it was one of our own. A teenager. Thought he was real smart. Turns out he's a dumbass. But, thank the Lord, he made it back to his folk's double-wide before any of the dogs got him. I've never seen anyone run so fast."

"I guess he didn't know the code?"

"Nope." Bobby chuckled. "I'll explain when we get there."

They walked for about fifteen minutes before Bobby paused and pointed to an outhouse.

Sam felt her eyes go wide. "That? That's it? An *outhouse?*"

"Looks like it, don't it? But it ain't. That little shed is just for... Dang. What's the word Edna used?

Theatrics? Eccentrics? Something like that."

"Aesthetics?" offered Sam.

Bobby clapped his hands. "That's it! That's the exact word she used. I don't got a clue what it means, but she sure thought it was funny. Me? I just thought it was an elevator."

Lenny didn't say anything. Instead, he forged ahead and opened the door.

"Don't do nothin' else!" Bobby cried. "Gimme a sec' to catch up."

When all three stood looking in the open door, Bobby pointed to a small, square keyboard with buttons labeled one through nine. A tenth button, marked zero, sat squarely beneath the bottom row: under buttons seven, eight, and nine.

"That looks an awful lot like the keypad from an old pushbutton phone," Sam said.

Bobby nodded his approval. "Right you are, young lady! One of the people Edna helped figured out how to make it work."

"So, what's the code?" Lenny asked. "How many digits?"

"Ten."

"Ten! That's nuts."

"Nah. It's pretty simple really. Watch." Bobby put his hand flat across all the buttons and pushed until something clicked. The floor of the oddball privy then dropped slowly down into the ground.

"It comes back up after a few minutes. There's a button on the wall at the bottom Edna used to get it back down when she needed out."

"What's down there?" Sam asked.

Bobby scratched his head. "There's just one square room as I recall—kitchen, bedroom, and bathroom—all in a space 'bout the size of a two-car garage."

"We need to get down there." Lenny pointed at the keypad. "Are there any other surprises we need to be aware of?"

Bobby shrugged. "Could be. I don't really know. Edna never talked much about what she did down there. She lost her husband, Max, several years ago, and she got a little stranger every year after that. Only came down here once in a great while. Far as I know, she lived in that rig y'all drove here."

"Wish I could've met her," Lenny said.

"She was sumpthin' Edna was. Had more friends than she could count."

Sam nudged Lenny as the floor of the false outhouse returned to the starting position. "It's time for us to check it out."

Chapter 25

"Politics have no relation to morals." –Niccolo Machiavelli

Clement retrieved Dak Heller's car from the impound, left it in front of a barber shop two blocks from the hospital, and texted him the location. He then called Senator Grovemont's private line.

Grovemont didn't bother with a greeting. "You got that damned camper yet, Clem?"

Clement grimaced. "Still working on it, sir. But I need your help."

"God damn it! I told you—"

"The situation has changed. Drastically. You need to hear what I have to say. That's why I called your private line."

"Listen to me, you idiot," Grovemont growled, "I can't be involved in—"

"You're *already* involved, Senator! It's your name on the endorsement for the PAC's contribution to Adrian McMichael's campaign."

"So?"

"He and his idiot brother-in-law, the Sheriff, damn near killed our investigator."

"All I know is that they put him in jail," Grovemont said. "They were going to let him out in a few days. How is that attempted murder?"

"Because," Clement said, trying to remain calm, "the jail cell they stuck him in was worse than a medieval dungeon. By the time I got to him, he was unconscious. His face, arms, and neck were swollen from all the bedbugs that bit him. He told the jailers he was highly allergic to them, but they had orders to ignore him. I'm telling you; he was near death. Now he's in a hospital, chained to a gurney. I told the DA, McMichael, that if Heller wasn't released, we'd withhold our donation to his campaign."

Grovemont groaned. "And you're just telling me all this now?"

"Obviously. I'm surprised McMichael hasn't called you." Clement paused. "He hasn't, has he?"

"Of course not. But, we *fired* this Heller character, didn't we? He's ancient history. Why should we care what happens to him, especially since he brought all this on himself?"

"Because he was still working for us at the time of the incident."

"Hrmph," Grovemont muttered. "Screw him, I say. He failed in his mission, and we cut him loose. That's all there is to it."

"So, you're not going to contact McMichael and demand Heller's immediate release?"

"Hell, no."

"And McMichael still gets the PAC's donation?"

"Absolutely! This is politics, Clem, not playschool. If what we need to find—what *you* need to find—is in Alabama, we may need all the local help we can get. McMichael undoubtedly has connections. We can't afford to get on his bad side. Now, is there anything else?"

Though Clement was no stranger to political hardball, Grovemont's reaction seemed way over the top. Unfortunately, Clement had little power. "No sir," he said. "That's it."

"Good. The next time I hear from you, I expect you'll tell me you've got your hands on that goddam camper. Understand?"

"Yeah," said Clement, "But—"

Grovemont snorted. "*Now* what?"

"Just one more thing," Clement said. "What's so important about the camper? Can't we buy—"

"It's not the damned camper; it's what's *inside* it that we're after."

"And what's that?"

"None of your goddam business! Now go. Just find it. And don't call me until you do."

Clement ground his teeth and forced himself

to relax. He'd need his emotions under control when he gave Heller the bad news. After a few deep breaths he went back to the hospital, parked, and walked to Heller's room. When he found the room empty, he went to the nurse's station for an update.

A nurse he didn't recognize gave him a disconcerting look when he inquired about Heller. "He's gone," she said.

"Gone? How?"

"I don't know; I wasn't looking after him."

"Did the police come for him?"

"I doubt it," she said. "His handcuff was still attached to the bed rail."

~*~

Dak felt a grin coming on when he reached his car. However, a glance at his reflection in the barbershop window next to the vehicle revealed a swollen face and a smile in search of a clown—a dead one. It fully restored his anger and his need for caution.

Gotta get movin.' Cops'll be looking for me soon.

He wondered, ever so briefly, if Clementine had made any headway on a legitimate release. It didn't matter, since he'd freed himself and gotten away without raising an alarm. The only thing that did matter, was vengeance. *A cop and a politician tried to kill me. Hadn't Clementine said as much?*

Focus, dumbass. Go somewhere safe. Now!

The car cranked right up, and Dak drove away carefully to avoid suspicion. *Don't look at me, folks. I'm just passing through.*

After a short drive, he reached a public park with few cars in the lot and plenty of shade. He chose a space as far from the other vehicles as possible and parked. He then hopped out, opened the trunk, and started working his way toward a hidden compartment within the upper padding of the back seat. There he kept his extra essentials.

After shifting his clothing and other material out of the way, Dak reached his goal. From within the dark compartment, he retrieved his back-up 9mm Glock, some duct tape, a small, unlabeled box, and a dart gun powered by a CO_2 cartridge. He resealed the hiding place and carried the material to the passenger seat. Once back behind the wheel, he used his phone to access the Internet and find the addresses of the DA and the Sheriff.

Once he had those, he opened the unmarked box and counted six syringe darts loaded with ketamine and God only knew what else. The dark agency that fired him had given him the anesthetics and the dart gun for a previous kill.

They'll be perfect for the job at hand.

He then searched the Internet for a good place to dispose of bodies. Lake Eufaula seemed to be the best option, though it would require a good hour's drive to get there. But the drive was worth it, especially because of the unique wildlife policies in place there.

Satisfied with his general plan, he left the park to find a motel where he could lay low until dark. It didn't take long.

~*~

Millie wasted no time on goodbyes as she exited Mel's car, grabbed her things, and headed for her own vehicle. They'd left it in the parking lot of the hotel where they'd spent their first night together. The hotel did not require a parking fee since Mel had used a company charge card that gave him added privileges. *It figures; he got a cheater's bonus.*

The interior of her car felt like a sauna, so she cranked the windows down to air it out. Eager to forget about the deceitful dirtbag, Millie focused on her original mission: killing Dak Heller. A quick check on her phone showed him on the move—an hour away in Montgomery.

She stuck her key in the ignition and turned it.

<click-click-click>

She tried again, keeping the key engaged a bit longer.

<click-click-click-click-click>

"Are you fucking *kidding me*?" she screamed, and pounded the steering wheel with both fists.

Most of the parking lot stood empty, but a maintenance worker from the hotel reacted to her shout. He set down the trash can he had just emptied into a dumpster and ambled awkwardly toward her. "You okay, ma'am?"

"I'm fine," she said, then gave in to her frustration. "No, damn it, I'm not. I've got a dead battery."

"Hit it again," he said.

She got the same result.

"I ain't a mechanic, but I 'spect yer right. It's deader than a hammer."

Millie bumped her forehead against the steering wheel. "That's just... swell."

"I got jumper cables in my truck," he said. "Want me to get 'em?"

She looked up at him and smiled. "Would you? Please? I'll keep my fingers crossed."

He strolled away, heavyset and limping, got in his truck, and drove it to a spot beside her. She released the hood latch under the dash, and he attached the cables to the batteries.

"All righty," he said. "Give it a try."

Millie held her breath as she turned the key.

<click-click> Silence.

He adjusted the clamps and told her to try again, but they got the same result.

"There's a tire and battery place nearby," he said. "I was 'bout to grab me a late lunch. I kin drop you off there on my way."

Having no other options, Millie thanked him and climbed into his truck, rather surprised by the neatness of the interior.

She ignored the seatbelt as he pulled away from the hotel.

What the hell else can go wrong?

~*~

Lenny waved Sam into the faux outhouse and asked Bobby if he wanted to join them.

"Nah," he said. "I'll leave that to y'all. But take Ebby with ya, okay? I'd hate for her to run into trouble out here."

"'Cause of the bears?" Sam asked, looking apprehensive.

"I dunno. Maybe. Hard to say when they'll show up."

Sam thanked him and called Ebby. Once inside, the dog shook herself, tossing water on both of them. Lenny suppressed a comment and then palmed the button array. When the floor began to drop, he frowned at Ebby, but didn't say anything.

"Good," remarked Sam. "You're bein' nice."

"I'm trying."

"Keep it up, and I'll give you a reward."

He brightened. "Really? Like what?"

"You'll just have to wait and see," she said, and pranced out into the subterranean room ahead of him. The lights came on automatically. He followed close after her, unwilling to give up the view of her tight shorts any sooner than necessary.

When they reached the center of the low-ceilinged room, they slowly scanned the interior. Bobby had been correct in his one-room assessment. A kitchen counter with a sink occupied one wall along with a compact refrigerator. Under counter storage seemed meager. A toaster and a two-burner electric range provided the only cooking options.

A single bed and a small dresser filled up the opposing wall, and a toilet occupied one corner. The wall through which they had entered featured floor-to-ceiling shelves. Most were filled with large, plastic bins. The other walls were unadorned, the furnishings spartan compared to those in the RV. Plain and depressing.

Sam made a face. "I guess we know why she didn't spend much time down here."

They looked closer at the storage boxes which had labels with odd names, though a few were familiar. All of them held dried plants in sealed, plastic bags.

"A few of the names I recognize from Edna's notes," Sam said. "They're in the recipes for different veils. Some of those names I can't read, much less pronounce. The writing is similar to what's in that really old book of hers."

"It's her stock of ingredients," Lenny said. "A great, big stock."

Sam agreed. "Edna's recipes all require fresh spring water. I suppose that's the spring Bobby mentioned. I hope Ebby didn't spoil it when she went swimming."

"Y'know what?" Lenny had his hands on his hips. "I'm tired, and this place is beginning to creep me out. Why don't we go back to the RV and relax for a while?"

"I'm okay with that," Sam said.

"And, uhm..." Lenny rubbed his palms together and tried not to look as horny as he felt. "Maybe you could give me my... the... uhm...."

"Reward?" Sam chuckled. "We'll see."

~*~

Clement sat in his car and struggled with his feelings. He could understand why Heller would want to escape, but the fact that he did would only make matters worse. He'd be caught eventually, and the escape would likely result in a longer sentence than what he would have gotten for his original offense.

And then there was Senator Grovemont, who'd earned Clement's utter scorn for abandoning an agent. Heller had come dangerously close to losing his life, and Grovemont couldn't have cared less. On top of that, Heller wasn't the only one the senator had chosen to ignore. Clement's efforts and assessments had been just as casually dismissed.

The pompous ass can't even get my name right.

Part of the reason for Clement's divorce had been his willingness to work for politicians, a class of people his ex-wife despised. What he and Heller had just experienced proved the wisdom of her beliefs. It was not a comforting realization. She had urged him not to commit himself to people who, by and large, were professionally shallow.

Yet, by accepting Grovemont's edict that he find the camper, Clement had recommitted himself to the same shady people, led by one of the shadiest.

That had to stop. He was done serving shitheads. But before he gave up the lucrative salary paid to him by the PAC, he wanted to find out what, *exactly*, Grovemont hoped to find in the Gianella woman's camper.

I'm working for myself now, Senator. I'm tired of you screwing me; you can go screw yourself now!

Chapter 26

"The most important issue for the killer is the ability to get a victim easily and successfully." –Pat Brown

True to his word, the maintenance guy from the hotel dropped Millie off at the tire and battery store. He spoke little along the way, but wished her luck as she climbed down out of his truck.

She met a man a few years younger than herself behind the store's cash register.

"How can I help you?" he asked.

"I think I've got a dead battery."

"Where's your car?"

She sighed. "It's in the parking lot of a hotel. But it's not far from here."

"Yeah, that's a problem," he said. "I can sell you a battery, and I can have one of our guys install it for free. But we don't make house calls."

"It's a hotel!"

His smile appeared sympathetic. "I get it, but it's the same thing as far as the company is concerned."

Exasperated, Millie held out her hands, palms up. "What am I supposed to do? Push the damn car down here? I can't afford a new battery *and* a tow!"

"My shift ends at six," he said. "If you buy a battery now, and you can wait 'til then, I'll drive you back to your car and install the battery myself."

Millie looked at her watch. She was eager to continue her pursuit of Dak Heller, and she'd already wasted time with Mel, but she had no other options. "Thank you," she said. "You say I can just camp out here until you're ready to go?"

He smiled. "Sure thing, ma'am."

Ma'am? Geez. That kid's only a couple of years younger than me. Okay, maybe a few years younger, but I'm no cougar! Well, not yet anyway. I only screw guys my age.

~*~

Clement spent the early part of the afternoon going over the material he'd received from Heller. Since the man took it upon himself to escape, Clement no longer felt any responsibility for him. Whatever happened to Heller from now on was his problem. Clement had a far different issue to occupy his time and talents.

Sadly, the notes didn't provide anything concrete about the camper's location. There was a notation which listed a license tag number and an address in Beulah, Alabama, but Clement had no idea where that was. On the bright side, Heller had told him the camper was parked at an RV dealership somewhere in or near Montgomery. He had his run-in with the cops on his way there, and by the time he spoke to Clement, Dak couldn't remember the name of the place. A quick search on the Internet provided Clement with a list of possible locations. He had no choice but to visit each one.

He spent the rest of the afternoon dodging salespeople at one RV dealership after another as he worked his way through all the sites on his list. The effort proved tiring and tiresome, but eventually yielded results. A salesman at the last dealership he visited remembered a customer named Gianella.

"He and some snotty hottie came through here a while back and claimed it," the man said.

"What can you tell me about it?"

The salesman rubbed his chin. "There's not much to say, really. It was mostly her attitude. She was hangin' all over the guy, and if ya ask me—"

"The *camper*," Clement said. "Tell me about the camper."

"Oh, right. Yeah. Lemme think. Uhm, it's a class C. Not too old, just a few years, but one of the bigger models. I tried to talk the guy into trading up to a Class A, but the girl... Sorry. Got carried away. He was content with the one he had. Our people had worked on it, so it was in great shape."

"I have no earthly idea what a class C camper looks like," Clement said. "Can you point to one like it out there?" He waved his hand at the sea of recreational vehicles parked all around them.

"I don't 'member the exact make or model, but for a class C it's pretty big. It's got an expandable section that you rarely see in an RV that size. It expands the bedroom by bumping out an exterior wall a few feet, maybe three or four. Different models, y'know are—"

Clement touched his shoulder. "Look, I'm in a bit of a hurry. Can you just point to one like it? I'll take a photo and be on my way."

"Oh, sure. Gimme just a sec."

The salesman began walking, and Clement followed behind. "These are all Class A jobs," he said. After touring three rows of parked behemoths, the man stopped and jabbed his finger toward a smaller version. "There's one. It's a different color, but I'm pretty sure it's the same model."

"What color was Mrs. Gianella's?"

"White, I think. Or maybe beige. Not flashy. Oh, and when they left, they were towing a little car behind 'em."

"Did you catch the make or model?"

"Nah. It was pretty old and kinda crappy. Prob'ly couldn't get much for it on a trade in."

Clement thanked him, took a snapshot of the RV, and started back to his car, then stopped and asked, "Do you have any idea where Beulah, Alabama is?"

"Not right off hand," he said. "But we've got a big ol' state map in the office. C'mon, I'll show ya."

~*~

While sitting in the customer waiting area of the tire and battery shop, Millie endured an interminable string of TV game shows, most of which were replays. Some of them, in black and white, must have aired before she was born. Having eaten nothing but a couple of Mel's croissants that morning, her dining selections came from a pair of vending machines.

The hours dragged by, but every time she checked on Heller's location via the tracker in his watch—rather, *her father's watch*—it indicated he hadn't moved. He remained in Montgomery.

The guy at the sales counter came by and tried to chat her up. He switched his approach from "Ma'am" to "Miss," but she'd recently had her fill of temptation. He eventually got the message.

When his shift ended, he clocked out, loaded her new battery in his car, and came to get her. The trip to the hotel was thankfully short, and he swapped out the batteries in a matter of minutes. She tipped him with the last five-dollar bill she had, said goodbye, and drove away as quickly as she could.

All that remained to figure out was whether she'd terminate Dak Heller before or after dinner.

~*~

Sam held Lenny's hand as they began their walk back to the RV. Ebby was thrilled to leave Edna's underground kitchen/warehouse. After running circles around them, she sniffed something that demanded her attention and took off as if possessed. They laughed about it at first, but when Ebby failed to respond to their calls, they grew worried.

"We've gotta go after her," Sam said. "Bobby talked about—"

"Bears. Yeah, I know."

Her voice revealed her anxiety. "And it won't be long before dark."

"We'll find her," Lenny said, trying to sound confident. "C'mon."

They broke into a trot, occasionally stumbling over roots, rocks, and other hazards. "Y'know," Lenny said, slowing to a walk, "if one of us trips and breaks a leg, it'll play hell with the search."

"You're right," Sam said, suddenly interested in the ground beneath their feet. "We've gotta be more careful. You don't think there are many snakes out here, do you?"

"You've been out here as much as I have," he said. "And so far, I haven't heard anything but birds and bugs."

Sam swatted at something on her leg. "Dad gum mosquitos!" She slapped at another on her neck. "D'you suppose any of Edna's sprays would work on them?"

Lenny chuckled. "You sure wouldn't want to use an attractant. And based on what dogs do when they smell the repellant, that's probably not a good idea either."

They stayed close together as they searched, walking farther and farther into the woods. When they located a small stream, they walked beside it in search of the source, Edna's essential spring.

"How long have we been out here?" Lenny asked.

Sam frowned. "An hour or so? I don't know, but I'm really worried. If we don't find Ebby before sunset...."

Lenny gave her a hug. "We should've brought a flashlight. If she doesn't show up soon, we'll go back and get one."

"We should grab the pepper spray, too. It'll work on bears, won't it?"

"Let's hope we don't have to find out."

Splashing sounds grew louder as they walked. They exchanged looks in the growing dimness of the woods and began calling for Ebby in ever louder voices.

The big, shaggy, totally soaked dog bounded toward them and vigorously shook herself once she got there. Sam scolded her for not coming when they called, but Lenny reminded her the dog had been cooped up a great deal lately. "She just needed to get rid of some extra energy."

Sam swiped her open hands on the water Ebby left on her shorts and t-shirt. "Yeah, I s'pose."

"Hey now. Be nice," Lenny said with a smile. "Seems like I heard that somewhere."

She squinted at him. "Are you gonna give *me* a reward now?"

He tried to look indecisive. "Maybe. But only if you're nice to me, too."

Sam grabbed Ebby's collar and turned back downstream. "Time to go."

~*~

Dak couldn't sleep and realized he didn't need to. *Rest? Yeah. Sleep? Later.*

His modest motel room was clean and free of bugs. The TV was old and small, but he found a channel that featured music, so he listened to that while waiting for dark.

He ordered a pizza, and though tempted to find a liquor store and get something with a kick, he opted for a soft drink from a machine in the hallway. It wouldn't be the first time he'd forced himself to be patient while prepping for a kill. He wouldn't be paid for the next two, of course, but he didn't care. Their deaths would be his reward.

Dark came later than it had in the spring. By the time the sun went down, he'd returned to his car, ready for the tasks ahead.

He knew McMichael had a wife, maybe kids, too, not that it mattered. He knew nothing about the Sheriff other than his address. Dak had never seen the man, but he knew the bastard was at least partly to blame for his torture. He decided to get the Sheriff first.

When he arrived, the only lights on were inside the house. Dressed in dark sweats, Dak approached the house in silence. He wore plastic gloves and a nylon stocking over his head. He might have dispensed with the head covering, but he couldn't take a chance on being filmed by a security camera somewhere.

With the dart gun ready at waist level, he knocked on the door. When no one answered right away, he knocked again, harder. A male voice from inside responded, "Hold your horses. I'm comin'."

The Sheriff was still in uniform when he opened the door.

Dak fired the dart gun, and the man grunted as he looked down at the projectile's pink, feathery stabilizer protruding from the end of the dart in his stomach. The ingredients from the syringe worked quickly, and the Sheriff slumped to the floor. He would stay unconscious for at least a couple of hours.

Dak grabbed him by the ankles and dragged him to his car; not an easy trick since the man packed a lot of fat. Nonetheless, Dak duct taped his hands and feet then crammed him into the rear seat and closed the door. He made a quick trip back to the house, slammed the front door shut, and returned to his car.

One down; one to go.

Chapter 27

"Love is love's reward." –John Dryden

By the time Sam and Lenny returned to the RV, both were sweat-soaked and grubby. After toweling off the dog, they walked to the tiny shower stall. Lenny suggested they could save water by showering together, but she promptly nixed the idea. There was hardly enough room for one person.

"Let me go first," she said. "I won't take long, 'cause I know we don't have a big water supply."

"And then?" Lenny asked.

"Then you take your shower while I prepare your… reward. Okay?"

"Absolutely! But—"

She couldn't imagine what he had in mind. "But *what?*"

"May I watch?"

She recoiled. "Watch me? *In the shower?*"

He quickly backed away, too. "In case you... I dunno... need me to scrub your back or something."

Suddenly, the reward she had in mind didn't seem like a great idea any more. "You're being creepy."

"I'm sorry," he said, a note of pleading in his voice. "I was just trying to make you smile. I didn't mean anything by it."

You were trying to make me *smile? Oh, right.* "You sure about that?"

He held up his hand with his first two fingers extended. "Scout's honor."

It didn't look quite right. "Were you really a boy scout?"

"Well, not exactly. I was a cub scout, but isn't that the same thing?"

She pointed to the main room. "Go. And be patient! Wait out there until I'm done. I'll let you know when it's your turn."

"Just don't take too long," he said.

"I won't. And see if your dear Aunt Edna hid some wine away somewhere. I could use a glass or three to unwind." She smiled and winked at him. "That's essential when it comes to rewards."

"No problem," he said. "I'll search the place. Maybe Edna stocked a wine rack or a liquor cabinet somewhere. And then maybe I'll spend some time reading her notes, and maybe run the vacuum, wash the RV, or blow dry Ebby; she's still a little damp. You won't even know I'm out here. Being quiet. And—"

"Patient?"

"Yeah."

"Good." She pulled the door shut and got ready for her shower. If she timed it right, and her nerve held, she'd be wearing the skimpy nighty she'd bought on her shopping trip. The thought made her smile. It seemed like that had been weeks ago instead of days.

But, by gosh, if he tries something dumb or creepy before I'm ready, he'll kiss that reward goodbye!

~*~

Clement took a long look at the map in the sales office of the RV dealership and finally gave up on finding Beulah, Alabama. Small towns littered the state, and the size of the lettering on the map appeared relative to the size of the towns. Having no idea where in the state Beulah might be, he kissed the map and the dealership goodbye.

Mentally kicking himself for not using the GPS program on his cell phone, Clement typed in the town name and got directions and an estimated drive time of ninety minutes. The route to Beulah appeared fairly straight but would require him to drive through a number of towns he'd never heard of along the way. He prayed they wouldn't have the sort of rush hour traffic he'd lived with near DC.

The trip took slightly longer than expected, though he encountered few obstacles other than slow drivers on the two-lane roads.

He pulled to a stop in front of a church in what he assumed was Beulah and dug out Heller's notes to get the Gianella woman's street address. All Heller had written down was a rural route and box number, an address meaningless to everyone except the postal worker who delivered mail to it.

Grinding his teeth, Clement went in search of a post office where, hopefully, someone could give him a street address. Or, more likely, a numbered horse or cow path, those being plentiful in the region.

Unable to locate anything that could be considered a "downtown" in Beulah, Clement went back to his cell phone. Eventually he learned that the Beulah post office had shut down about the time Teddy Rosevelt led the charge up San Juan hill. A bit of additional research revealed that the post office in Valley, Alabama, handled the mail for Beulah. The drive there and back would add another half hour, plus however long it took to get the info he needed from a postal worker. He checked his watch and wondered if any post office in the country stayed open past 5 pm. He'd already missed that mark by an hour.

Having no other choices, Clement made his way to Valley and verified that the post office had indeed closed for the day—no lights, no people, no traffic.

Veils

Tired and hungry, he drove around looking for a restaurant. Like his search for a post office in Beulah, he couldn't find a place to eat in Valley that offered adult beverages, something he felt he'd earned. That prompted a drive across the border into Georgia where he stopped at a liquor store called Frisky Whisky and bought a bottle of Scotch.

Even though the sun was going down, he allowed himself a leisurely dinner. The restaurant had few guests, and his waiter seemed eager to do something to kill the time. "You doin' okay?" he asked.

"I'm getting by," Clement said, "but I haven't accomplished what I set out to do."

"Which is... what?"

Clement snorted and shook his head. "It's prob'ly an impossible task. I'm trying to find the address of someone in Beulah."

"You're a bit north of there," the server said.

"I know. Are you familiar with Beulah?" He focused on the man's name badge which offered up initials instead of a name: PD.

"Grew up there," he said. "I was on the football team, the Beulah Bobcats."

"No kidding?"

PD replied with a smile. "Nope. No kidding."

"Have you ever heard of a woman by the name of Gianella?"

His smile grew even wider. "I reckon just about everyone in Beulah knows Miz Edna. But gosh, I haven't heard that name in ages. How's she gettin' on?"

"I'm told she passed away. I understand she has a relative who might be living in her place. That's who I'm trying to find." He quickly worked up a phony reason. "I have some information that could be very important to him. Possibly life-saving."

PD pursed his lips. "I never knew where she lived, to be honest. But I think she was in or near where some Yankee outfit wants to mine granite. Some folks, Miz Edna included, didn't take kindly to the idea."

Clement felt a ray of emotional sunshine. "D'you suppose you could show me where that is on a map?"

"I can try."

Clement pulled up a map of Beulah on his cell phone and showed it to the young man. The server examined it briefly, scrolled the map over and down, then tapped his index finger on an area that appeared uninhabited. "It's in there somewhere. Not too many folks live nearby. It's pretty... what's the word? Iso—"

"Isolated?"

"Yeah. A few small houses. Old ones. Maybe a couple trailers. Unless it's changed a lot since I lived there, that's about it. Trees. Lotsa trees. Animals. Oh, and old people."

Clement thanked him, finished his meal, and got back in his car.

Beulah, here I come.

~*~

Pleased by how easily he'd snagged the Sheriff, Dak proceeded to the address he had for District Attorney Adrian McMichael. Located in a posh neighborhood, the big, colonial style house had a long, straight driveway leading to a circular area surrounding a fountain and a statue of some ancient naked cutie. Dak left his car at the curb and walked toward the mansion, pausing only a moment to admire the physique of the stone nymph, or whatever it was.

The exterior lights were on, so Dak kept to the shadows. Fortunately, the property boasted huge evergreens, magnolias, and hardwoods making that task simple. He worked his way around the house toward a spacious swimming pool with an equally spacious patio. Lights were on there, too.

A man Dak recognized from online photos sat alone, smoking a cigar and drinking what appeared to be whiskey. Dak briefly envied him those luxuries. The bastard wouldn't be enjoying them much longer.

Positioning himself beside an enormous bush with white, pineapple-sized blossoms, Dak took aim with the dart gun. As McMichael rested his glass on his leg and took a puff on his cigar, Dak pulled the trigger. The dart hit the DA an inch or so below his right ear. It startled him enough to make him inhale and choke on cigar smoke—very briefly—before he dropped both his smoke and his glass and slumped in his recliner as if dead.

Dak took it as a good sign that McMichael's glass landed in his lap rather than shattering on the patio floor. He left the smoking cigar where it fell. Dressed exactly as he was when he nabbed the Sheriff, Dak took pains to be quiet as he dragged the unconscious attorney through a gate and across the yard to the car. There he bound McMichael's hands and feet as he'd done with his previous target.

Loading McMichael on top of the Sheriff proved to be a challenge, but eventually he got it done.

Good thing I got fatso first.

The next step meant a drive to Lake Eufaula, but he suddenly realized he needed one more thing before he got there. After leaving McMichael's fancy-ass neighborhood, Dak drove to a wayside store he'd passed earlier that evening. It may have once been a gas station; now it offered bait, fishing tackle, and souvenirs. Though his car was the only one in the lot, he parked as far from the entrance as he could. His passengers wouldn't be waking up anytime soon, but he didn't have anything to hide their bodies on the back seat.

Once inside he headed straight toward a rack of folding lawn chairs. The one McMichael was in when Dak shot him would have been superb, provided Dak had a pickup truck and a frontend loader. The damn thing probably weighed as much as the Sheriff. Instead, Dak chose a sling chair in the colors of the University of Alabama. The seatback featured a cartoon elephant and the words "Roll Tide." He had no idea what it meant, but because the elephant looked ridiculous, it made him smile. It would do just fine.

He paid for it, tossed it on top of his still-sleeping passengers, and headed for Lake Eufaula. The place seemed perfect as it was the only one in the whole state which maintained a strict catch and release policy for alligators.

It seemed only appropriate that he should find a place that was both convenient for gators and fairly easy for humans to access. There he would strip the cop and the DA down to their undies and drag them partially into the water.

Meanwhile, he would relax in the "Roll Tide" chair and wait for the two men to wake up and realize what was in store for them. If the gators didn't show, Dak planned to shoot them both and disappear.

He sincerely hoped the gators wouldn't disappoint him. In fact, the prospect of watching them eat the men responsible for his torture pleased Dak no end. He was eager to serve the meal.

All it would take to get to the lake was an hour or so behind the wheel. Plus, he'd need to spend a little time looking for the perfect dinner spot once he got there. A quick check of his fancy watch showed he had an hour and a half before the pair in the back seat started to come around. It would take a little longer for all the grogginess to wear off.

For Dak, it was crucial that both men were fully awake when the toothy dinner guests arrived for their meal.

Chapter 28

"Self-doubt is real. Everyone has it. Having confidence and losing confidence is real, too, and everyone has been in that position." –Venus Williams

Sam wrapped herself in a bath towel, exited the shower, and scooted into the tiny bedroom. Lenny had already expanded the RV's only extra room, so the double bed no longer completely filled it. She shut the bedroom door with a breezy, "Shower's all yours, Len!"

And then she locked it.

A built-in dresser with three drawers provided what little storage there was in the cramped bedroom. She'd placed all but one of the clothing items she'd bought in the top drawer and crammed her impulse purchase, the slinky red nighty, in a back corner in case Lenny went snooping.

She dried her hair, applied her makeup, and considered giving herself a quick spritz of Edna's attractant. While looking at herself in the mirror, she let the bath towel fall to the floor and made a decision.

I don't need Edna's help. If the nighty and I aren't enough for Lenny, nothing is.

It took more time to remove the sales tags than it did to slip into the sexy negligée. The garment simply didn't consist of much material. If not for two strategically placed, dark red bows and a dainty wave of glitter, the all but transparent garment left nothing to the imagination. Staring once again at her reflection, Samantha realized she had never felt so thoroughly naked in her entire life.

And instantly, her confidence plunged like a cliff diver.

Have I gone nuts? Am I crazy? This is the most insane idea I've ever had! I look like a stripper. Well, what I imagine *a stripper looks like. For starters anyway. And now what? Open the door, walk out like I'm on stage, and do a bump and grind?*

She attempted to make a slight adjustment to one of the bows, but when it wouldn't cooperate, she closed her eyes and chewed on her lower lip.

Oh, my God! Lenny's going to think I'm a total bimbo! Or a slut. Or something even worse—he'll think I look stupid.

She wanted to cry but knew it would only spoil her makeup and make her look worse. *I've gone too far. He'll never think of me as just his girlfriend; he'll think I'm just... easy. A hook-up, a throw-away.*

But I'm not! I love him; that's all. I only wanted to do something nice for him. Maybe I should've bought chocolates instead. Or ice cream! Everybody likes ice cream. But this?

She stared at herself in the mirror, as if she were someone else, someone who worked the streets, selling herself to any horny old goat with a little extra cash in his pocket.

What if Mom and Dad saw me like this? I'd be dead. Disowned. Kicked to the curb and into the sewer. What if Lenny feels the same way? Oh, dear Lord, what in the world am I supposed to do now?

And what if—

Lenny knocked on the door. "Hey! You okay in there? I'm outta the shower, and I'm wearin' my Sunday best, what little of it there is." He chuckled. "Oh, and I found a bottle of something called prosecco tucked away on the shelf over the stove. Ever heard of it? Tastes a lot like champagne."

Sam held her face in her hands. *Oh God. It's time.* She cleared her throat. "I... Gimme a minute, will ya? I need to... uhm... figure something out."

"Well, don't take too long," Lenny said. "I've already poured each of us a glass of this bubbly stuff. And darlin', I can't even begin to tell you how much I'm looking forward to my reward."

~*~

Millie had stopped for gas somewhere between Auburn and Montgomery. She prayed her credit card wouldn't be denied, and it wasn't, though she knew the balance had grown disastrously since she began her quest to hunt down Dak Heller. For dinner, she bought a bag of trail mix and a soft drink, an enormous shift in her diet after the disaster in New Orleans.

Before going on, she had checked the GPS locater on her phone and was surprised to see Heller had left Montgomery and was nearing a lakeside town called Eufaula. After finding a more-or-less direct route, she took off in pursuit. The sun had set by the time she reached the lake. Fortunately, her GPS program didn't care. It led her to a two-lane road through public land close to the water.

She nearly ran into Heller's car rounding a bend and pulled to a stop just off the road in front of it. Heller was nowhere in sight, but her tracker pointed her through the woods. Moving slowly and making as little sound as possible, she proceeded until the ground became squishy. She could make out the lake through the trees. Heller was close by.

Moving carefully, she regained dry ground and edged closer to him. She could hear his voice, but couldn't make out his exact words, nor could she imagine who he might be talking to.

The mystery unfolded as she got closer. Heller sat on a cheap lawn chair looking down at two men in their underwear lying half in the lake and half in the muck on shore. Both were face-up and bound with their ankles together and their hands behind their backs. Neither wore a gag.

"It's nearly suppertime," Heller told them. "And guess who's coming to dinner?"

He must've thought that was hilarious since he broke into laughter at his own wit.

"'Course, you already know who's on the way. They oughta be nibblin' on your toes any minute now."

The men pleaded for mercy, but Heller merely laughed more. "You didn't think about mercy when you had me tortured, did ya?" He checked his watch and waved his gun at them. "If those toothy bastards don't start chewing on you soon, I'll just have to shoot you. But I'd really hate to do that. I'd much rather hear you scream as they drag you into the water."

"We were just doing what we were told," McMichael said. "We had orders. Grovemont—the U.S. Senator—he made us do it. I swear!"

"A senator? Seriously? You think I'm stupid enough to believe that?"

Millie used the time and the distraction from Heller's taunts to find a better shooting position. She had no intention of missing him again. Her shot in front of the post office in Camp Hill must have been deflected by the car's window. There were no such obstructions here beside the lake.

She had no idea what the two men had done to earn Heller's wrath, but whatever it was, she knew they wouldn't survive unless she acted first. *It shouldn't be too hard to find a place to hide since the*

*woods are choked with undergrowth, and the sun is
no longer up.*

Millie finally located the perfect spot. She
knelt between two trees and steadied herself next to
one as she took aim. Heller, in his chair, occupied a
slim open slot in the thick brush between them.

Suddenly, Heller stood up and walked closer
to the two men. A tree now blocked Millie's aim. She
shifted to get a better position while Heller
continued to taunt his victims.

"Time's up, gentlemen, and the gators are
late, damn it. But I'm outta time." He then fired a
round into each of the prostrate men at his feet.

Millie hurriedly stood and fired at Heller,
hitting him in the upper back and spinning him
toward the lake. He didn't go down, however; he
stayed on his feet looking for his assailant.

She fired again before he could locate her, but
she hurried the shot and missed him.

An adrenalin rush helped her duck behind
the tree as Heller fired back and yelled, "That you,
Clementine? It was you shot me before, wasn't it,
you two-faced piece of shit? How'd you like to join
the two assholes over here? The gators can eat all
three of ya."

Clementine? Mille grimaced. *Who the hell is
that?*

She backed away, and though she made noise
doing so, *she* wasn't the one who'd been wounded.

Lying in wait for Heller near their parked cars made sense, provided she got there first. She wanted an ambush, not a wild west gunfight.

Heller was nowhere in sight when she reached the cars. She looked around for a good hiding place, rejected the first couple as too obvious, and then settled for some bushes lining the road in front of Heller's car. There she sat and waited.

Other than the buzz of insects and the chirp of an occasional bird, Millie heard nothing. She figured that either Heller had died, or his wounds prevented him from leaving the shoreline. While waiting, and contemplating the situation, her conscience began to bother her. Not because she'd tried to kill Heller, but because she'd ignored his victims while planning another attack.

What if they're still alive? They'll need a doctor. And I abandoned them! Instead of trying to help, I let my obsession with Heller take over. What in the name of God is wrong with me?

Using far more stealth in her return to the shore than she had when leaving it, Millie kept her gun at the ready and scanned the woods for any sign of Heller. She found none. From a hiding place in the woods near the scene of the shootings, Millie peered at the bodies, the surrounding trees, and the underbrush, but saw no sign of Heller.

Creeping away from the cover of the woods, Millie made her way to the two men. Both had been shot in the head, their deaths brutally guaranteed by Heller. Remembering his words about alligators, she tried dragging the men away from the water. She made some progress with the smaller of the two, but she couldn't budge the other.

She called the police and reported the murders, doing her best to describe the location. Though tempted to tell them she'd seen who did it, she didn't want to reveal any details about herself, or why she just happened to see a crime committed in such an out of the way location. When they asked her for additional details, she ended the call.

Using the surprisingly bright light built into her phone, Millie scoured the area for the victims' clothing, anything to identify them. She ignored the ejected shells from Heller's gun but found two things of interest.

The first was his stupid lawn chair now lying on its side with the stupid cartoon elephant smiling at the dead men. The image disgusted her, but she left the chair the way it was. Hopefully, the police would be able to get a clue about the killer. A fingerprint, perhaps? A shoeprint? Maybe DNA from the chair or the shell casings he'd left behind.

The second item was disappointing on one hand, but satisfying on the other. Her father's watch lay on the ground beside the chair. She assumed Heller had figured out how he'd been followed.

She took the watch with her as she made her way back to the cars, slowly and as quietly as before. Gun in hand, she approached the parking spot. Heller's car remained where it was. Her car appeared undisturbed.

Veils

What if he's in my car? He could be in the back seat! I can't see a damned thing in the dark, and I don't dare use the light from my phone.

She crept back through the woods until she could approach the car from the rear. If he were in there, he wouldn't have a good shot. But then, neither would she.

And if he is in there, and I manage to shoot the bastard, he'll bleed all over my stuff in the back seat. What do I do then? Ditch the car? Burn it?

Ultimately, she opted to walk away and hide. She'd return later when the police were gone. With any luck, they wouldn't impound her car, but they'd sure as hell search it and either catch Heller or drive him away.

She found a spot that provided a sheltered view of the cars and tried to get comfortable. The mosquitos hadn't bothered her during her efforts to kill Heller. Now, however, they'd arrived in force. She swatted as many as she could knowing the cops would arrive soon. At that point, she'd either have to suffer in silence or move farther away. Neither option appealed to her.

She decided to tough it out. And maybe, just maybe, if Heller got out of her car, or strolled in from the woods, she'd have another chance to take him out, provided the police didn't get there first.

Chapter 29

"Sometimes, if you want to see a change for the better, you have to take things into your own hands." –Clint Eastwood

Lenny's impatience grew as he waited for Sam to come out of the bedroom. He felt more than a little stupid dressed only in boxers and a T-shirt. The underwear Sam had left him outside the bathroom was clean, however, and he'd shaved and showered, too.

"By the way," he said almost like an announcement, "I took another look at those photos Edna left me. You'll never guess whose faces I recognized."

When Sam didn't respond, he took another sip of his prosecco and turned on the radio, hoping to find some music to enhance the mood. He settled for The Beach Boys' "God Only Knows" and took a few, slow dance steps in time with the tune. He turned the volume up so Sam could hear it as well. The mood needed to be for two.

Veils

"D'you remember that redneck who said Edna helped him get a job as a physics professor? Well, his picture is in that box, and so is Bobby's. You know, the guy with the booby-trapped outhouse?"

"Yeah," she said from within the bedroom, her voice still unsteady.

What's she up to? Why the delay? Why can't we just jump in the sack and—

A knock at the door derailed his erotic train of thought.

Now what?

"Hey, Mr. Gianella! You in there?"

Lenny recognized Bobby's voice and moved nearer to the RV's passenger side door. "Hang on," he said. "I'm not dressed." He then looked around for his jeans or anything else to put on over his boxers. He settled for the bath towel he'd left on the sofa.

At that moment, Samantha exited the bedroom with a huge smile on her face.

Lenny's jaw dropped, but only long enough for his mind to register the stunning vision in front of him. Then he swallowed. He'd never imagined Sam could look so incredibly sexy, so amazingly wonderful, so—

"C'mon, Mr. Gianella! It's Lenny, right? I've got people waitin' out here."

Sam's expression instantly changed from passionate to panicked. "I— What the hell is—"

"It's okay," Lenny said, still clutching the bath towel around his waist. He shook his head and rolled his eyes toward the ceiling, then added, "I'll take care of it. Why don't you hop back in the bedroom? And would you grab my pants, and toss 'em out here, please? I'll join you in there as soon as I can."

Sam looked down at her negligee and then at Lenny. He thought she might break down and cry.

"You look absolutely stunning," he said, his voice throaty. "Fantastic! Astonishing, even. I— I don't know what to say except maybe that you've totally blown me away, and I can't wait—"

"Lenny! It's dark out here," Bobby said, once again pounding on the door. "And the skeeters are eatin' us alive!"

Sam rushed back into the bedroom, grabbed his jeans, and tossed them on the sofa before slamming the door behind her. Lenny abandoned the bath towel and quickly slipped into his pants.

Zippered and belted, he opened the passenger side door. Bobby and three men he didn't recognize quickly piled into the RV and shut the door.

Lenny glared at Bobby. "Would you mind telling me what the hell's going on here that couldn't wait 'til tomorrow? Or maybe Christmas? Or just—I dunno—next goddamn summer?"

Bobby sighed heavily and jabbed his thumb at a man in neatly pressed street clothes wedged between two others who looked like they'd just finished plowing a hundred acres without a mule. "You know him?" Bobby asked.

After a quick look Lenny said, "Hell, no."

"I can explain," the man said. "My name's Clement Bess—"

Bobby elbowed him to silence then looked at Lenny. "Don't matter what his dang name is if you don't know him."

What Lenny had heard of the name sounded vaguely familiar, so he told the two men hanging onto him to let go. "And let him speak."

"Thank you," the man said, rubbing his belly. "I'm Clement Bessemer, and I'm currently employed by the Patriots for Progress Political Action Committee."

Lenny frowned. "So? You want a donation? Good luck with that."

"No, it's nothing like that. We need to talk."

"About what?" Lenny glanced at a clock on the wall.

"I— *We* think you may have something of great interest to one of the candidates my PAC represents."

"Seriously? You came here in the middle of the night—"

"It's barely eight o'clock!"

Lenny scowled. "Some folks around here like to go to bed early."

"I'm sorry! I had no idea. Perhaps—"

Lenny waved him to silence, wandered back to the radio, and shut it off. The sounds of The Beach Boys faded to nothing.

Sam re-entered the room dressed in shorts and a t-shirt. Though her outfit lacked the sexy glitz of her five-alarm nighty, Lenny still struggled to take his eyes off her, and only at the last moment did he notice she had her can of pepper spray by her side.

"What's going on, Len? Why are all these men here?"

"That's what I'm tryin' to find out." Lenny thanked Bobby and his friends for having their backs and wished them well. "We'll be okay. Y'all have a good evening." As they left, Lenny turned to the only remaining stranger. "Mr. Uh... Bessemer?"

He smiled. "Call me Clement."

"Let's cut to the chase, okay, Clement? 'Cause if you beat around the bush, my girl here will hose your ass down with pepper spray. Now, what *exactly* do you want from me?"

"Just one thing," Bessemer said. "And I apologize for my unannounced arrival. I'm not here to cause any harm or inconvenience."

Lenny opted not to say anything about the unbelievable amount of inconvenience he'd already caused. "And?"

Bessemer cleared his throat. "I need to find out why my employer is so determined to have me beg, borrow, or steal this camper. He swept his arm in a broad gesture to include the entire RV. What's in it that's so damned important to him?"

"I can answer that," Lenny said, still irritated. "Just don't know why I should. My aunt Edna was a remarkable woman. She helped people, all kinds of people, and I wish she was here now to guide me."

Sam stepped forward and stopped by his side. "What Lenny is saying is that we can't share any of Edna' secrets without knowing who's asking about them or needs them. It doesn't sound to me like you're the one in trouble."

Lenny put his arm around her shoulders and gently squeezed. "Exactly."

The man exhaled in frustration. "I can't imagine what your aunt had that's got the senator so hot and bothered."

"Which senator?" Sam asked.

Bessemer hesitated, looking from Sam to Lenny and back. "You have to keep this confidential. Understand?"

"No," said Sam, "we don't understand. It's a simple question; we aren't asking you to give away any state secrets."

Lenny grinned at her. "Exactly!"

"Okay, okay," Bessemer said. "I guess it can't really hurt anything." He hesitated a moment before adding, "It's Senator Grovemont who's interested. And I mean *very* interested."

"I've heard of him," Sam said. "Terry Grovemont?"

Bessemer was quick to correct her. "It's Terrence. Terrence Grovemont."

Sam snickered. "My Dad says he's a real piece of—"

"Ah," said Lenny, "easy now."

"—piece of... work. My Dad listens to talk radio, a lot, and your senator pal is a prime topic. They call him 'Hairy Terry' 'cause of his stupid hairstyle—all white and fluffy, like Louis XVI or Marie Antoinette or something."

Bessemer pursed his lips, and Lenny wondered if the man had similar thoughts.

"Yes, but—" Bessemer began.

"And," Sam went on, "it seems he claimed to be a war hero, and that he fought in Afghanistan. Turns out he had a desk job the whole time; he was some sort of lawyer."

"You know," said Lenny, "I remember hearing something about that on the news, but then the story just went away."

"Listen," Bessemer said. "I'm not here to discuss the Senator's failings; I'm here—"

"He lied in college, too," Sam said. "He copied a bunch of stuff from someone else's Master's thesis, and used it in his own. No one knew until a few years later."

Veils

Lenny chuckled. "I guess it's only natural that he went into politics." He stared at Bessemer. "Did you know all this?"

"I heard some rumors. It all happened long before I got involved with the PAC. We support a number of candidates, not just Grovemont. But—"

"He gets the lion's share, right?" Sam asked. "He's running for President, isn't he?" She shook her head. "For the life of me I can't think of any reason I would ever vote for him."

"Me, either," said Lenny.

"To be honest," Bessemer said. "I don't like the man. He's done some terribly underhanded things. The thought of him being President, being the leader of the free world... Well, frankly, I find the idea appalling."

"Then why the hell are you working for him?" Lenny asked. "If the man makes your skin crawl, why stick with him?"

"Because," Bessemer said, "I'm hoping there's something in this camper I can use against him."

~*~

Dak felt like roadkill and figured he probably looked like it, too. The bullet wound in his shoulder hurt like hell, and though he tried to ignore it, that proved impossible. Nevertheless, he forced himself to focus on an escape. Clementine was still out there, still trying to kill him. The sneaky bastard must've figured out how to track him via the fancy watch

Dak acquired from a previous kill. He couldn't recall much about the job, but the watch had been nice. *Exceptionally* nice. Right up until Clementine used it to betray him. Dak had no choice but to discard it.

By now Clementine would be waiting to ambush him out by the road. So obvious, he thought. And so easy to evade—at least for someone with two working arms. Dak was down to one. The shoulder wound hurt worse when he tried to move his left limb, although he was able to hold his gun in his right hand. That meant if he could get to his car without being shot again by the asshole stalking him, he could get away. If and when the cops came, he'd be long gone.

He hadn't had time to collect his spent shells near the bodies by the lake. That meant he'd have to discard his gun once he got away in case the cops managed to track it back to him. That wasn't likely, but he couldn't leave it to chance. Then again, if he played his cards right, he could take out Clementine before he ditched the weapon.

He also knew he needed medical attention, and soon. He could feel the blood dripping down his back, and probably leaving a trail of his DNA behind. He shrugged that off knowing there was nothing he could do about it.

Moving slowly, which was the best speed he could handle without screaming, Dak made his way back toward the cars. He hoped to catch Clementine unaware, though that didn't seem terribly likely. Before he reached his vehicle, however, flashing blue lights on a patrol car cast their glow through the woods. Dak lowered himself to the ground as the car came to a stop.

Oh, great. Just what I fucking need, a goddamn cop. And you called 'em, Clementine! What kind of idiot are you?

Once the state trooper got out of his car, Dak fired two rounds into the dirt, an action guaranteed to draw the local LEO toward him. From his hiding place in the woods, Dak shifted enough to peek around a tree and watch the officer's approach. When he got close enough, Dak shot him in the head.

Chapter 30

"Revenge is sweet—and not fattening." –Alfred Hitchcock

Millie slipped back into her hiding place when the state patrol car rolled to a stop. She watched the officer exit his vehicle and look at the license plates on the two cars next to his. He pulled a pen and notepad from his pocket and had just begun to jot something down when two gunshots rang out from the woods between the cars and the lake.

The cop stuck his notepad in a breast pocket, drew his weapon, and advanced cautiously into the woods in the direction of the gunfire.

Leaving the safety of the trees, Millie made her way toward her car hoping to drive away before the cop returned. She scurried roughly half the distance when she heard yet another gunshot and instinctively dropped to the ground. Rethinking her options, without knowing who was shooting or if anyone had been hit, she left the road and slipped into the nearby foliage to hide.

Veils

Within moments, Dak Heller crept out into the open and went directly to his vehicle and fussed with the driver side door.

Millie stood up and tried to get a shot at him, but he was bent over, and his car stood in the way. When she heard his car door close, she fired at him anyway.

He revved his engine and sped off on the dirt road.

Millie fired twice more as he drove away, but neither had an effect. She was torn between checking on the officer in the woods and going after Heller. Having seen how efficiently Heller had killed the two men by the lake, she felt sure he'd done the same to the lawman. It only took a moment to make the decision, and she sprinted to her car.

With any luck, I can follow the bastard wherever he goes. And after all, how far can *he go with a bullet in his back? He definitely needs at least one more.*

~*~

Clement had no clue why the young woman Gianella addressed as Sam seemed so unhappy about him being there. Her attitude shifted somewhat when he admitted he was no fan of Senator Grovemont, but it was more a case of tolerance than friendship. That felt odd; he usually got along with everyone.

Her partner—*Husband? Boyfriend, maybe?*— was definitely less standoffish, and perhaps that contributed to her discomfort. Clement had missed something, and it hung in the air like a condemnation soon to be voiced. He knew better than to let it unnerve him.

"I'm at a loss for how to proceed," he said. "I don't know where we go from here. I don't know anything about what your late aunt has that's got Senator Grovemont in such a dither."

"Go ahead and tell him," Sam said. "He's bound to find out sooner or later anyway."

Lenny gave him a brief introduction to Edna's veils, focusing on the most popular one, the attractant, while giving little play to the others.

Clement quickly realized what Grovemont had in mind, though it wasn't a sexual lure he desired, rather it was something to make him likeable—make his popularity rise. Just in time for the primaries and ultimately, the general election.

"You can see," Lenny said, "why your peckerheaded PAC player would want to get his hands on that particular veil. I'm certain my Aunt Edna never intended for it to be used to get someone elected."

"Grovemont's a fraud," Clement said. "I knew that, but I didn't realize just how much of a fraud he was. He'd rather use a veil than bother trying to be someone worthy of a following."

Sam nodded in agreement. "The thing that gets me though, is how he found out about the veils in the first place."

Clement shrugged. "He wouldn't say anything to me about them, but he must've known about them and just assumed Edna kept some in her RV. That's why he wanted to get his hands on it."

"Hang on," Lenny said. "I've got an idea." He stepped away and retrieved a box of photos which he handed to Clement. "I got these from my Aunt's attorney when we first discussed my inheritance. I didn't know any of the people in those pictures at the time."

"But we've recognized a couple of them since then," interjected Sam. "You met one tonight: Bobby."

Clement responded with a half laugh. "Not exactly a pleasant introduction. I thought he and his pals were going to give me a beating."

"Nah. They were just trying to protect us," Lenny said. "Bobby's a good guy. I imagine the other two are as well."

"Wish I could say that about the guy I replaced." Clement shook his head. "He's an honest to God nightmare. And as far as I know, he's still on the loose."

Sam and Lenny exchanged worried looks.

"What and who are you talking about?" Lenny asked.

Clement suddenly wished he'd kept quiet. "It's not important. The guy's running from the police. I can't imagine he'd try anything with you."

Sam's distress slipped into anger. She still held a can of pepper spray in her hand, and Clement feared she might use it on him.

"Who the hell is this guy?" she asked. "If it wasn't important, you'd never have mentioned it."

"I can explain," Clement said. "See, I'm not the first one the PAC used to find your camper. This other man was hired because of a contact Senator Grovemont insisted we use. I didn't understand the connection or how Grovemont knew about it. All I knew was that the guy sent by Grovemont's contact was the kind of person capable of doing literally anything, legal or otherwise."

"Like kill someone?" Lenny asked.

"Yes. I've no doubt," Clement said. "But you must understand, he *wasn't* hired to do *anything* like that. He was only supposed to track down your RV."

"What's his name?" asked Sam.

Clement shrugged. "Does it matter?"

"Hell, *yes* it matters!" Lenny's voice surged on the second word.

"It's Heller," Clement said. "Dak Heller."

"What does he look like?" Sam's expression was cold and could have belonged to a prosecutor.

"He's white. Average height, average weight. And, well, he has average looks, too. No obvious tattoos or other distinguishing characteristics."

"That's it?"

"Well, actually, no. There is something else. He's highly allergic to bedbugs, and he was bitten repeatedly by them while held in jail. His hands, arms, neck, and face are probably still a little red and swollen even though he was treated in a hospital."

"So, he was *released* from jail?" Lenny asked.

"Uhm, no. He escaped," Clement said. "And I might have… *inadvertently* helped him."

Sam leaned in, close to his face. "And you didn't think to mention this when you first got here? What the hell is wrong with you?"

Clement stammered, "Well— If— I mean, if I thought he was a real threat—"

"He was hired to find us!" Lenny bellowed.

"But we fired him!" Clement yelled back. "Why would he still come after your camper?"

"Let's all just calm down a bit," Sam said. "Maybe Len and I have gotten worked up over something that isn't really a huge deal."

Lenny obviously disagreed but said nothing.

"Let's go back to where this started." Sam pointed at the photos Clement held. "Why don't you go through those and see if you spot anyone who might have a connection to Senator Asshat?"

Feeling some relief, Clement quickly turned to the task she suggested while the two of them retreated to the back of the vehicle and engaged in a whispered conversation.

Clement felt sure he wouldn't recognize a single face, other than the man named Bobby, but he didn't let that keep him from examining each photo with care. He'd worked his way through roughly two thirds of them before he stopped and stared at a face he knew he'd seen before—in a frame on the wall of Grovemont's office. "Oh my God!"

That brought Sam and Lenny hurrying back to him. "What is it?" she asked.

Clement held up the photo so they could see the face. "This guy. He's Grovemont's son. I heard he went to school somewhere in the South, but I didn't know where."

"There's an Auburn University logo on his shirt pocket," Sam said.

Lenny nodded. "That'd put him smack in the middle of Edna's turf."

"And," said Clement, "if this kid needed your aunt's help, he probably told his father about it, and that it worked. That would explain how Grovemont knew about the camper."

~*~

Dak resisted the urge to race away from the lake. He knew the state trooper he'd killed wouldn't be the only one to respond to the emergency call Clementine made. There would be another patrol car, and more once they found the dead cop.

What aggravated him further, besides the excruciating pain in his back and shoulder, was the fact he hadn't killed Clementine as well. He had three kills that night, a fourth would've been the home run of executions, the most he'd ever bagged in one day. There was still time, however; he could still get Clementine, but he had to hurry. His wound needed attention; he could bleed out, or the bullet could move, though he doubted it had hit an artery. Aiming at someone's shoulder rarely resulted in a kill shot.

For the time being, he had to drive as far from the lake as possible. He didn't know where Clementine was, but he still had one thing to go on—the tracker he'd installed in the Gianella kid's phone. Clementine had all Dak's notes, including the registration info for the camper his former employer was so hot to find. If Dak could get there first, he could wait for the traitorous bureaucrat to show up.

And as soon as he does, I'll put him down like those other two dogs, the sheriff and the DA. The only one left will be Grovemont, and I can't wait to make that asshole suffer.

~*~

Sam felt as if her world—the one with Lenny, Ebby, and a promising future—was about to dissolve into nothing. Lenny would be gone, and she'd have to go back to Atlanta and a life of drudgery in some crappy file room somewhere. They didn't know Clement Bessemer, and they sure as hell had never heard of Dak Heller. And Senator Grovemont, a dirty politician if there ever was one, tied them all in a knot of crime.

Except that she and Lenny had done absolutely nothing wrong—not a damned thing, and yet now they were involved up to their necks.

Or are we?

She signaled for Lenny to join her once again at the rear of the RV. Their previous session there had ended prematurely, and she was eager to restart the conversation. When Lenny leaned close, she let her voice drop to a whisper. "Based on everything I've heard, we've done nothing wrong. There's no reason—no reason at all—why we should get involved."

Lenny lowered his voice, too. "I think you're right, and I know we haven't done anything wrong; certainly nothing illegal."

"Yet," she said.

"He hasn't asked us to do anything!"

"He will. It's just a matter of time." Sam grimaced. "At the very least, he's going to ask us to supply him with Edna's repellant. He'll want to use it on Grovemont."

Lenny seemed puzzled. "How would that do anything?"

"Oh, come on! How many times have you seen video of politicians surrounded by supporters? All those people with their campaign buttons, signs, and banners—they're all part of the show. You can see it in the politician's eyes; they're all but shouting, 'Look at me! Look at this adoring mob! Everyone should want to vote for me. I am so damned great! How can you *not* vote for me? Get on board. Get in the groove—with Grovemont!'"

Lenny bit his lip to keep from laughing. "'Get in the groove'? Seriously?"

"If you've seen one video of a political rally, you've seen 'em all."

"Yeah, but—"

He was interrupted by someone pounding on the RV's door.

"Aw geez, Bobby. Not again!"

Chapter 31

"We all lose somebody we care about and want to find some comforting way of dealing with it, something that will give us a little closure, a little peace." –Mitch Albom

Millie trailed behind Heller's car, no longer caring if he noticed. Most of the roads held little traffic anyway. Heller drove almost due north from the lake, and once he'd put it a few miles behind, he increased his speed dramatically. Millie's car was a poor match for his, but she managed to follow him all the way to the little town of Beulah, Alabama.

She could tell by the way he drove that he knew he was being followed.

With the needle on her gas gauge hovering over the empty mark, she prayed he'd soon stop his insane getaway. He may have had more petrol, but he had to be running low on energy. Not that it mattered if she couldn't continue to chase him.

She was about to give up hope when Heller slowed his frantic pace and rolled into a heavily wooded area far outside of the little town. He slowed when he spotted what must have been his ultimate destination, a nice RV with a car hitched in back. She recognized the car; it belonged to Gianella.

Heller hit his brakes and stopped a few feet from the camper. Millie pulled in a little later. Heller had already staggered to the door of the RV and was pounding on it with the butt of his gun.

Millie hurriedly parked, made sure she had a round chambered in her gun, and got out of her car.

By then, a man had opened the door, and Heller stared up into his face, totally shocked. "*Clementine?* What—" he rumbled, his chest heaving. "How..." He turned to face the person who had been trailing him, and was shocked again. "*A broad?*" He shook his head.

When Millie raised her weapon, Heller dropped to the ground at the feet of the man from the RV. That man, unknown to her, stepped in front of the prostrate killer and began waving his arms and telling her not to shoot.

"No," she screamed. "*You* get out of the way. He's a madman! He's already killed three people tonight. Don't let him—"

During their brief exchange, Heller rolled to his injured side, and while emitting a low groan, raised his good arm and took aim at the man protecting him. His arm wavered, and he appeared weak, but not so weak that he wouldn't be able to kill again.

Unaware of what Heller was doing, the man from the trailer moved toward her.

Millie couldn't wait any longer. She took aim and fired.

Heller's arm dropped, but only for a moment. It was enough; Millie fired again, hitting him squarely in the chest.

~*~

Lenny and Sam heard the yelling and the gunfire outside the RV, but neither wished to make themselves a target. Ebby had curled up in a tight ball in the bedroom, unwilling to join them.

Lenny couldn't help but worry that Bobby or some other neighbor had gotten into a shooting match with one of the quarry peddlers. Or maybe someone else had followed Clement. He could tell Sam was equally worried.

When the shooting stopped, Lenny peeked through the passenger side window and saw Clement talking to a woman. Based on their casual stance, he figured the danger had passed.

When he and Sam stepped outside, they both reacted to the body on the ground. "What the hell just happened?" Lenny demanded. "And who's she?"

"I'm trying to sort all that out," Clement said. He turned back to the woman. "Who—"

"My name's Millie Abraham." She poked the dead man with her toe. "And I've been tracking this murdering bastard for a long time. Way too long."

"But why?" Clement asked. "What did he do to you?"

"He killed my father for starters, and nobody claims to know why." She squinted from Lenny to Sam, took a second look at Sam, then nodded in recognition. "He also killed your lawyer friend."

"*Mr. Putzkin?*" Sam cried out in surprise. "He never hurt *anybody!* All he did was write wills and do estate planning. Why would—"

"My guess," Millie said as she glanced at the dead man, "is that he was looking for information, probably about you. But I have no idea why."

Lenny knew. "He wanted the RV."

"And I can explain all of that," Clement said. "But let's do it inside. We need to contact the police anyway."

Millie looked deeply concerned about a call the police. "Listen, I think I'd better go. The cops—"

Clement held up his hand to stop her. "It's going to be all right. I can take care of this."

"But—"

"Hang in there. I'll explain."

Sam was still visibly shaken, so Lenny kept his arm around her as they sat on the sofa. Clement went to make the call, and Millie sat beside them.

After staring at Millie for a few seconds, Sam loosened up. "I know I've seen you somewhere."

Milie smiled. "I've been thinking the same

thing. It dawned on me outside. I saw you two together in a coffee shop in Atlanta, and I bumped into you again in Auburn. You let me use your perfume."

"That's it!" Sam exclaimed. "That's exactly it, only... Uhm. It wasn't exactly perfume."

Millie dipped an eyebrow. "Oh? What was it?"

"Ah, that's the crux of the whole situation," Clement said, having finished his call to the police. He looked at Lenny. "Would you care to explain?"

"You might as well," Sam said.

"They're called veils," said Lenny. "My aunt concocted them. The one you borrowed from Sam is an attractant." He tried, but failed, to squelch a guilty smile. "They can be kinda strong."

"Meaning what?"

Sam piped up. "It means if you're in some kind of personal relationship, the attractant can sorta... You know, ramp things up. If you're with someone who's interested in you, and you get close—" She paused and swallowed. "Things can get... intense."

"Like *sexually?*"

"Yeah," Sam said as her face turned a pale shade of crimson.

Millie appeared to be groping for words when Clement broke in. "As much as I'd love to hear more of this discussion, I'm sure the police will soon be here, and that'll likely put an end to all our conversations. At least, until the cops are done."

"About that—" Millie began.

"Relax," Clement said. "You saved my life; it wasn't an execution or a murder. It was a form of self-defense. If he hadn't been aiming at me, he would've gone after you. That's something I'll swear to, and gladly."

"Thank you." Millie sighed in relief.

"I do, however, have one question for you," Clement said. "Have you any idea why Dak Heller might have been hired to kill your father?"

"All I have is a theory," she said. "My dad was very outspoken. He was especially concerned about corruption in politics, and there was one man in particular he talked about on social media. Dad was a featured guest on a number of talk radio shows, and lots of people listened to him."

"Who was he talking about?" Lenny asked.

Millie frowned. "A bigwig named Grovemont. Senator Terrence Grovemont."

~*~

Six weeks later....

Lenny and Sam sat together on the sofa in the RV, the remains of their dinner spread out on the pop-up table before them. Ebby lay sprawled at their feet. They stared at a newscast on the TV; the story held them transfixed.

"It's working," Sam whispered. She squeezed Lenny's hand. "They did it."

He grinned at her. "But *we* made it possible." He pointed at a video on the screen. "Senator Septic Tank looks scared to death. The crowd might as well be getting ready to lynch him."

Sam snorted. "If that were so, it's only because he deserves it."

They fell silent until the program paused for a commercial break. Sam leaned close against Lenny, her head resting just shy of his chin. It was something he dearly loved about her. "Have you heard anything from Clement or Millie lately?"

"Not since the last shipment of repellant. I don't know how they did it, but from the way the crowd at that rally is acting, they must've gotten Grovemont to bathe in it. Too bad there weren't any dogs nearby."

"Or bears," added Sam.

Lenny picked up the TV remote, turned the machine off, and faced her. "I've got an idea."

"Me, too," she said. "It's a gorgeous night. Why don't we take Ebby for a walk?"

Lenny had a much shorter walk in mind, one that led straight to the bedroom in their tiny RV. "I, uhm—"

"Ebby needs the exercise," Sam said. She kissed him and took a quick glance at her engagement ring and smiled. "C'mon. Let's go."

Veils

Lenny sighed. "Okay. But maybe later you could model that hot little red outfit for me? The one you said you packed away?" He raised his brow in anticipation.

"Hm," she said. "We'll see."

"Seeing—what a coincidence! That's exactly what I had in mind. And then—"

"Easy, Tiger. Let's not get ahead of ourselves." She waved her index finger in the air. "We're walking Ebby before we do anything else. And while we're outside, we really need to talk about some of the letters sent to Edna. There are quite a few folks who need us, y'know. I think it's time we seriously tried to help them."

"Okay, okay," he said. "But... uhm... I could use a little help, too, y'know."

~End~

About the Author

Josh Langston writes books that amuse, anger, enlighten, and entertain, qualities you'll find in *Veils*, his fifteenth solo novel. His short fiction has been published in a variety of magazines and anthologies, and two of his short story collections have placed in the Amazon Top 20 for genre fiction.

In addition to writing, Josh loves to teach, especially to students aged 50 and over. His classes on novel writing, memoir, and independent publishing are quite popular. A great sense of pride for him is the number of his students who have gone on to write and publish books of their own.

If you are a member of a book club and would like to arrange a chat with Josh for your group, you may contact him at: **DruidJosh@gmail.com**. And be sure visit his website, too: **JoshLangston.com**. His blog is called "Sage of the South" for a reason!

And now for an added bonus: Chapter One of *Hyde and Zeke*, a crafty, crazy step back in time to the 1980s. Get ready to have a wonderful ride!

Cutie and the Beast

Hyde & Zeke

Be Wary
of Those
You Meet
in the Woods

Bestselling author

JOSH
LANGSTON

You're just one page away....

Chapter One

"I am fond of pigs. Dogs look up to us. Cats look down on us. Pigs treat us as equals." –Winston Churchill

Granville, Georgia. 1981 — It began during my senior year in high school....

Despite everything that's happened over the years, and that's saying a lot, Zeke is still my best friend. I couldn't have said that in the beginning, of course, because... Well, let's just say we got off to a weird start.

I remember it clearly. Malindi Moore had just announced we were through, and I was in a desperately rotten mood. She claimed it wasn't anything I said or did. She "just needed her space." She "needed to experience more of the world." I think what really happened is that she heard the school yearbook layout was done, and she no longer needed to spend time with the yearbook photographer, me.

I shouldn't have been surprised. Malindi made being shallow an art form. When I no longer proved useful, she discarded me like an old lens cloth. Zeke would have tried to warn me if we'd known each other back when Malindi and I first got together. But, of course, that didn't happen.

Sorry. I'm getting ahead of myself. I do that a lot, so rather than apologizing all the time, you'll just have to get used to it.

So, Zeke. He came into my life right about the time Malindi left it. And if she hadn't dumped me as cruelly as she did, he and I would never have met.

When Malindi dropped me, I headed straight for the woods. It was right next to my house, and I'd spent plenty of time there in the past experimenting with nature shots. But I didn't bring a camera then. I just needed some privacy. I figured if I shed a tear or two, nobody would see it and realize what a complete loser I am—well, was. See, Malindi was my first real girlfriend. She wasn't my first big crush; that was Miss Lovingood, my World History teacher. She wasn't a bad teacher for someone fresh out of college, but she'd have been an absolutely awesome swimsuit model.

Malindi wasn't in the same league as Miss Lovingood, but she was really cute, and that should have been a warning sign. Back then, really cute girls just didn't dig guys like me. It's not in their genes. Zeke could have told me that. Not then, of course, but later, when he learned to communicate.

So anyway, there I was in the woods, sobbing and sniffling, and doing the love-sick moron thing. That's what you're supposed to do after a cataclysmic breakup, right? Weep. Moan. Eventually pour out your tale of woe in song lyrics. Constantly relive the misery in a ballad. With harmony. Make it sound really good. Get a recording contract. Achieve stardom, and then get revenge by marrying your former true love's best friend.

To be honest, I doubt Malindi had a best friend, and if she did, he or she would probably have been just as shallow. Birds of a feather, right? Probably vultures.

Whatever. Anyway, there I was, firmly embedded in nature and busy agonizing over the demise of my love life. I'd settled myself on the trunk of a fallen tree, head in hands, and figured I could bask in my wretchedness a while longer, though I needed to get back to civilization before dusk. Folks have seen bears in those woods. I'm not a fan of omnivorous critters bigger than gerbils, especially not after dark.

Which, when I think back on it, makes my introduction to Zeke even stranger.

He was a whole lot smaller than he is now, and not in the least bit intimidating. He looked as pitiful as I felt. I didn't know he was a "he" at the time, and I've got to admit, I'm still not sure that label is accurate. It probably doesn't apply to his species, whatever it is.

Way back then, he gave off a sad puppy vibe. We've all seen it—mournful eyes, trembling lip, soft fur. Okay, I may have imagined the trembling lip thing; I haven't seen him do it since. Anyway, just looking at him, I felt absolutely sure he'd been dumped, too. Abandoned. Probably by someone like Malindi. Kindred spirits, no?

"What are you doing out here?" I asked.

He didn't vocalize, but looked right at me. The eyes got me. They were... I dunno, soulful.

I reached out to him, slowly. Scaring him wouldn't do. But he didn't seem intimidated at all. He sniffed my hand and must have sensed I didn't intend to eat him because he wiggled close enough to rub himself against my knuckles.

He didn't look anything like a mink, probably because of the extra legs, but I imagined he felt like one—maybe on steroids. He wrapped himself around my outstretched hand like a mitten of stunningly soft, thick fluff.

And then he sighed.

"My name's Denver," I said. "Most folks call me Denny, 'cause I think they know I hate it."

And then he sighed again, and it sounded like he said, "Zeke" in a quiet, breathy kind of voice that dwelt on the vowel sound.

That clinched it; we were formally

introduced. He had a name, and he had me. No way could I leave him there, all alone in the woods. With the bears. Or worse. If Malindi found him, she'd have him skinned and turned into ear muffs or something. So, I took him home.

And that's how Zeke and I got started.

~*~

To keep this in perspective, I need to step back a few months. Bear with me; it'll all make sense eventually.

Miss Lovingood asked me, "How'd you like to join the *Gangway* staff?"

The question took me totally by surprise. I never thought Miss Lovingood would say two words to me outside of class. I had no idea she was the faculty advisor for the school yearbook.

I'm not much of a joiner, but the thought of working alongside Miss Lovingood had me all but drooling. "Uh, doing what?"

"Some of the kids say you're a whiz with a camera," she said. "We need someone with skills like that to create a photographic record of all the cool stuff that goes on here at Herbert Hoover High."

Cool stuff? I wasn't aware of anything like that. Mostly, I suspect, because the cool stuff was committed by the cool people, and I definitely wasn't one of them. The cool people did cool things and had cool nicknames for all of it. They never said Herbert Hoover High; it was always H3. So... *cool.*

"Well, what do you say?" she asked, all smiles. Dazzling smiles; narrow-waisted and D-cupped.

Dazzling smiles mind you; dazzling *me*. There wasn't a microscopic chance in hell that I'd pass up an opportunity to spend time with the most desirable female on planet Earth. "You bet," I said. "That'd be... Uhm. Cool."

I couldn't believe that was the best thing I could come up with. But then, I'd been ambushed. It wasn't like I had time to think of something clever.

"Excellent!" she said. "Our first staff meeting is at three this afternoon, in the library, right after school."

I watched her walk away, mesmerized by the sight of her retreating figure—a graduate-level course in celestial mechanics. Utterly awe inspiring. At that precise moment, Malindi Moore stepped between us, and my focus abruptly shifted back to the real world.

She actually batted her eyelashes at me, and she had the cupid lips thing going full throttle. "So," she said, her smile accentuated by bright lip gloss and perfect, brace-free teeth, "you're going to take pictures for *The Gangway*?"

"Yeah," I stammered. "I guess so." Master of the understatement, that's me.

"Do you know if they'll use pictures students provide? I've got some really good ones."

I could only imagine how good they were,

and suddenly I realized she was posing for me: pouty lips, hair "just so," one hand parked strategically on her hip. "Uh, maybe," I said. "I don't know how anything works yet. I just—"

"But you have a camera, right?"

"Sure! It's a Nikon with—"

"Great—you can take some pictures of me!" She fluffed her hair and did some kind of wiggle thing that left me distinctly short of words. And breath.

"Okay," I managed. "You wanna do it... here?"

She looked around, slowly, as if hoping to spot something interesting, a virtual impossibility on the ground-floor hallway of H3. "Here would work, I guess. Provided you can do some special effects stuff; you know, like make the hallway out of focus."

Finally, something I was good at. "I can do better than that! With a little planning, I can change the background completely. How does a beach in Hawaii sound?"

"With me dressed like *this?*" She waved the idea off, thought for a moment, then said, "Have you ever looked at a fashion magazine?"

I didn't want to admit that I hadn't. "I'm more into... you know... *Photography Today* or maybe—"

"I'm talking about fashion, Denver." She paused, thinking. "It *is* Denver, isn't it? Like, in Wyoming?"

"More like the one in Colorado," I said, immediately wishing I'd said something cool instead, but she didn't seem to notice I'd corrected her.

"So, where's your camera? I'm ready."

"Uhm. Well... See, I don't usually bring it to school. The halls are always crowded, and if somebody knocked it outta my hands or something, I—"

"Well, bring it tomorrow, for sure. Okay?" She winked at me.

Oh, my God, she winked at me! "Uh, right. No problem."

"I'll meet you here," she said tapping on one of the five zillion identical metal doors that lined the hallway. "My locker. Right after classes."

I'd miss the bus, but I didn't care; I'd walked home before. Now however, I had a reason: Malindi Moore, locker number 1222, wanted to pose for me. Life was good.

Of course, back then, I was pretty stupid.

~*~

I figured out later that luscious Miss Lovingood got saddled with the faculty advisor job on *The Gangway* because she had less seniority than anyone else at H3. Barely four years older than me, she had no idea how to organize a yearbook. For some reason, the girls on the staff picked up on that before the guys did.

She stumbled through that first meeting appointing students to various tasks based on—who knew? Maybe hair color or shoe size. And class, definitely class. Seniors got all the choice spots. Juniors got left-overs. Sophomores and freshmen need not have applied. "Come back next year," she told them. "We'll really need you then." Unless, of course, you still hadn't aged up to one of the privileged ranks.

It turns out I was the only person who knew how to operate a camera. Remember, this was back in the day before everyone had one buried inside a cell phone. And anyone who could actually develop their own film was considered some kind of wizard. Polaroids? Ha! For the first time in my life, I was in demand.

Most of the people on the staff were okay. None of us were in the cool crowd—make that "cool but cruel" crowd. We took pictures of them, and wrote about them, and some of us probably wished we *were* them. Not me.

And then there was Burt Boeheim. Most of us thought of him as Burt Bovine due to his size. The biggest guy on the H3 football team—"Go Explorers!"—he had an equally oversized ego. I think his plans for the future required proving to everyone what a badass he was. He got as far as proving what a dumbass he was, not that anyone had the nerve to tell him.

Miss Lovingood made him *The Gangway*'s

liaison for sports. It took some effort to translate that into words Burt could handle. Single syllables seemed to work best for him. Sadly, the library had no English-Neanderthal dictionaries.

Anyway, between dodging Burt and taking photos of Malindi at every venue she could think of, I found myself hard pressed to shoot the stuff Miss Lovingood and the rest of the staff wanted me to shoot.

You're probably wondering what Zeke was doing all this time while I was running around taking pictures of cool people doing cool stuff. The best way I can think of to describe it is simply to say he was evolving—*from* what and *to what*, exactly, I'm not sure of. But I'll get into all that soon enough. Bear with me.

~End of Excerpt~

Hyde and Zeke is available from Amazon.com in both paperback and ebook formats.

Hyde & Zeke

www.ingramcontent.com/pod-product-compliance
Lightning Source LLC
Chambersburg PA
CBHW071520260626
47170CB00002B/441